TWISTED DECEPTION

TWISTED DECEPTION

ISABELLA

SAPPHIRE BOOKS

SALINAS, CALIFORNIA

This and other Sapphire Books titles can be found at
www.sapphirebooks.com

Dedication

To Schileen

Forever my love!

Acknowledgments

It takes a village to put out a book.

Thank you to that village - Shelley, Peggy, and others who wish to be just part of the process.

To my family, Sapphire and personal. You make it all worthwhile.

To the readers who keep reading my stories. Thank you just doesn't seem to be enough for all you've given me.

Prologue

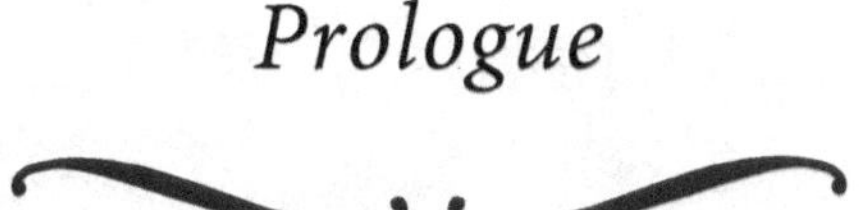

Six minutes left to get this done before security made their rounds on the floor. His fillings tingled as he shoved a penlight between his lips and traced paths on the diagram. He snuck a glance at his watch. Three minutes to finish.

With surgical precision, he wove the tips of the snips between the assorted colors of wires, pulled two, and cut them to the camera system. Attaching a new set of wires, he pulled a remote from his pocket to test the box he'd subbed in. A green light flashed to red, then back again, as he reset the signal. Two minutes to spare.

Pocketing his tools, he slipped the door closed and gently set the latch in place. He tossed the plans, flashlight, and snips into his briefcase, adjusted his tie, then looked out the slim window in the door. One minute.

As he eased out into the hallway, he pulled the door shut behind him and casually walked down the hall as if he worked at Integrated Financial.

Chapter One

Time wasn't on Addie's side and Paul wasn't helping. Neither were the texts from her girlfriend.

10:30—Geez I'm starving. When r u getting home?

"Is that Drake?" Paul asked, stuffing papers into his already bulging briefcase.

Addie wondered how much longer the poor imitation snakeskin could take the abuse. Only one latch kept the battered beast closed. The hinges often popped open at will, and Paul had strewn his work all over more than once when they were walking to work. Addie had to keep pedestrians from stepping on his client prospectuses. He probably didn't have a better briefcase for the same reason he didn't have a girlfriend. Paul was usually a little clueless. Addie liked him in spite of it. Or, perhaps, because of it.

She stared at the glowing screen of her cell, then hesitantly tapped it. If too much time went by, Drake would text again. The second one would be a shouting text.

10:40—Leaving now. ☺

"You want to get a drink?" Paul asked. "Or

doesn't your ball and chain stretch that far?"

Addie rolled her eyes as she shut down her computer and gathered her purse. If she sat, she couldn't see over the half wall that kept her and Paul separated. She bumped her hip against the file-cabinet drawer, closing it. While it wasn't an office per se, the walls offered enough privacy from prying eyes that Addie could shop for her favorite shoes online every once in a while. "This from the man who'd kill for a ball. Or a chain," she said as she cast Paul a glance that, if he *had* a wife, he would have recognized instantly as a *don't fuck with me* look.

Heading home to Drake, the girlfriend who could barely afford to take her out for sushi, made her headache from a long day of crunching numbers even worse.

"I'll take that as a yes. O'Malley's Pub?" Paul pressed his luck. "You know you love their fries."

"Twist my arm. Let me tell Drake I'll be late." Even as Addie typed, she had a feeling what the reply would be.

10:42—Change of plans. Meet me at O'Malley's pub.

10:43—WTF? Are u kidding me. I'm going to bed. Don't wake me when you get in. Pillow on couch.

Addie sighed and Paul stole a look at the reply.

"Shocker." He groaned. "Aren't you tired of her crap yet? Or just tired of sleeping on the couch?"

Drake worked hard and had no problem staying out late with the guys from the garage. But if Addie did the same, Drake hit the ceiling. Besides, it was her apartment. And she'd had it with the couch.

"Guess it's just us."

"Good! We always have a better time without your little grease monkey." Paul threaded his arm around Addie's waist. "God, are you losing weight?"

"No, not really," she lied. Drake had made some harsh comments about Addie's figure, and she had made a point of not eating around Drake, who watched everything she put in her own mouth. Addie had been proud of her swimmer's body. Soft in all the right places but fit. Yet she didn't compare to the pin-up girls that draped themselves on Drake when she was at a race. She didn't have a clue what Drake saw in her, and it was starting to be painfully obvious that Drake had a type and she wasn't it, yet.

Paul smiled and tapped his watch. He wasn't a man's man. He was the type that would make your mom happy. Slim, well-groomed, and polite as hell. Why couldn't she like guys, or at least guys like Paul? What did they call a man who hung around lesbians?

"Bullshit. Ever since you've been dating Motor Girl, you've gotten skinnier and skinnier. By next month, you'll be down to your birth weight. Don't make me stage an intervention."

Addie's phone vibrated in her hand, as if Drake had overheard them.

10:48—Goin 2 my place instd. Gotta race 2mrrw.

10:48—Fine. Maybe you'll be in a better mood tomorrow.

The bomb she'd just lobbed would probably blow up in her face tomorrow after Drake's race, but she was beyond caring at the moment. It was Friday night, and she'd worked over sixty hours that week. She needed a glass of wine. Or a shot. Or both.

Addie found herself stuffing her own briefcase past the point of closing too. It didn't matter. She'd broken the zipper a long time ago.

Taking work home was requisite if you wanted to keep your job at Integrated Financial Services. They weren't just the top brokerage firm in San Jose. Integrated Financial had practically predicted the economic collapse within a few weeks. That alone placed them in the top ranking of stockbrokers.

Above Addie, a bank of clocks set to times around the world loomed, ticking silently. They were critical. If someone wasn't careful, it was easy to put the wrong time down on a sell order and screw a client out of major money. Addie had sat there on many a night, watching the bright-red second hand crawl slowly around the face of the clocks, just waiting for them to hit a sell time.

But not tonight.

"Let's get out of here," Addie declared.

Paul summarily pushed his desk chair in. "Don't have to tell me twice. Let's make a night of it. We'll stay up late, then go to the Waffle House in the morning and get fried chicken and gravy."

"Is that another hint about my weight?"

"I'm pretty subtle, right?" he said, snapping off the lights to the office they'd shared for over a year and leaving Addie in the dark.

"Yup. Subtle."

Paul could be a pain, but he was always good to her. They were both hanging on by their fingertips to every rung they'd climbed on the corporate ladder at

Integrated. However, he'd never tried to edge her out for a promotion, cut her out of a deal, or even hit on her. Addie knew she had a true friend in him so she wanted to return the favor.

Following him out into the hall, she added, "Tell you what. I'm going to text my friend Tara. She should be getting off work right about now."

11:00—Heading 2 O'Malley's pub. Join? Want u 2 meet someone.

11:01—You finally dumped that biiiooottccch, Drake?!? Can't wait to meet your new squeeze. C ya in a few!

Misunderstanding aside, Addie announced, "You're welcome."

"For what?" Paul asked.

"Tara will meet us at O'Malley's. She's just your type. Hard-working. No life. Likes Chinese takeout right out of the box. And doesn't like commitment."

"My dream woman!"

Her phone vibrated in her hand again. Afraid it was Drake, Addie ignored it.

Paul pushed the office's main door open, the Integrated Financial logo's emblazoned boldly on the glass, and waited for Addie to walk past. "Bet Motor Girl doesn't do that for you, does she?"

Addie elbowed him in the stomach. "Stop. She's not that bad."

Suddenly, she remembered that she'd forgotten the file she was supposed to work on that weekend. Drake hated it when she brought paperwork home, as if it was an insult to her and the quality time they were supposed to be spending together. But the days of Saturday-morning hikes and fun Sunday brunches were long gone, replaced by arguments over leftover pizza and pretending to still be asleep when the sun rose so they didn't have to talk.

"I'll meet you in the garage and we can argue who gets to drive."

"Not if I'm already in the car waiting for your slow ass. Besides, I'm the designated driver tonight. I don't want to make a jerk out of myself if your friend is hot."

"She's definitely hot. And you'll make an ass out of yourself regardless. Meet you in the garage in five after I get that file."

Paul strode down the long corridor and hopped into an open elevator as Addie's phone vibrated yet again. Steeling herself, she tapped the screen.

11:14—Leaving now. C u in a few.

At the sight of Tara's text, Addie relaxed.

11:14—C u in about 10.

Addie typed in her pass code at the main door for reentry. Integrated had become serious about security after a hacker had nearly breached their firewall earlier that year. She looked up at the new security camera pointed right at her. She should feel safer, but the idea of Big Brother watching, well, it had people talking. Padlocks on the supply cabinet wouldn't have surprised her. Things had been tense at the office since then, but it was more because of the merger rumors swirling. She didn't want to think what that would mean for her job.

She had heavier things on her mind at the moment.

Snaking through the darkened offices and half cubicles, she reached hers, snatched the file from her desk drawer, then tucked it under her arm and read another text from Tara. Was this what her life amounted to after so many long hours and grueling days on the job?

11:15—I need a double. C u in five.

Addie slipped her head through her briefcase strap, shrugged it across her chest, and tucked her purse under her arm so she could keep texting. Lately, it was the only way she could keep up with family and friends. Lucky for her, her mother had recently started to respond to texts. Little snippets of niceties between them throughout the week had replaced the long Sunday phone calls. Nice!

Addie rushed out of the office for the elevator. Lucky for her it was waiting.

11:16—Not intro-ing you to a girl. Want you to meet my coworker, Paul. Nice guy.

The elevator dinged, stopped, and the doors slid open. Addie caught sight of a man out of the corner of her eye but didn't give him a second thought. Integrated had a reputation. Staying late wasn't just the norm. It was almost mandatory. You worked long hard hours and hoped your boss took notice.

"Good evening," he said in a deep voice she didn't recognize.

"Hey." She didn't bother to look up from her phone. She kept it brief, not wanting to encourage more conversation. Addie read Tara's latest text.

11:18—He better be. That last guy you wanted me to meet was a d-bag.

"So, working late, huh?" the man said.

Addie cast a glance in his direction, discreetly checking him out in the highly polished brass wall of the elevator. His suit stretched across the huge expanse of his chest, the buttons of the vest looking like they'd pop at any minute. Spit-shined wingtips looked out of character for some reason. His beefy hands clenched and then relaxed. No briefcase. Odd. Everyone had a briefcase at I.F.

Not wanting to be rude, she answered, "Yeah. You?"

"The hard-ass boss, but I'm sure I don't have to tell you. You work on the twenty-third floor, right? I've seen you in the cafeteria a couple of times."

Addie could feel his gaze crawling over her from head to toe. In that tight space of the elevator, it was unnerving.

11:19—Gotta stop txtn. A guy got on the elevator and he's looking over my shoulder, TTYL.

"It's a job, right?" he said.

Addie tucked her phone in her pocket as the man shuffled closer. She stepped back as he crowded her at the panel. As he stuck two fingers out, a scar across the first two knuckles caught her attention. She heard a loud click at the same time he pushed a floor that meant he would get off before her. His hand lingered on the panel and she caught a whiff of a strange scent. Mothballs, she thought. She remembered her grandmother's house smelling the same way.

"Wow, you smell good. What's the name of that perfume you're wearing? I'd love to get some for my wife."

He still stood too close for her comfort, so she started to step to the back of the elevator. Before she could put space between them, Addie felt herself pushed up against the wall.

"Think you're too good to talk to me?" He was close enough that she smelled stale nicotine on his breath. Without warning, he bashed her against the wall, instantly splitting her lip. Blood seeped into her mouth. "You should've been nicer."

She tried to push off the wall, but he forced his body against hers. If she could get turned around maybe she had a fighting chance. She felt herself being pulled back by the strap of her briefcase. In a second, she was thrown down to the ground. The pain from her face making contact with the floor almost made her black out.

Her mind was screaming, Fight, Addie! Fight!

Arching her back, she shifted her hips as she tried to roll her attacker off her. A glint of silver briefly caught her eye. Next, she felt the pressure of the briefcase strap release. He tossed the case into the corner of the elevator and jerked her around on her back, face-to-face with her attacker. Her phone buzzed.

Reaching up, Addie tried to shove his massive weight off her, but he grabbed her wrists and pushed them back. His face was close, sweat dripping on her. Without thinking, she rammed her head against his nose. Her forehead made contact with something that snapped. His blood splattered all over her cheeks as he bellowed, "You little bitch…"

She bucked her hips, trying to toss him off, and he let go of one of her hands to clutch his wounded nose. Instinctively, she raked his face with her fingernails.

"Uargh," he screamed, reaching for the furrow marks her nails had drawn. He straddled her hips, waving the knife blade in front of her. "Fight me and I'll kill you. Understand?" He lowered his face closer. "I know where you live."

He reached across her, grabbed her arm, and flung her onto her stomach. His thick fingers threaded into her hair, yanking her head back. He pushed her dress up, and the snap of the elastic waistband being cut echoed in the small confines. The tip of the blade caught the flesh of her butt, and she yelped. A trickle of hot blood rolled down her thigh.

"Stop struggling and you won't get hurt."

"Fuck you."

"Oh, I plan on it. You just made it interesting."

A meaty fist clocked the side of her head, and the edges of blackness started to encroach on her. Fighting to stay awake, she heard her phone buzz again. It was always in her hand, except now when she needed it most. The elevator jerked from its stop and started moving, and then everything went black as more excruciating pain lanced through her skull. Black and quiet.

A scream wrenched her from the darkness.

"Addie! Addie, what happened?" She could hear Paul but couldn't see him. Her eyes were practically swollen shut.

She tried to sit up, but her body wasn't cooperating and her head was throbbing.

"Don't move. An ambulance is on its way. Addie, who did this to you?"

Flickers of memory like the ticking frames of a silent movie flashed behind her closed eyes. Her aching body confirming what she could imagine was only a nightmare. The stranger had attacked her.

"Christ," she heard him mutter under his breath. "Stay with me, Addie. Help's on the way."

Two minutes, she'd just needed two minutes to get that file and they could have been sitting at the bar. Paul pulled his coat off and covered her as she started to shake. "Oh God, Addie. Who did this to you?" he said again. Behind him stood two women in cleaning aprons, their carts full of maintenance supplies pushed to the side by the bank of elevators. Addie didn't know how she'd gotten into the foyer of the building.

Her vision cleared, and she licked her bloody lips. "I don't know. I've never seen him before."

"Can I do something, sir?" one of the cleaning women asked, standing at a respectful distance. Her graying hair was scraped up into a hasty bun, a concerned look on her aging face.

"I think we all just need to stay here and wait for the police to show up."

The second one piped up. "Yes, yes, but I have to do my job, or I could get fired." She was younger, a dark ponytail swinging as she whispered something to her coworker that neither Addie nor Paul was meant to hear.

"I'll talk to your boss. Besides, you found her, and the cops will want to talk to you both. Did you see anyone get off the elevator?"

The cleaning women swapped glances and shook their heads at the same time.

"No, no, we didn't see anything. Sorry." The younger one nervously twisted a rag between her hands, wringing it out as a siren pierced the tension.

"Oh, the police are here. I'll go and bring them, yes?" one of the women said.

Addie dug her nails into the back of her arms as she rocked back and forth. Pain suddenly felt good. It kept her focused in the moment, keeping some modicum of clarity from slipping away. Footfalls echoed in the distance. Not the rushed steps of someone in a hurry to get away, but the casual pace of someone daring them to find him. The doors swished open, pushing the smell of nicotine into the small gathering.

Chapter Two

"How are you?" It took everything Greyson Hollister had not to return the vise-like handshake from the man she knew was spreading the takeover rumors. The conference center hummed from all the glad-handing going on around her. She was sure her next comment would pass without notice, except for its intended target.

"Good to see ya, Greyson. Sorry about your father."

"Thanks." She pulled her hand back and gently jerked him toward her. "Cut out the bullshit takeover rumors." Her voice was menacing now that no one could hear them. "You know I own controlling interest in Integrated Financial, and I'm not selling," she whispered. For good measure, she pecked him on the cheek. "Otherwise, I'll go to the FCC on that little trade issue with Markham Holdings." He paled as she patted him on the shoulder. Squeezing his hand harder, she wished she could crush it and the man at the same time. "Didn't think I knew?"

"It isn't me, Greyson." He dropped her hand and stepped back, putting some critical distance between them.

"You've been warned."

Greyson walked past him and toward the bar. She needed a drink. All of this pressing the flesh, as her father called it, left her with a sore hand, indigestion, and the need for a shower to get the scum off her.

"The price of doing business, princess," he said. She watched him soak in the energy of the hive as people milled about schmoozing and puckering.

It was a memory best left to yesteryear.

Flexing her hand, she nodded her thanks to the bartender as she tipped her two fingers of bourbon and savored the fire coating her throat. The burn was more refreshing than a cool drink of water and just as soothing. She'd accomplished her mission tonight: kill the takeover talk.

"Ms. Hollister, there's been an incident at the office," a man whispered in her ear.

For Greyson Hollister, men were like earrings or purses: nothing more than an accessory that she could switch out from time to time. Lately, though, she'd forgotten to trade her latest accessory for a new one. Jarrod Bennet, her pseudo-date for the night and her never-late assistant, always had bad timing.

She didn't let her smile waver as she scanned the room and waved at someone without missing a beat. She never lowered her guard, and the recent economic troubles only made her persevere. Bad news rarely ruffled her feathers. She poked a strand of hair back into a tight all-business bun that was giving her a splitting headache.

"Did you hear me?"

"I did. You said there's been an incident at the office. What kind?" Taking another sip of her bourbon, she let its peaty taste linger on her tongue. "I assume you can handle this, Jarrod. I pay you enough."

"I'm afraid this is a little out of my wheelhouse, Ms. Hollister." Jarrod pulled at his necktie, trying to loosen the knot. Clearly he *was* out of his element. "The police called and would like to speak with you."

Greyson narrowed her eyes. A sideways glance at Jarrod's sullen face almost made her smile. "Police? Was there a break-in?" Briefly exchanging niceties as another patron slid past her, she said, "If so, call the insurance company. They'll send a rep out—"

"There was a rape."

"What?" Greyson straightened as if her spine had suddenly fused itself. She tried to conceal the shock as another constituent approached. Now Jarrod had her full attention as she finished the handshake and pulled him away from the crowd.

"Someone was raped in the building," he repeated, pulling his necktie looser.

"When?"

Jarrod peeked down at his watch. "Around ten thirty. They're taking the victim to Mercy General."

"Who?"

"Addie Blake. She's an analyst down in accounting. Seems she and Paul Winston were pulling a late night to bring in the quarterlies on time."

She knew Addie Blake from division meetings. Addie Blake was a mouse of a gal. Soft-spoken, hard worker, smart. She didn't speak often during meetings, something Greyson appreciated when others were too chatty. What she did contribute was thoughtful and concise. Just the kind of worker Greyson liked. She'd taken an interest in Addie Blake, especially after seeing her leaving just as many a late night as Greyson did. Greyson found that admirable in a cutthroat world of corporate suits who'd knife their coworkers, especially if it meant a bigger piece of the pie or face time with the boss. Corporate greed. It fueled the world of high finance. Towers filled with testosterone, scotch, and bitches. Greyson wasn't the corporate bitch, but she was the top bitch.

Greyson suddenly felt sick. "Please tell me they have the suspect?" Setting her drink on the table, she glanced at Jarrod but knew his answer wouldn't be good.

He shook his head, cast his eyes down, and buttoned his jacket. "I'll get your coat and have the car brought around if you want to make your apologies to the guests."

"Excuse me?" Greyson furrowed her brows. She didn't tolerate a man telling her what to do. Especially a subordinate. Jarrod kept other men at bay and provided enough cover that relationship questions were nonexistent. Lately, though, he'd tried to cross the line into paramour. She'd been on track to yank the proverbial rug right out from under him tonight before he shared this tragic news. "Are you telling me what to do?"

Jarrod shrank. "No, no, of course not. I'm sorry. I just…I mean…I thought you'd want to handle this personally. I mean, we've never had something like this happen at Integrated Financial. I can call someone from Legal if you'd rather not be bothered."

"We?"

"I don't mean 'we' as in you and me. I just meant the big 'we.'" He was blathering, making a small circular, almost unnoticeable, gesture with his hands.

"Have my car brought around and find out what hospital Ms. Blake is in."

"The police have asked to speak with you."

"Call Legal and let them know what's going on. I'll ask Neil to meet me at the hospital."

Neil Harris was her personal attorney. He was cutthroat, efficient, and well-connected—the only person she trusted. His advice had become invaluable of late.

"Of course. Would you like me to drive you?"

Greyson spied an opportunity and pounced on it. "Jarrod, there is no 'we.' You're my assistant. If I've led you to believe anything else existed between us, that's only in your head," she said sternly as they walked toward the coatroom. She'd shot him down repeatedly and almost felt sorry for him—almost. She compensated him well for his extracurricular help. If she knew Jarrod, they would do this dance again in about a month.

She really should let him go, and eventually she would, but at this moment she was kicking it into damage control. She'd handle Jarrod later. "Now, I'm sure you can find a taxi home. Can't you?" She pushed through the doors, leaving him fumbling for a response. Snatching her keys from the valet, she raced to her car, barely hearing Jarrod curse and then respond.

"Of course." The venom dripping from his voice might have concerned her if she'd hesitated a moment longer.

※ ※ ※ ※

The fog wrapped around the departing SUV like a protective cape. He smirked. It would only be a matter of time before he took a bite out of that apple. Until then he would just have to satisfy his appetite with another juicy morsel. Walking back into the convention center, he fingered the razor-sharp stiletto in his pocket. It was begging for release, and he was more than happy to oblige.

"Hey, did you forget something?" asked a waitress loaded down with a tray of dirty glasses.

She'd been shaking her ass in his face all night, and he'd more than noticed. He'd waited patiently until they could be alone.

"Yeah. I think I left my cigar case inside. Mind if I check?"

Her eyes smiled as she looked him up and down. Clearly she was appreciating his tailored appearance.

"Sure. If you can't find it there, go to the coat check. It's also the lost-and-found." She pressed the button on the service elevator.

As it opened, he followed her in. "Here. Let me help you with that," he said, pressing the down button and watching the door slide closed. If only she could see the feral grin spread across his lips. Tonight was going to be a great night, he thought as he caressed his stiletto.

Chapter Three

I want to go home, Paul. *Please*, take me home," Addie pleaded before curling into him as she sat on the cold marble floor.

"Addie, I'm so sorry."

A loud commotion sounded outside the foyer of Integrated Financial. Cleaning carts being pushed and a woman's command to stop made everyone freeze.

"Charlie One on scene. Can you send Medical? I have at least one female vic—roger."

Addie caught a flash of the badge on the woman's dark-blue uniform. "Can I have everyone step back, please?"

Addie jerked Paul down, keeping him rooted next to her

"You too, sir."

"I'm her friend, Paul Winston. I'm not leaving her alone," Paul said. "Besides, the other officer that was just here told me to stay where I was."

"What other officer?" The cop looked around the small confined area.

"He just went that way." Paul pointed to the lobby of I.F. "Said he saw someone running out of the building."

The cleaning women parroted Paul's actions and pointed toward the front, too.

"Dispatch, do you have another officer reporting

on scene?" Before she got a reply she reprimanded Paul again. "Sir, you're standing right in the middle of a crime scene that you've just contaminated. Step out." It wasn't a request. It was a command that demanded action.

"Actually, I think the crime scene is in there. We found her lying here." Paul's tone deepened as he stood

"Paul…" Addie needed a lifeline.

"Ma'am, he'll be right over there. Okay? I need him to leave while I ask you some questions." The officer pierced Paul with a glance.

"I'm not going anywhere. This is one of my closest friends, and she needs someone." Paul planted his hands firmly on his hips.

"I'll arrest you for obstruction. Is that how you want to help your friend?" The officer took a step closer to Paul, but he didn't waver.

"Paul, it's okay."

"Okay, but I'll be right over there. You just yell if you need me. I'll call Drake."

"No…no…I…I…don't want you to." That was all she needed. Her mind was already reeling. An out-of-control girlfriend would only add to her anxiety. Besides, Drake wasn't the warm-and-fuzzy type. She'd witnessed Drake scrape layers of skin off her knuckles working on her car and barely let a curse word fly, then continue working. If the sight of Drake's own blood didn't get a response, Addie doubted seeing her battered face would.

"Ma'am, can you tell me who did this to you?" The officer glanced away before Addie could say anything, pulling at the mic on her shoulder. "I need additional units to Integrated Financial. Perp could still be in the building."

"We told you there was another policeman here a few minutes ago," Paul reminded the officer.

Addie stiffened as the words connected. She hadn't thought of that. Her attacker could still be nearby. A scream sat poised on her lips.

"Ma'am, I'm Officer Torres." The woman ignored Paul and softened her voice this time. "I'm sorry, but I have to ask this. Were you raped?"

Addie flinched. She couldn't bear to look at the officer, much less answer her question. She'd asked for this, hadn't she? The man had said as much when he attacked her.

"Think you're too good to talk to me?"
"You should've been nicer."

Addie trembled. He'd wanted to kill her.

"Fight me and I'll kill you. Understand?" His face had been inches away from hers. *"I know where you live."*

"Oh, God. He knows where I live." Addie's shrill voice punctured the vibrating air in the foyer.

"We're not going to let that happen, Ms..." Officer Torres stumbled for a name.

Addie didn't offer hers, so Paul piped up. "Addie, Addie Blake."

"Ms. Blake, we aren't going to let anything happen to you."

"How can you stop him? You couldn't protect me here." Addie looked around the room and pointed at the cameras. "They couldn't protect me." Addie screamed, "Paul, get me out of here." She tried to stand, but her body wasn't cooperating, and her jerky movements kept her from getting any purchase on the floor.

"Ms. Blake, please. You're safe now. Let me ask you some questions, and then we can get you out of here the minute the ambulance arrives. Okay? Can we do that? The sooner I can get a B.O.L.O. out, the better our chances of catching him are. You don't want him to do this to someone else, do you?"

Glancing down at her clothing, she saw that her stockings were shredded and there was blood all over. The floor was littered with her belongings—coat, shoes, and briefcase. Her mouth was dry, and her lips were cracked and bleeding. She ran her tongue over her teeth just to make sure none were missing and felt the stinging pain where his knife had nicked her ass. Addie shook her head. No, she didn't want another woman to go through this hell.

"Are you sure?"

Addie could only nod.

"Okay. So, did you lose consciousness at any point in the attack?"

Addie searched the elevator as if it would cough up the answers it had witnessed. Her mind wandered. What had just happened? "Could you repeat the question?"

"Did you black out at any point during the attack?" Officer Torres spoke more slowly this time.

Addie focused on the officer's shoes and blew out a painful breath before answering.

"At one point he hit me so hard…" She grabbed her head. "I think I blacked out, but…" She squinted, then shielded her eyes. The bright light of the foyer was making her headache worse. "But only briefly, I think."

"Okay, can you give me a description of the man who attacked you? I'm assuming it was a man, correct?"

"Yes."

"Did you recognize him?"

Addie shook her head.

"So, he didn't look familiar? How about hair color? Identifying marks? Tattoos? Scars? Anything?" Officer Torres sounded desperate.

Addie could only stare down at her bloodstained hands. How had this happened? She'd worked late tons of times and never had a problem. Why now? Why?

"Ma'am?"

"Big."

"Big?"

"The buttons on his vest looked like they were about to pop."

"So he was fat?"

"Muscular." Addie picked at the blood under her nails.

"Don't." Officer Torres grabbed Addie's hand and pulled it away. "You might have evidence under your fingernails. Don't."

Officer Torres's voice brought her back to her harsh new reality. She'd been attacked, brutalized, and for what? She looked over at the elevator again. Her purse was missing. Was robbery the motive? It didn't matter. She didn't keep anything of value in it. Her briefcase was still there and closed. So why her? Why?

"I'm not sure I can be of much help. It all happened so fast, and I was…" God. Why hadn't she been paying attention instead of texting?

"You were what?"

"I was texting, and a man got on the elevator.

I guess I wasn't really paying attention." Addie's eyes welled up with tears. She was her own worst enemy right now. It had all happened in a flash.

Officer Torres peppered her with questions again. "Can you tell me anything? Height? Weight? Hair color? Anything that can help us look for this guy?"

Addie wracked her brain. Squeezing her eyes shut she forced herself to remember what had happened after she texted Tara. The smell of her gran-gran's house flashed in her mind.

"He smelled like an old person?"

"Huh?" Officer Torres stopped writing on her small pad. "Old person?"

"Yeah…he…mothballs." She tried to cough, her throat constricting as the partial memory flashed. "The smell reminded me of my grandmother's house."

Paul knelt and tilted the water bottle so Addie could take a drink.

"Sir." Torres lanced him with a commanding look. "Crime scene." She pointed at the pool of blood he'd just knelt in.

"She needs some water," he said.

Addie shrank under the weight of everyone staring at her, gagging at the taste of blood mixing with the water as she gingerly sipped from the bottle. She covered her mouth, trying to keep the liquid down, but backwashed into the bottle. Red swirls mixed with the pure water.

She pushed the bottle away and whispered, "Thanks."

Paul stroked her head and then placed a soft kiss on her forehead before he stood and rejoined the cleaning women still gawking at her. She suddenly wished Drake could be more like Paul.

"Okay. Did he have dark hair?"

Addie nodded.

"Black or brown?"

"Brown."

Torres scribbled on her pad. "How about height? Was he as tall as you?"

Addie shook her head.

"Taller?"

Addie nodded. "I think so." She couldn't help the sob that escaped, so she covered her mouth to muffle any more that might slip out.

"You're doing fine, miss." A gentle pat on the shoulder was her only comfort from the officer.

Addie nervously bit her lip and cringed in pain as blood oozed into her mouth. Another memory flashed.

"Blood," she blurted out. "I hit his nose with my forehead. His blood splattered on my face." She reached up to touch her battered face, but the officer grabbed her wrist, stopping her again. Addie flinched at the contact, her bruised wrist still gripped in Officer Torres's hand.

"Sorry," Torres said. "But don't touch anything. Maybe we can get something from his blood." The officer turned Addie's wrist over and examined her hand. "Did you hit him or scratch him?"

"Scratched."

"Okay, good. You're a fighter."

Addie closed her eyes. She could hear the pencil being pushed against the paper of the notepad. Someone said something about a *suit* leaving the elevator earlier. Just the mention of a possible suspect made Addie shake so violently, she could barely control her movements. Looking over, she caught the outline of three people as her vision started wavering. She recognized Paul's familiar form but barely made out the two women in cleaning uniforms.

"I'm...cold." Addie pulled Paul's jacket tighter around herself.

"You're pretty pale. You're probably going into shock, ma'am." Officer Torres spoke into her mic. "ETA on that ambulance. And did you find out who was here earlier?"

"Two minutes. Negative. I think it was Travers."

"Roger." Turning back to Addie, she repeated the message. "The ambulance is close, ma'am. Can you remember anything else? Anything?"

"Spit shine," she blurted out. She'd spent four years in the army and recognized a spit shine when she saw it.

"What?"

"His shoes. They looked brand-new."

"What color were his suit and his shoes?"

"Black."

"Anything else?"

Addie shook her head, squeezed her eyes shut, and curled further into herself, wishing she could disappear. She just wanted to go home and hide behind the protection of her locked door. She wanted to take a hot shower, crawl under her covers, and forget about what had just happened.

Boots squeaked on the clean tile floor, and the noisy jiggling of wheels caught her attention. She tensed at all the commotion surrounding her.

"It's okay. It's just a few more officers and the ambulance arriving." Officer Torres gently touched her arm, and she opened her eyes. "Don't worry. You'll remember more later. A detective will probably come to the hospital to take your statement."

"Can't I just go home? I want to go home."

"I'm sorry, but I can't let you do that, miss. You've been assaulted, and I recommend you get checked out."

The offered smile was weak at best. Addie almost felt bad for her but suspected the officer was trained to see people at their worst. She definitely fit the bill, especially if the reaction of the cleaning women was any indication of how bad she looked.

"You've been through a very traumatic event. You'll remember, and when you do, write it down. Every little bit helps."

The jiggling sound of wheels grew nearer, and Officer Torres stepped away.

Addie focused on a blood smear on the back wall of the elevator. Her blood. She couldn't bring herself to make eye contact with the enthusiastic medic gauging her. Thankfully, he made quick work of taking her vitals, assessing her injuries, establishing an IV line, all without disturbing possible evidence on her body.

"Okay. Let's get her loaded and to the hospital."

"Paul." Addie reached out toward him. Grabbing his hand, she pulled him closer. "Don't leave me, please."

"I'm right here, Addie."

"Sir, we have to leave."

"I want him to ride with me in the ambulance."

"But ma'am—"

"Get me off this thing then." She started pulling at the straps that anchored her on the gurney.

"Addie, it's okay. I'm right here. I'm not going anywhere. Right?" Paul asked the EMTs.

"Yes, ma'am. He can ride with you to the

hospital."

"Thank you," he whispered.

One nodded and pulled the gurney sideways, lining it up to pull through the doors.

Addie caught a brief snippet of the conversation between the cop and the cleaning women. It didn't sound promising. Not that she could blame them if they opted not to say anything. They'd always been friendly with Addie when they came up late at night to clean. The conversations had always drifted to their large extended families that depended on this job.

"Thank you, ladies," Paul said as he passed them.

"I'll need to speak to you, too, sir," Officer Torres said.

"I'll be at the hospital." Paul still held Addie's hand.

"Fine."

She couldn't focus on anything going on around her. She lay on the gurney paralyzed with fear. *Why me? Why?* Like a record needle that was stuck, the question played again and again in her head. Then the smell of mothballs wafted past her again. The sound of a door shutting made her freeze.

"It's him," she whispered.

❧ ❧ ❧ ❧

Greyson slid her SUV into the tight confines of the parking slip of Mercy General like a skilled valet and then sat frozen there behind the wheel. She'd raced across town, her only deterrent the dense fog that hugged everything. The red and blue lights of an ambulance bounced off the drifting moisture, making the building appear more like a disco lounge than a hospital. She couldn't move. It had only been a year since her life had been tossed upside down, but this place had played a big part in the series of events that still haunted her.

While her professional life was a straight-up rocket ride, her personal life had been a series of tragic events, starting with the sudden death of her wife after the birth of their son, Ben.

"I'm sorry, Greyson. I'm…I just don't know how to say this, but something's happened—"

"Ben? What's wrong with Ben?" Greyson's heart raced. She started for the elevator, but Dr. Madrigal stopped her. She'd been gone only for a moment, grabbing some flowers for Cate. They were her favorite, white roses. How could anything have happened?

"It's not Ben." Dr. Madrigal pulled Greyson out of the traffic pattern and set her down.

"I need to get up to Cate's room, Millicent."

"Greyson…it's Cate."

"What about Cate…" Greyson looked at Millicent and knew it was bad. "What about Cate, Mill?"

"She passed, Greyson."

And that was it. It had been a textbook C-section, and moving into recovery they had discovered Cate's blood pressure had risen dangerously high, but they'd given her a shot and waited. When she was out of danger, the nurses had moved Cate to her room and brought baby Benjamin in so she could see him. Greyson's heart had fluttered when she'd watched Cate and Ben together.

A picture-perfect moment she hadn't captured on her phone camera. She'd thought they would share a lifetime of picture-perfect moments, so she didn't want to ruin their first minutes together. What was one missed opportunity? Greyson would regret her decision for the rest of her life. A day later, Cate had died from an aneurism. A sharp pain, a moment of relief, and suddenly Cate was gone.

Barely having time to mourn Cate, Greyson had found out by accident that her father had stage-three liver cancer. Another gut punch. She had been to the hospital every day, sitting with him and watching him wither away before her eyes. Ben had given her father such joy at the end of his life that she was happy he'd held on long enough to see him.

Greyson smiled. Ben was the glue that kept *her* together.

Peering over the steering wheel, she looked at the stalwart structure that had not only been her second home, but also the source of her deepest misery. Could she force herself to go inside one more time? This time it wasn't her drama to shoulder, or was it? As she yanked the door handle, the cool, wet mist of fog sent a chill through her. She pulled her collar up, bracing for what was to come.

She cast a quick glance around the Mercy General parking lot as she slipped past the sole ambulance in the emergency bay off-loading its human cargo. Again she noticed the red and blue lights taking turns doing an erratic dance in the fog and relaxed when she didn't see any of the requisite reporters' vans with antennas scratching the sky. If they already had the story, they would have swarmed her, sticking microphones in her face, blinding her with camera lights. She'd seen video of herself. Most of the time she looked like a spider under a magnifying glass, the light burning a hole right through her. She wasn't under any illusions; they were coming. It was only a matter of time.

Pulling her phone she checked the time.

12:10.

Too early for a call to Neil Harris, especially when she didn't know what she was dealing with, yet.

Emergency personnel greeted her by name. Enough time hadn't elapsed for her to be just another face in the always crowded room. She inquired about Addie Blake and received the typical hospital response: *Our apologies, but we can only talk to family members. However, if you'd like to have a seat in the waiting area, I'll see what I can do.* That was the hospital's way of saying, Don't bother us.

Her heels clicked on the sterile floors on her way to the waiting room. The smell of hospital disinfectant burned her nose. She passed the same window that faced the parking garage. The same dying potted plants still offered little hope for a diversion. Too much nervous energy had her pacing the floor in front of the window. Efficient use of space, she thought, glancing back at the plants. She wouldn't be able to stay in the claustrophobic area for much longer. In fact, she'd been there five minutes too long already. She made her way back to the ER desk. She wasn't above requesting a favor from the head of emergency medicine, Doctor Millicent Madrigal, if it hurried them along.

On a mission, Greyson marched down the hall but froze just as she rounded a corner of the emergency-room hallway. A woman's frantic voice carried down the hall. She thought she recognized one of the voices, and the other had bitch language floating off it like a trash can being emptied. Standing off to the side, she watched the scene unfold in front of her. A woman and man stood almost nose-to-nose, and from the looks of it they were ready to come to blows. She recognized Paul Winston. He worked for I.F., at least she thought he did. The woman, no clue, but she was a hulking creature, wearing a mechanic's shirt with *Drake* on the name patch.

"Look, I'm not built for this kinda thing." The woman ran her hands through her short black hair and then stuffed her fists into her pockets. "I mean, God, Paul. She's gonna be a wreck, and I gotta work. I can't sit home and hold her hand all day."

"She needs you, Drake. She was attacked and she's…well, she's in bad shape."

"Yeah, she was attacked at work, right? So the company's responsible. They gotta have deep pockets, right"

"Where are you going with this, Drake?"

Greyson watched as the woman called Drake leaned against the sterile surface and nervously twitched her shoulders. "They have a duty to keep her safe, and they didn't do that, did they? So they need to answer for what happened to her."

"Jeez, Drake. She's in there hurting and all you're thinking about is revenge?"

"Look, this happened at work. I need to call and get her a good lawyer. Integrated Financial needs to pay for their lack of security. They need to pay for what happened to my girlfriend."

The ultra-clean floors squeaked as the woman heaved herself off the wall and paced back and forth. Greyson knew people like her. Event opportunists, she liked to call them. The kind of people who took advantage of a tragedy, a circumstance, or a problem and made a quick buck off it.

"Let it alone, Drake. You're only going to make matters worse. Think of Addie," Paul pleaded. "Besides, you should prepare yourself for how she looks."

"Looks? What do you mean?"

"Greyson?"

Greyson stiffened as a hand grabbed her shoulder. Drake and Paul went rigid and looked at her.

"Is that Addie's boss?" Greyson heard Drake yell.

Shit! Shit! Shit! She didn't want a blowout here in the waiting room.

"What are you doing here?" Greyson recognized the smooth tone of Dr. Madrigal's voice. She turned, ignoring the pair, and smiled at the tall African-American woman, hugging her.

"Millicent. How are you?"

"Good. Everything okay with your mom?"

Pulling Dr. Madrigal's elbow, she guided her down the hallway and out of the reach of prying ears.

"Yes, yes, Mom's fine. I ah...I was notified that an employee of mine was attacked and brought here. So I was just checking in on her condition." Greyson moved Millicent farther away from the conversation that was starting to roll out of control over her shoulder and back toward the nurses' station.

"Oh, that's awful." Millicent lowered her voice. "I've just been called to emergency on a possible rape."

"I think that's her. Her name's Addie Blake. Is it possible for you to check?" Greyson positioned herself between Dr. Madrigal and Drake.

"I need to get to the emergency room, but I'll let you know."

"That wouldn't be breaking any rules, would it?"

"I can't give out personal information, but I can see how she is."

"Thank you so much. I appreciate it." Greyson smiled.

"I can't promise anything, but I'll see what I can do."

"Thanks."

Greyson could feel eyes crawling all over her, so she casually turned to confront them. Her gaze instantly locked with Drake's. The hair on her neck stood, and she felt an instant aversion to the woman. Drake flashed her a cocky grin. If they'd been somewhere else, she might just knock it off her face. She shot Paul a glance, and he instantly looked away and grabbed Drake's arm as she started for Greyson.

"I'd listen to Paul if I were you." Greyson stepped into Drake's personal space. The action froze Paul where he stood.

"You ain't me, and I don't need someone telling me what to do. If I was you, I'd watch my back."

"Well, what you lack in brains, you make up for in moxie." She returned Drake's cocky smile, lifted her finger, and broke the ultimate taboo. Greyson touched her. Pushing Drake's chin up with just the tip of her index finger, Greyson made sure she recognized their difference in stature. She looked down at the human brick wall.

Drake cocked her arm back, but before she could shoot it out, Paul grabbed it, almost unable to keep Drake from striking Greyson.

"I wouldn't be threatening me, if I were you. I don't take threats lightly. I'm like that junkyard dog you have chained to the fence in front of your shop. He hates you like a bat hates daylight. And one of these days, he's gonna snap a chain and even the score."

Greyson flicked her wrist, jerked Drake's head to

the side, and whispered, "Yeah, feel me?" She glanced at Paul, then strutted past Drake without so much as a sideways look. This was war, and nobody came into I.F. and screwed with the boss.

Nobody.

Pulling her phone from her Chanel bag, she tapped the screen and texted.

12:34—Shit just went sideways. Pack accordingly.

Chapter Four

M s. Blake, I'm the SAFE nurse for the hospital. SAFE stands for sexual assault forensic examiner. I'm trained to look for forensic evidence after a sexual assault."

Addie pulled the paper-thin drape tighter around herself, clutching her cell phone. It vibrated in her hand as another text message came through, but she couldn't turn it loose. "I told the officer I wasn't raped."

"Did your attacker ejaculate on you or rub himself against you with his penis?"

The nurse sounded so clinical, so detached, that it frightened Addie. Had he touched her with his... well, she wasn't sure. All she could think about right now was getting up and finding the nearest exit and running until she couldn't run anymore. Her heart raced. She couldn't remember. Why couldn't she? She tried to recall, to fill in the blank spots.

Nothing!

She did recall being in the elevator. It had started to move, and he'd hit her again, but this time so hard she saw lights and then the inky black of a nightmare as it sucks you into its maelstrom. Then a bright light had pierced her consciousness, and Paul was next to her calling her name. Fuck, she couldn't remember.

"I...don't remember."

"We should do a rape kit just in case. I'll be honest. This is almost as intrusive as the rape, but I'll try to be as gentle as possible. I'll explain everything as I do it, and I'll tell you why I'm doing it. Okay?"

The nurse laid her hand on Addie's shoulder, and she flinched away from the contact. As if the paper could protect her, she jerked the thin gown tighter around herself. "I've bagged your clothes for the police. A detective has arrived, and she'll be taking your statement."

"But I already gave one to the other officer."

"I'm sure they're just being thorough. It's pretty standard procedure. I'll send her in when I'm done. Okay?"

"Do I have a choice?"

"You always have a choice, Ms. Blake. I can only tell you that if you want to find this guy and prosecute him, we need all the evidence we can find. What would you like me to do?"

Addie contemplated her choices. What if she didn't do this, and they could have found evidence that could catch him? What if he did this to someone else and she could have stopped him? Every victim contemplated these questions, she was sure, right? Could she live with that possibility?

I don't think I can live with myself if I don't do everything I can to catch him.

"Yes, let's continue with the examination." Addie lowered her head, hanging her shoulders in defeat and letting a sob slip past her pursed, trembling lips.

True to her word, before she began, the nurse explained every step of the process with such clarity that Addie almost stopped her. Each step promise to be more of a violation than the last. Only one other woman before Drake had ever touched Addie intimately. Yet here she sat, exposed, the second time in only a few hours. Had life become that cruel? Only a few hours earlier she'd been dreaming of a beer, a bar stool, and some fries.

"I'm going to need to cut your fingernails, so why don't we start with that?"

Addie nodded as she held out her right hand and then her left. The snap of the clippers, eating away in a simple manicure, broke the dead silence of the cold room. The manicure was her first in months. Addie didn't have them often, so the luxury of a mani-pedi always made her feel special. She peered down at short, red reminders of the trauma. She'd never again in her life wear red nail polish. It had proved to be a foolish splurge.

"Okay, if you could scoot down and put your feet in the stirrups."

"What?"

"I'm sorry. We'll need to do a vaginal swab and comb your pubic hair for fibers or pubic hairs he might have left behind. When was the last time you had intercourse?"

Addie stared at the nurse, stunned at the implications. She would need to be violated again to find the person who violated her. She couldn't shake the feeling that she was in a bad dream and would wake up at any moment. If she woke up right now, her life would be just as she left it when she went to bed last night, normal.

"Ms. Blake, when was the last time you had intercourse?"

It took a minute for the question to settle in. *Intercourse?*

"With a man?" she asked softly.

"Uh-huh."

She swooned a bit as the nurse helped her lie down. Like a brain-teaser puzzle, the table contorted itself to accommodate Addie in a position she hated seeing during her annual exam. Stirrups popped up, like a gift every woman should enjoy receiving once a year, as the hospital staff scurried around gloving up and unwrapping sterile items.

"Never."

"You're a virgin?" The stunned look on the nurse's face was surreal.

If Addie had been anywhere else, she might have enjoyed shocking the woman. In fact, she'd take perverse pleasure in the knitted eyebrows, followed by a surprised look, and then the *oh* that always came when they realized she was a…well, it didn't matter now.

She was shivering so hard she could barely utter the word. "Lesbian."

Chapter Five

Greyson guarded the door like a sentry. She wanted to talk to Addie Blake before Drake could poison the well. Greyson didn't leave things to chance.

She reached for the door just as it opened, but a peek was all she caught. Enough to see past the curtain and a small, frail woman clutching a paper sheet to her chest as she lay on the examination table. If that was Addie, and she suspected it was, she definitely needed to do damage control. In just a few minutes, two at most, she could convince Addie that it would be in *her* best interest to stay quiet until Greyson had a chance to talk to legal counsel.

A rape at the company would cause a ripple effect, reverberating out into the larger business community. Part of her couldn't believe how insensitive she was being. Poor Addie had just endured the worst moment of her life, and the second worst moment was walking up to Greyson right now. Drake had turned the corner and had that *I'm coming to getcha* look on her face. Poor Paul followed her, his own face a map of pain.

"Aw, you're still here," Drake said as she propped herself against the wall, a foot perched on it, her hands once again stuffed in her pockets.

"I see you're still here, as well." Greyson wouldn't be intimidated, and if Drake was trying, she would have to be a lot better at it than that.

"Yeah, well, she is *my* girlfriend and all. So—"

"A minute ago she sounded more like a meal ticket. Or did I misunderstand that inference? You do know what inference means, don't you? Maybe I misunderstood the whole check comment. Perhaps you meant chick," Greyson quipped.

"I bet you think you're smart, don't you? Standing there in your thousand-dollar suit. The cost of that bag alone could feed a family of four for at least a month."

"What do you have against hard work?"

"Nothing. I work hard every day. What would you know about working hard?"

Well, nothing like a verbal sparring match with the ill-equipped, thought Greyson. Under different circumstances, this would be fun. But now wasn't the time to inflame someone who'd just threatened to sue her on her girlfriend's behalf. At least that's what Neil would say if he were here. *Where is he, by the way*? She sneaked a peek at her watch. Casually, she tossed out, "Nothing, I suppose."

"Yeah. I didn't think so."

Greyson wanted to slap that smug little smile right off her face. What did *she* know about hard work? *Bitch.*

A woman in scrubs poked her head around the door, barring anyone from looking in.

"Which one of you is the girlfriend?"

Drake jumped from the wall, raised her hand, then looked at Greyson. "Me."

"She's asking for you. I have to warn you that she's pretty banged up, so prepare yourself."

"No problem."

The arrogance of the woman who had just

moments ago proclaimed she wasn't built to deal with this astonished Greyson.

"Is it possible for me to see Ms. Blake?" Greyson inquired.

"I'm sorry, but she's asking for her girlfriend only. What's your name? I can tell her you're waiting to see her, but it's up to her." The nurse escorted Drake into the room and shut the door.

"Jesus Christ," Greyson heard Drake say before the door closed completely.

Greyson cringed. Obviously Drake wasn't as prepared as she thought. "Tactless wonder," she whispered.

Greyson rooted herself to the wall by the door, waiting for her chance to talk to Addie. The door swung wide, and a pale Drake rushed out and over to the trash container, threw her hands on the wall, and puked.

"Oh, Christ," Greyson whispered just as she peeked into the exam room again.

Addie looked closer to death than anything living. Her face had clearly been mistaken for a punching bag. Black rings around her eyes were beginning to form, and she had so much blood in her hair she looked more like a redhead than a blonde. Greyson's own stomach took a dive, and Addie's gaze locked with hers for a moment before the door squeezed shut. Greyson suddenly wanted to walk in and scoop Addie up, hold her tight, and let her know everything would be fine. She did it with Ben and he calmed right down. Only Addie wasn't Ben, and Greyson wasn't Drake. She'd find whoever did this to Addie and make him pay.

"Shit," she whispered. "Fuck."

Greyson hadn't seen someone so badly beaten

since her childhood, and now, looking at her, she was shocked. This was beyond damage control. Someone had violated her employee, her business, and, in a twisted way, her own reputation. Greyson almost ripped her pants pulling her cell phone from her pocket. She hit speed dial and waited for a voice to answer on the other end.

"Harris here."

"Neil, where the fuck are you? Did you get my text?" She turned toward the wall and cupped her mouth over the phone, hoping Drake wouldn't hear her. She walked down the hall and waited until she was out of earshot to say anything else. "Neil, I told you there's been an attack at the office. We have an employee who's been raped in the building. I'm at the hospital now, hoping I can get a word with her. But I doubt they'll let me see her. She looks bad, Neil. Really bad. I need you to do damage control. Get down here. The victim's girlfriend has been making noise that she wants to sue us. She's a money-grubbing little bitch who's already said we need to pay for what happened to her girlfriend."

"Jesus, Grey. Just got the text now. Calm down and take a breath. Have the police talked to you yet?"

"They called me, but I told them I wanted my lawyer present." Greyson didn't usually sweat stuff, but this rattled her. "The sergeant asked me why I want a lawyer. I told them I don't talk to anyone these days without one. So can you get your ass down here?"

Neil Harris had been her college roommate and her friend forever, so it had been an easy decision to hire him. He was a shark when needed and very effective when it came to making sure anything illegal was tied up in a nice tight little package.

"I'm on my way, Grey. Don't say anything to anybody. Do you understand?"

"No shit. You know me better than that. Like I said, I don't talk to anybody unless I have to."

"All right. Give me twenty minutes and I'll meet you in the hospital lobby."

"Thanks. Tell Emily I'm sorry."

"You owe me, and I'll figure out how you'll pay me back."

"Yeah. What's this? The thirtieth dinner I owe you at Geno's?"

"At least. See you in a few."

"Yep."

Grey closed the phone, tucked it into her pocket, and looked back at Drake. Paul was standing next to her, apparently trying to calm her, but Drake looked like she was steaming. She glared at Greyson, snarled, and stalked back into the examining room. Paul walked over to Greyson, chewing his lip.

"Ms. Hollister, I'm so sorry about tonight."

"Why, you didn't have anything to do with this. It isn't your fault." Greyson looked at him and almost felt sorry for him, but she didn't usually waste much time on emotions.

"No, you don't understand. I went down to get the car. I should've waited. I should've been there with her in the elevator."

Greyson patted him on the back. "Look, don't beat yourself up. You couldn't have known. Besides, we have those new cameras and the alarm system. I'm sure we've got him on tape."

Greyson spotted Dr. Madrigal walking back down the hall toward them. "Paul, will you excuse me for a moment?"

"Sure. I'll just wait here and see if I can get in to see Addie."

Greyson raced down the hall, meeting the doctor. "Dr. Madrigal, any word?"

"She's pretty beat up. Whoever did this to her… well, let's just say she's lucky to be alive."

"Can I see her?"

"I'm not sure I can get you into an examining room. She's undergoing an extensive procedure. I don't think she'll be in any condition to talk to you. I mean, I'm the attending. I'm sorry, but I've got to finish the examination and make sure the evidence doesn't get contaminated. I *can* tell you what she's going through isn't any fun."

"Christ."

"After I get in there, I can't tell you anything when I come out. So please don't ask me. I'm sorry. I wish I had better news." Millicent patted Greyson's arm.

Could tonight get any worse? All she could do now was wait for Neil Harris to get to the hospital, advise her, and try to keep the incident out of the press.

The nurse poked her head out. "Dr. Madrigal, we're waiting."

Greyson stuffed her hands in her pockets. "I understand, Millicent. I'd never ask you to compromise your position."

"Thanks," the doctor said, walking away. Before she hit the door, she looked back at Greyson. "We should get the kids together and have a play date."

"Sounds good. I'll call your office next week and see what we can schedule."

"Take care." Dr. Madrigal pulled the door handle just wide enough to squeeze through.

Looking at Paul, Greyson wondered if she should go and sit with him until Neil got there. He was worrying the edge of his paper cup so much it was ready to split, spilling its probably cold contents all over himself. Again, she couldn't begin to fathom the guilt he was carrying. If she were more like her father she would have sat next to Paul and said something comforting. Instead, she would leave him to exorcise his own demons. She wasn't her father.

Pulling her jacket tighter around her, she walked in the opposite direction, toward the lobby. Neil would be there any minute, and they needed to come up with a game plan to keep Integrated Financial out of the newspapers.

Chapter Six

He stood over her body. She was so beautiful, with her mousy brown hair splayed out like the wings of a bird. He loved birds. The marks around her neck were just starting to turn a pretty shade of purple. The slow rise of her chest assured him that she wasn't dead. *What does it feel like to extinguish a life?*

He pulled out his wallet and removed a slip of paper. Yanking his pen from his pocket, he licked the end, ink staining his tongue. A visceral jolt sliced through him at the taste. He could add another name to his list of women who wanted him. Peering over the paper, he noted the woman's name on her nametag and scratched it onto the list, then added hair color since he'd forgotten to get her last name. He wrote an eight behind the information. She was good, but she wasn't a ten.

Greyson Hollister, now she was a ten. He tucked his wallet back into his pocket, wiped the stiletto on her service uniform, and pulled off his latex gloves, tucking them in his pocket. With his elbow, he hit a button on the elevator for a floor that he knew would be empty and left via the stairs. Where was Greyson right now? Maybe he'd drive by her house and see if she was home.

Addie shivered in the paper gown. The clock on the wall had to be lying. It couldn't be two a.m. The second hand of the clock seemed to barely be moving. She was used to eking out time at work, but now she just wanted to go home and take a hot shower, wrap herself in her favorite blanket, turn off all the lights, and never get out of bed. The door opened a little, and a petite black woman poked her head around it.

"Can I come in?"

"Dr. Madrigal, we've been waiting for you. If you're ready, we've started the preliminary examination." The nurse snapped on a pair of latex gloves, opened a box, scribbled on the lid and took out a comb and handed it to the doctor.

"Hi, Addie. Do you mind if I call you that?"

Addie shook her head and squeezed her eyes shut, tears seeping out. Her bottom lip quivered. The room was biting cold, and she couldn't stop shivering.

"I need you to sit back and try to relax. This will take some time, and we can't rush it. It's part of the evidence chain in your case, and we want to make sure we don't miss anything."

Addie fought lying back. A gentle push on her shoulder and she relented. Staring up at the pulsing fluorescent lights, she forced herself to ignore the feel of the comb being run through her pubic hair, as the doctor pushed, scratching her pubis. If she had any dignity left, it was gone now. The snap of the clippers pierced the silence as the nurse continued to clip her fingernails, dropping them into a plastic zip bag. Out of the corner of her eye she watched as the nurse wrote something on the bag and placed it in the box.

The nurse pulled out long cotton swabs,

motioning to Addie to open her mouth. Without thinking, she did. The rough cotton swished around inside her cheek and was then placed inside a small plastic vial, which was labeled and put inside the box with her fingernails. With methodical precision, each member of the team moved quietly through their routine. With each click another second ticked off on the ancient clock. How would she ever get that time back?

"Addie, I'm going to have to do a vaginal examination now. If you could just let your knees rest open and try to relax, I'll be as gentle as possible," Dr. Madrigal said, tapping her knees.

"But I told you he didn't rape me. I mean...I don't think...oh God, I don't remember."

"You said you blacked out, that you didn't remember whether he did or not. So let's not take any chances. I'll take a sample with the swab, just in case there's any seminal fluid."

Addie nodded. "Quickly, please."

She just wanted all of this to be over. She tried to lose herself in a memory from her childhood, but nothing would come to mind. *Oh God, I can't tell my mom*, Addie thought as the cold speculum violated her. Another scratch. She winced.

"Sorry." The doctor replied automatically, without conviction.

The rest of the exam played out in slow motion. Her body felt it, her mind relived it, and her heart froze. It was as if someone had amputated it and she could only feel it beating at a distance. That was all. Coolness engulfed her, threading its fingers through her body.

Suddenly, she tried to remember what the man

in the elevator looked like, but he was still a blur. What was preventing her from focusing on his face? But something about him, something about the way he talked to her made her feel like she knew him. Maybe she'd seen him before and not realized it. At the coffee shop? Maybe the bookstore she frequented? Hell, she could have passed him on the street every day, but she wouldn't know him from Adam. Then she remembered something—that smell, that god-awful smell of mothballs. It wouldn't be enough. Wracking her brain, she tried to retrace her steps up to the moment he entered the elevator.

She keyed in the code at the door.
Looked up at the camera.
She was at her desk, grabbing the file.
She coded the door again.
The elevator was waiting for her. Why was it waiting for her?

She closed her eyes, and suddenly a pair of dark, angry eyes met hers. They were his, calculating, cold. She could feel his wrath all over her body.

Trying to push the memory away, she thought of Drake. Where was she? She'd seen her for just a few minutes before she darted out of the room. Oh, that's right. Drake had taken one look at her and bolted for the door. Some girlfriend she was. When Addie needed her most, she bailed.

Addie shivered again, cold air eating at her. Why couldn't they at least give her a blanket? Suddenly, she felt sick to her stomach. Sitting up, she clutched it and covered her mouth. Bile crept up her throat and threatened to be expelled. The nurse was by her side in seconds with a small pan, holding it under her chin.

"Go ahead, sweetie," the nurse said, pulling her hair out of the way so she could puke.

"We're almost done, Addie." The doctor pulled off her gloves, tossed them into the trash, and walked to the head of the examining table. "We'll have to give you some drugs that will keep you from getting pregnant and hopefully treat any possible STDs. I'm truly sorry you had to go through this. Hopefully, they can catch the man who did this. I'm pretty confident we got some of his DNA."

"Did he rape me?"

"We don't see any signs of trauma to the vaginal area. So that's a good sign."

"So where did you find DNA?" Addie struggled to sit up and cover herself.

Dr. Madrigal hesitated. "It looks as if he ejaculated between your posterior cheeks. Also, the blood splatter on your face and the skin under your nails."

Another memory flashed before Addie's eyes—she was on her stomach. She could feel his weight as he rode her. She closed her eyes and gave them a vigorous rub, as if she could wipe the memory away. Spikes of pain assaulted her, yet the memory played again. She remembered the cold plate of the elevator against her face, the feel of a knife sliding along her stockings, ripping them. His warm breath threatening her very existence. He huffed as he spewed all over her backside.

Those moments would be etched into her brain and never fade. She would wear them like the shame of a bad tattoo you never wanted anyone to see. Never shared with anyone, but always there.

Could she go home now?

Greyson noticed a tall, lanky woman wearing a fashionable but conservative business suit walking through the hospital like she owned it. She had a purpose, and it looked like it was Greyson. She held a reporter's pad and pen in one hand, her cell phone raised to her lips with the other. Her mouth moved in a way that looked almost seductive as she talked. Before Greyson could look away, they locked eyes. In one fluid motion the woman clipped her phone to her hip, transferred the notepad to her other hand, and stuck her right hand out toward Greyson.

"Ms. Hollister. How are you?"

Greyson couldn't help but be suspicious of the overly familiar way the woman greeted her. Clearly a reporter had found out what had happened. That meant the hospital would be swarming with reporters and Greyson would be fodder for the society pages, again.

Greyson hesitated. "Do I know you?"

"Detective Nancy Hill. I'm part of the rape task force."

"There's a rape task force?"

"Unfortunately. We've seen an increase in activity lately, and the mayor wants to get a handle on it." She finally dropped her hand when it was clear Greyson didn't intend to shake it.

"What can I do for you, Ms. Hill?"

"Detective…"

"Detective," Greyson said reluctantly. She didn't dislike cops; she just didn't like them at this moment. Neil Harris hadn't arrived yet, and she wouldn't be making any statements about the attack until he arrived. The police department had its leakers, so she wasn't under any illusion that what she said would be kept confidential.

"What can I do for you?" she said again.

"You? Nothing. I'm here to interview the victim. A..." She flipped open her pad and moved her finger down the page. "Addie Blake. She's the victim, right? An employee of yours, if I'm not mistaken." She flipped the pad closed, pushed it in her jacket, then stuffed a hand into a pocket of her slacks. The shiny gold badge on her belt caught Greyson's attention. Without thinking, she looked up to the officer's chest, searching for her gun. The bulge wasn't there.

"Waistband," the detective said.

"Hmm?"

"Looking for my gun, aren't you?"

"What? No, I was just—"

"Checking me out?" Detective Hill smiled.

"What? No."

"It's okay. I get that a lot." She widened her smile.

"God, you *are* arrogant, aren't you?"

"We've met before, but you probably don't remember."

"I doubt it, Detective. I don't usually forget arrogant women."

Detective Hill hooked her thumbs in her waistband and tapped her nails against the gold badge.

"Really? St. Patrick's Day, 2009."

Greyson searched her brain but shook her head. "I've got nothing, Ms. Hill."

"Detective."

"Detective."

The door behind them opened, and a uniformed officer peered out.

"Detective, we're ready for you," she said, then ducked back in.

"Well, duty calls." Detective Hill started to walk away but stopped. "Oh, I've got a forensic team at Integrated Financial. I'd suggest you tell everyone the office is closed tomorrow, so they don't get in the way. And another thing." Detective Hill stopped. A manicured finger brought Greyson's attention to Detective Hill's lips as she tapped them. "It seems your camera system has a problem. You might want to check that out. I'll need to ask you some questions, so I'll be in contact. Have a nice evening, Ms. Hollister."

With that, she disappeared behind the door Greyson was even more desperate to get through.

Nice evening? What the hell?

Greyson grabbed for the door but heard someone calling her. Neil Harris was waving her down.

"Finally," she said, still not able to remember having met Detective Hill.

"Who was that?"

"Detective Nancy Hill."

"You didn't say anything, did you?"

Greyson didn't have to respond after the look she shot him.

"I..." He touched her elbow. "The lobby."

"I want you to find out *who* Detective Nancy Hill is."

"Any reason?"

"She knows me, but I don't know her."

⁂

Detective Hill shivered. The cold environment of the examination room always took her by surprise.

Unfortunately, she'd been here too often lately, and she suspected they were dealing with a serial rapist. No, she knew they were dealing with one. Slowly, she approached the victim. Her battered face almost made her sick. The whites of her eyes were red, blood smeared over her face, hands, and hair.

"Have you taken photos, Sergeant?"

"Getting ready to, ma'am. They just finished with the kit." The officer pointed to the box Dr. Madrigal was scribbling on.

"Hey, Doc."

"Detective. Is that a new suit?"

"Finally, someone calls me detective." Nancy pulled on the lapels of the secondhand Armani she'd picked up. She always nabbed a gem or two while shopping in the upscale Twice as Nice shop. It amazed her how quickly the rich and wasteful dumped this year's fashion just so they could clear their closets for next year's designer duds. "New to me," she whispered.

Dr. Madrigal didn't look up as she pushed the box away and grabbed a chart. Not wanting to interrupt, Nancy returned her attention to the victim. Addie's eyes were closed, tears clearing a path through the blood that covered her face.

"Can we get her a warm washrag?"

"Not yet," Dr. Madrigal said. "I want to take a few more swabs to help make sure we have enough evidence to catch this bastard. She thinks she bloodied his nose."

"Oh, got a shot in? Good for her and for us."

Detective Hill moved toward the victim. "Do you mind if I ask you some questions, Ms. Blake?" She pulled a rolling stool over and sat down by Addie's head.

"I've already answered the other officer's questions."

"I'm sure you have, but I'm taking over the case, and you've had some time now to think about what happened. Maybe we can get something fresh."

"Sure. Why not? It isn't like I have any privacy as it is. I mean, look at me."

"I'm sorry, Ms. Blake. I know this is tough." Nancy felt awkward every time she had to question a rape victim.

"She wasn't raped," Madrigal interjected.

"She wasn't?"

"No."

"What happened?" Nancy asked, looking at Dr. Madrigal.

"You sound almost disappointed, Detective," Addie whispered

"I'm sorry, Ms. Blake. I didn't mean to sound callous. I—"

"I understand you're just doing your job." Addie still hadn't looked at her.

She'd seen the pattern before. The victim could rarely make eye contact with anyone right now because she was scared, ashamed, or embarrassed about what had happened to her. She owned the attack or rape. No matter how hard Nancy tried to tell victims it wasn't their fault, they always blamed themselves.

She stood and strode over to Dr. Madrigal, leaned down, and whispered, "What do you mean she wasn't raped?"

"No seminal fluid in the vagina, no trauma to the vaginal area. Don't confuse what I'm saying, Detective. She was attacked, and she does have seminal fluid on her. His blood—or at least I think it's his blood—is on her clothing, and she looks like she got his skin under her nails. So he left his DNA behind." Dr. Madrigal snapped off another set of gloves, stepped on the trash-can lever, and tossed them and her gown into the trash.

"Can you get those pictures now, Sergeant?" Nancy walked back to the examining table and patted Addie on the shoulder. "I'll be right back. Can I see you outside?" Detective Hill held the door and waited for Dr. Madrigal.

"What's up, Nancy?"

"This has all the earmarks of the elevator rapist, but no rape?"

"She has injuries similar to the other women's, so I wouldn't cross her off the list. She's in bad shape. I know you need to do your job, but go easy on this one. If you hadn't noticed, she's got a high-powered friend over there." Dr. Madrigal nodded at Greyson Hollister as Greyson walked away.

"As if I hadn't noticed." Nancy rolled her eyes and then looked back at Dr. Madrigal. "Something's not right about this one, just doesn't feel right."

"Since when does rape feel right?"

"I don't mean it like that. I just mean…he didn't rape her, but he beat the crap out of her? The cameras are off, and he left behind seminal fluid. Something's wrong with this picture."

The other victims had been beaten, just not this bad. This one was torn up. She absent-mindedly ran a finger around the metal of her badge and tapped her leg with her notepad, then looked around the room.

She caught sight of Hollister again, walking away with a man. Maybe Hollister wasn't telling her something. It was one thing for the cameras to not be working. It wasn't a convenience store, after all. But this was Integrated Financial, and they were in their brand-new glass mausoleum. Each cubicle had a view of the outside world, when most offices were lucky if they had good circulating air. Just her little pass through the downstairs and the elevator had given her pause. No, Integrated Financial had big bucks behind it. Someone had gone to a lot of trouble to avoid being seen. Disabling the camera system, timing it so no one would be at the company to see them. But who had that kind of access?

"Let's be real careful with those results, Dr. Madrigal. I don't want anything screwing up this case." Nancy turned around and looked back at Madrigal. She'd said the wrong thing, and from the look Millicent flashed her it was clear that she'd just insulted the doctor.

She put up her hands in a defensive posture. "I didn't mean anything by that. I'm just saying that we've had way too many rapes, and I want to catch this guy. We give out too many details and could be facing a copycat."

"Good. Glad you're not making a comment about my medical skills, Detective Hill." Madrigal opened the door and slipped back into the examining room.

Nancy waited and searched the room, thinking she might be able to snatch a clue. Maybe the attacker would come to the hospital, right? Seven rapes, seven victims—six identical, and one victim who didn't fit the profile. She just couldn't shake the feeling that something was definitely wrong with this case.

Slapping her notepad against her thigh, she pulled the door open, entered the examining room, and watched as Madrigal wiped the blood from Addie's blank face. God, some days she hated her job.

"Sergeant, are you done?" She couldn't look at Addie anymore. Her heart ached. Maybe she needed to get out of sex crimes. "Dr. Madrigal, are *we* done?" She looked over at Addie. "Is there someone I can call?"

"I...I think that...I mean, my friend Paul's here. I think he can take me home."

"Do you have family I can call to come get you? I mean, I'd feel better if you were with somebody—"

"Paul's my coworker. I was supposed to go to a bar with him, and then...I mean...before this happened and so, I..."

Nancy opened her pad and scribbled her pen across the paper to start it again. The fountain pen had a habit of drying out. Maybe it was time to get rid of it, she thought as she pushed harder on the tip, practically digging through two pieces of paper. "This Paul guy, what's his last name?"

Nancy wasn't shocked by Addie's expression. It was routine to look at the people closest to the victim. She could tell Addie didn't think this guy might be a suspect.

"He didn't do this, if that's what you're thinking. I've known Paul for a long time. Ever since I started working at Integrated Financial, and I can tell you there's no way he would do something like this. Besides, you think I'd recognize him. Right?"

"Well, you're the one who said you didn't get a very good look at him."

"No. I said I didn't recognize him. This guy was much taller. He had a smell to him that reminded me of my grandmother. Paul doesn't remind me of my grandmother. And I hit him. I mean...I mean...my head. My head hit him in the nose...and his voice...his voice was...it wasn't Paul..."

"I'm sure you understand I have to look at everyone."

"Yeah, but I'm telling you it wasn't Paul." Clearly Addie was agitated at the inference.

Nancy closed her pad, jabbed her pen into her shirt pocket, then jerked it back out, remembering she hadn't closed it. The blue line across her chest meant she'd have to buy another shirt. She wasn't even moderately good with laundry, so she'd quit trying to clean the ink stains. Instead, she opted for a laundry service and her usual bulk purchase of button-downs. She clicked the top several times to make sure the fountain pen tip was closed and slipped it inside her jacket this time. At least if it leaked there she wouldn't waste another shirt and no one could tell.

"I understand, Ms. Blake, and the sooner I can talk to Paul, the sooner I can eliminate him as a suspect." Tapping Addie's hand gently she got up, gave Addie a half smile, and started to leave the room.

"It isn't him." Addie started to sob uncontrollably. "I'm telling you, it isn't him. I would know. I was the one that was attacked. Why won't you believe me?"

Nancy sat back down and steadied herself. Most times she could control her emotions, but when a victim had been brutalized this badly, they were usually dead, and Nancy rarely had a conversation with them. Nancy's cell phone went off with the special "impending danger" soundtrack she'd downloaded. She'd thought it was funny at first, but now—it always meant impending danger. Holding up her finger, she said, "Could you give me a minute?"

She moved to a corner in the room and answered the call. "What's up?"

"Detective, we have another rape," a nondescript

voice said.

"Jesus Christ, where?"

"The convention center."

"I'm on my way." She groaned. Two in one night. What the hell? Their rapist was stepping up his game, assuming it was him. Returning to his first victim of the night, she worried for Addie Blake's safety.

"Ms. Blake, where will you be staying? I'll need to ask you more questions when you're up for it."

Addie studied her face and sighed. "My apartment."

"I don't think that's a good idea. From what I understand from the officer on scene, you confirmed that your purse was missing. Is that correct?" Nancy couldn't let Addie return to her apartment alone.

"Oh, shit. Will this night never end? What am I going to do?" Addie said to no one in particular.

Nancy couldn't have agreed more. What was *she* going to do?

Chapter Seven

Greyson chewed the inside of her lip, anxiety starting to eat away at her. She worked hard to put Integrated Financial on the map, and now she could almost feel it sifting through her fingers. Her daddy would be proud of what she'd accomplished, but he'd be pissed as hell if he could see what was happening right now. She tried to take a deep breath, but it felt like someone was sitting on her chest.

She paced the lobby, rolling her Montblanc between her fingers. She'd given up smoking years ago, but the tactile sensation of fingering something had stayed with her. A nervous habit she'd tried to break but couldn't. Once or twice she'd even raised the pen to her lips and accidently bit the end. Maybe she should switch to pencils? They would be easier on her dental work.

Greyson plopped down next to Neil and slapped his knee. "Did I wake you up?" she asked, looking at her watch.

"Sorta." Neil gave Greyson a sheepish look.

They had gone to the ICU waiting room hoping for privacy, but it was packed with despondent families. So Greyson suggested going back to the waiting room closest to the emergency department, just in case she was needed. This room was buzzing with hushed conversations, as they were sitting on one of the only empty couches there.

"So, Grey, what do we know?"

Greyson got up and started pacing again, but Neil pointed to the seat next to him and patted it. It took everything Greyson had to sit down. She was a pacer. At least that's what her mother told her. She paced when she was stressed; she paced when she was thinking; hell, she paced in the middle of the night when she couldn't sleep. It had been a bonus when Benjamin was young. His late-night feedings had kept her up, and she'd liked tending to him. It had given her something to focus on other than the crap in her life.

"Hold on, Neil. I need to call my mom and let her know I'll be late."

"Take your time. I'm here now."

He put his feet on the small coffee table littered with magazines and newspapers.

"Hi, Mom. How's Ben doing? Great. Uh, I've been called to an emergency at the hospital. No, I'm fine, but can you make sure Ben gets his medicine? Yeah. I'll stop in and kiss him good night when I get home. Thanks. You too, Mom."

"Everything okay at home?"

"Everything's fine. At least that part of my life is finally going great."

"How's Camille?"

Greyson took a long, deep breath. "She's doing okay. I think she's missing Dad more than usual lately."

"She's always been a strong woman, but I guess being diagnosed with multiple sclerosis isn't helping."

Rolling her pen between her fingers, Greyson teared up. "No. It threw both of us for a loop. I'm just glad she agreed to move in with Ben and me. I don't think I could handle worrying about her being alone in that big house."

Neil patted her knee and offered a smile. "She'll be fine. Okay, so getting back to the situation at hand. Look. What happened doesn't reflect on you. Integrated has a top-notch security system, ID scanner, cameras, the whole nine yards. We'll find this guy. He's left an image of himself, a fingerprint, something behind. Now let's look at how we get in front of this story." Neil pulled a pad from his case.

"I've called Mackenzie in PR, and she's waiting for your phone call to discuss a press release about all of this. She asked me if you should talk to the media, and from a legal standpoint, as long as you watch what you say, I don't see a problem. We want to present I.F. as a caring company that puts its employees' safety first. We want to emphasize our distress and our willingness to help the police no matter what the cost."

"Neil, we've been battling those merger talks for weeks now. Any chance this could be connected to Global Financial?"

"You mean, do I think they would do something like this to get I.F.? That's pretty risky. Besides, they've been waging the takeover war. Pulling a stunt like this would hurt them too."

"Just trying to think of every potential situation." Greyson wasn't as sure about Global Financial as Neil was. She'd had the unfortunate opportunity to turn down Global's offer and see a side of the CEO she doubted anyone else had. The bastard was a downright pig. He'd hit on her the minute he walked into her office. The asshole had some nerve. "Okay, what's the bad news?"

"A lawsuit."

"I figured as much."

"You said the girlfriend is already rumbling about suing?"

"Yep. I overheard her talking to Paul Winston about how the company should pay."

"Great! Well, we need to try to shut her up."

"How do you propose to do that?"

"You'll think of something. That's what you do. You're a problem solver."

"Thanks," she said, letting a long sigh punctuate what had already been a crappy night.

"Just run anything you decide to do by me first. Okay?"

"Of course."

They sat for the next twenty minutes strategizing before a disruption caught their attention. Drake pushed through the double doors yelling at Paul, who was frantically trying to quiet the raging beast of a woman.

"Wait, Drake. She needs you. You can't leave her like this."

"Have you seen her? Jesus Christ, she's all fucked up."

"Drake." Paul's voice commanded the attention of everyone in the lobby except the person he was directing it at. She'd just pushed through the automatic doors, almost shoving one of them off its slider.

A security guard dashed up to Paul and grabbed his arm. "Sir, I'm going to have to—"

"Shit, I need to take care of this," Greyson said as she ran and stood by Paul's side.

"I'm sure it's just a misunderstanding, Officer…" Greyson looked at his name badge closer. "Grey." The irony wasn't lost on her.

"He needs to be quiet. This is a hospital."

"You're absolutely right. I'll take care of it. Come

along, Paul. Let's get some coffee." Greyson nodded toward the bustling kiosk.

"But—"

"Coffee. We could all use some. Oh, look. Neil from Legal is here."

"Oh, shit. Is Addie getting fired? Am I getting fired?"

"What? No, no one's getting fired. Calm down and tell me what happened back there."

If Greyson was looking for an opportunity to see Addie and talk to her, this might be it.

Paul stirred his coffee, added two creamers and took a long sip, then finally said, "Drake's a bitch."

"Hmm." Greyson nodded in agreement. "Is Addie safe at home?"

"Well, she's all alone now. That fucking bitch kicked her to the curb. Seems she couldn't handle seeing Addie like that."

"What? Who could be so shallow…so…callous?" Greyson was shocked. *Bitch.*

"Now I have to go in there and tell Addie that Drake doesn't want to have to deal with all this." He spread his hands wide, as if he was laying something out before them.

"What about your place?"

"I'd love to have her, but I live in a tiny studio apartment. There's not even enough room for me, and I sleep on a pullout couch."

"I see." Greyson didn't want to seem too accommodating, so she waited a moment before she made her next suggestion. "Why don't you let me handle this? I'll make sure Ms. Blake is safe and has a roof over her head."

"You'd do that? Why?"

"Why? Because her girlfriend has just tossed her away like a piece of trash, and you don't have the space to make her comfortable. Besides, she's an employee, and I feel responsible for what happened."

"I don't know…" Paul squirmed in his seat.

"You can come too, if you think it would help. I know you two are close friends. Maybe she'd feel safer with you there."

"You mean go to your house?"

"Well, if that makes you uncomfortable, I can get you both a room at the Regency."

Greyson had a corporate account at the Regency, one of the most expensive hotels in San Jose. She put up high-value clients there, and it hadn't failed to impress them, yet. She wanted to assure clients that they were in good hands at Integrated Financial, so dropping a dime or two didn't hurt.

"Oh, I don't know. I mean, Addie wouldn't…I mean she's pretty much a simple gal. She might—"

"Well, it's either my house or the Regency. You decide for her."

Paul appeared to be wrestling with the choice. Greyson hated indecisiveness, so she said, "My house it is. She can get a shower and a fresh set of clothes, and no one will bother her. She'll be safe at my place."

"But—"

"Look, from what I understand, her purse was taken. So that means the attacker knows where she lives. It's a done deal. Now go home, pack some of Addie's things, and don't say a word to Drake. It will only inflame an already bad situation. Don't you agree?"

"I just don't know what Addie's going to say about all this."

"I suspect her mind is someplace else." Greyson was interested in damage control at the moment, and if she had to take control, she would. It's what she did.

Turning toward Neil, she looked at him, hoping for feedback.

Neil only shrugged and said, "I hope you know what you're doing."

"Do you have a better idea?"

"Not at the moment."

"Her girlfriend kicked her out and left her here. Who does that?"

"Grey—"

"It'll be fine. Don't worry. She'll stay with me a few days, and then we'll figure out a better place for her."

"Grey," Neil said, still sounding rather dubious.

She put up a finger, stopping him.

"Okay." He returned to his computer.

"Paul, here's my address. I'll make sure she gets home, and you can meet us there."

"Okay." Paul sighed.

Greyson sat back down with Neil, effectively dismissing Paul, and started to go over their game plan for tomorrow. She tried to listen intently as he mapped out what the next few days would look like, but all she could think about was how bad Addie looked. No one deserved what had happened to her, especially not Addie. She'd fix that. She'd take care of Addie no matter the cost. She owed her that much, considering where the attack had happened.

⁂

Nancy pulled at her watch, twisting it around and around. But the time didn't change. It just emphasized the need to get to another crime scene before the evidence was contaminated.

"Dr. Madrigal, can I speak to you?" She gently guided the doctor away from Addie and behind the curtain, as if it would conceal her. "We have another victim," she said, a slight tremble in the low tenor of her voice. Two in one night was unheard of for this guy, but clearly he was stepping up his game.

"Another?"

"Yep, so I need to leave. But I'll be back."

"But what am I going to do with…" Dr. Madrigal pointed toward the curtain.

"I'll contact the girlfriend and she can take her home."

"Jesus, Detective. Two in one night?"

Nancy nodded. She didn't need someone stating the obvious. As part of the task force, her ass was on the line. Now the mayor would be calling the chief, and the chief…well, shit rolled that way, and she was at the bottom of that shit pile.

"You better go. I'll prep the room and get another kit ready."

"Thanks. See you in a couple of hours. Hopefully this victim isn't as bad as her."

"Crazy, isn't it? We're praying that a victim isn't as badly beaten as another."

"Sometimes it's the best we can hope for until we catch the bastard." Nancy twisted her watch again. Time wasn't on her side.

"Unbelievable." Dr. Madrigal smoothed her scrubs. "Let's see if we can catch a break with the DNA."

"Fingers crossed." Nancy held up her hands. Pulling back the curtain, she looked at Addie's vacant expression. God, some days it sucked to be a cop.

"Ready to go home, Ms. Blake?"

Chapter Eight

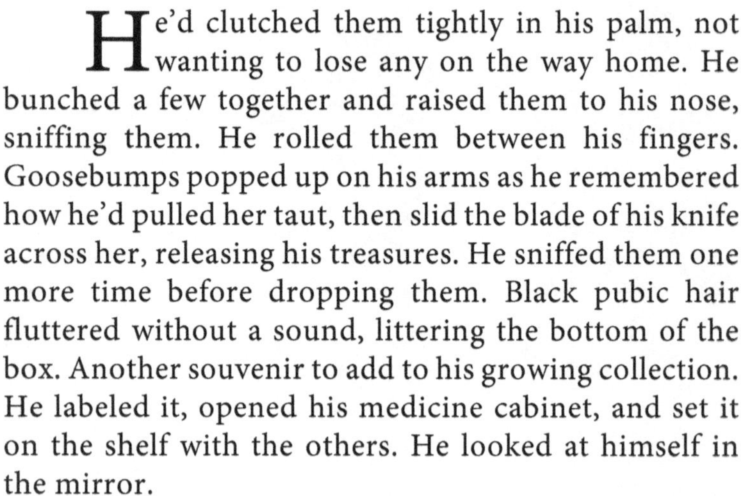

He'd clutched them tightly in his palm, not wanting to lose any on the way home. He bunched a few together and raised them to his nose, sniffing them. He rolled them between his fingers. Goosebumps popped up on his arms as he remembered how he'd pulled her taut, then slid the blade of his knife across her, releasing his treasures. He sniffed them one more time before dropping them. Black pubic hair fluttered without a sound, littering the bottom of the box. Another souvenir to add to his growing collection. He labeled it, opened his medicine cabinet, and set it on the shelf with the others. He looked at himself in the mirror.

Blowing a kiss, he said, "Soon, Greyson, soon."

A reporter and cameraman darted past Greyson as she was talking to Paul. Erin Green was vicious and tenacious when it came to a story. The sanctimonious bitch had never met an issue she didn't like. She'd been run out of her former station after covering the downhill slide of a congressman caught with a prostitute, having forgotten to mention she'd had an affair with said congressman for six years. Walking away after she'd ruined his marriage, she'd dragged his adult kids through the same mud she'd slung all over him.

Getting dirt on someone was a contact sport for Erin Green. She didn't care who got hurt as long as she received the ratings and the accolades. Only this time, she'd managed to offend the right wing. Their reach and love of the congressman had pushed her out of Oklahoma and into liberal San Jose, California. Starting at the bottom again, she'd covered every hard-luck story available, putting enough distance and time between her and her tarnished silver spoon.

She'd dogged Greyson for days about the takeover rumors. A quick phone call to the station manager and tickets to the Sharks game had gotten the bitch off her back, for now. But like a cobra ready to strike, Erin had showed up ready to devour a quick story. Only this time, Greyson was sure Erin wouldn't stop till she had *this* story. It was too juicy to pass on.

Greyson glanced at Neil and nodded toward Erin Green. He packed up his stuff and slid on his jacket, and then they slipped out of the hospital, stopping in front of the emergency-room doors.

Neil pulled Greyson aside. "Want me to play interference?"

"No. You should probably go. She sees chum in the water, and she's going on a feeding frenzy."

"Are you referring to me as chum?" He was clearly trying to joke.

Greyson didn't even look at him. "Go, before she sees you and thinks I have something to worry about."

"Relax and just remember, no comment. Got it?"

"Go," she ordered Neil. "And take Paul with you. I don't want any accidental statements."

Greyson adjusted her jacket and ran her fingers

through her hair. If she was going into battle, she wanted to be as poised as possible. Pulling out her lipstick and mirror, she colored her lips, pursed them once, and tossed everything back into her bag. She was the head of Integrated Financial and ready to scuffle with Erin Green.

Cutting a straight path through the still-crowded lobby, she never lowered her gaze when Erin caught sight of her.

"Ms. Hollister. I'm surprised to see you here tonight. Care to make a comment about the event at Integrated Financial?" Shoving the mic in Greyson's face, Erin kept pace, walking sideways as if she were born to it.

"Ms. Green, it's late. Did you get demoted to the crime beat?"

"I go where there's a story, Ms. Hollister. You didn't answer my question. Are you here about what happened at Integrated tonight?"

"I don't have a comment for you, Ms. Green."

"So someone gets raped at your company, and you don't have a comment for me. Interesting. Good thing a…" Erin flipped her reporter's notebook open, still walking sideways, and fingered a line across it. "A Drake Hogan called us about a rape at Integrated Financial. Seems her girlfriend…" Again she glanced at her notes. "Addie Blake, the victim." Turning toward the camera, Erin Green pulled the mic to her lips and reported, "Ms. Greyson has no comment about a possible rape at Integrated Financial. I'll have more news as soon as I speak to…" she looked at her pad, "Detective Nancy Hill, head of the Elevator-Rapist task force. This is Erin Green reporting for Channel 11 News. Back to you, Hunter."

Greyson whipped around and pinned Erin to the wall. "Stay out of my business, Green, or you'll be covering the water board down in South County."

A grin sliced Erin's face as she turned to her cameraman. "Did you get that, Bob?"

Fortunately for Greyson, Bob had dropped his heavy camera to the floor. Jerking it back up, he cupped the viewer to his eye and shook his head.

"Sorry." He set it back down and walked over to the coffee stand.

"Guess tonight just isn't your night, is it?" Greyson straightened and smiled back at Erin.

"Oh, I wouldn't be so sure, Ms. Hollister. I have an interview tomorrow morning with Drake Hogan. I have a feeling she's going to give me everything I need about this story."

Greyson needed to get Addie out of there as soon as possible. Before she could put her plan in motion, Detective Hill walked out of the room with Dr. Madrigal.

"Detective Hill, I understand the Elevator Rapist has struck again. Care to make a comment?"

Erin shoved the mic at the detective, who twisted away from her. "No comment."

Before any of them could move, the cameraman ran up to Erin and said in a hushed tone, "There's been another rape. We gotta go."

"What? No shit?" A wicked smile creased her face. "I better get out of here. I'll contact your office for a comment, Ms. Hollister."

"Call my lawyer," she said before she whispered, "bitch."

"Addie's ready to go home. Is someone here to take her?" Detective Hill looked around the room.

"I'll be taking Ms. Blake home," Greyson stated matter-of-factly.

"You?"

"Yep. Do you have a problem with that?" Greyson bored a hole through the detective. "Seems her *girlfriend* couldn't handle her condition, so I offered to take her somewhere safe. Can I see her now?"

Greyson could see the wheels twisting in the detective's head. What was she having a problem wrapping her mind around? The girlfriend part or that Greyson would be caring for Addie? It didn't matter. Greyson would finally get a chance to talk to Addie and do the best she could at damage control.

Walking past the detective toward Dr. Madrigal, Greyson asked, "I suspect you've taken her clothes as evidence? Is it possible she could borrow a set of scrubs or something, Millicent?"

"You two know each other?" The detective looked at Dr. Madrigal and then at Greyson.

"Not that it's any of your business, Detective, but we've been friends for a while. Now, if you'll excuse me, I'd like to get Ms. Blake home. I'm sure she'd like a hot shower and a safe, warm bed." Greyson grabbed the door handle but Nancy stopped her.

"Ms. Hollister, she's pretty fragile, and I don't think she can handle twenty questions tonight. Why don't you let the police ask the questions, and you just be a friend tonight?"

"Excuse me, Detective. What are you implying?" Greyson's face heated. Yanking her arm from the detective's grasp, she turned and faced her squarely. "I don't like what you're suggesting. So if you have something on your mind, spill it."

Millicent stepped between them and put her

hands on Greyson's shoulders.

"I'm sure she didn't mean anything by it, Grey. We don't need any drama. Ms. Blake has been through a lot, and this isn't helping. Why don't you go in and talk to her, explain what's going on, and yes, I'll scrounge up an extra set of scrubs."

"I've gotta go anyway," Nancy said, pushing through the door.

"Come on. I'll take you in to see Ms. Blake." Dr. Madrigal said, trying to turn Greyson.

Greyson stared at the detective until she was out of sight. Greyson was the alpha bitch here, and she wasn't about to back down to someone who wasn't even in the kennel.

"Breathe," she whispered, closing her eyes and trying to let go of the negative energy the detective had just piled on her. She had a job to do, and she didn't want anyone or anything getting in her way.

"Ms. Blake, is it all right if I come in? I'm Greyson Hollister, and it looks like you'll be coming home with me."

❧ ❧ ❧ ❧

Addie clutched the paper gown tighter around her. Had she just heard correctly? The head of Integrated Financial, aka the Ice Queen, was standing in front of her offering to take her home. There had to be a mistake.

"Where's Drake?" Addie looked past Ms. Hollister, expecting to see her girlfriend leaning against the doorframe, her trademark smug smile planted firmly across her face.

"Ms. Blake...I...may I sit down?" Ms. Hollister

motioned to the small stool still at the head of the examination table.

Addie hesitated, glanced at the door one more time, and then nodded. She couldn't look at her boss. In fact, she was embarrassed that Ms. Hollister was seeing her like this. She shuddered again and pulled the blanket tighter around her.

"Ms. Blake, I've offered to take you home. I want to make sure you're safe. It's the least I can do, considering what happened tonight."

Out of the corner of her eye, Addie could see Ms. Hollister's hands shake. As if she knew Addie was watching, she shoved them into her pockets and continued.

"I can't tell you how sorry I am that this happened to you. I just…well, I came as soon as I heard." Ms. Hollister's head was bowed and her voice barely above a whisper. Was this an act, or did the Ice Queen really feel bad for her? How was that possible?

Addie wished she could say something that would make Ms. Hollister feel better, but she couldn't. In fact, she didn't know what to feel at this moment. She was numb inside. Her body ached and her mind… well, her mind was overloaded.

"Ms. Hollister—"

"Please call me Greyson."

"I don't think I can do that, Ms. Hollister. I just want to go home. If you can take me there, I would be forever grateful."

"Of course, but I think it would be better if you came home with me since the man who attacked you took your purse."

Christ, was tonight ever going to get better? Addie remembered telling the cop the only thing missing was her purse.

"I have security and an alarm system. Besides, I'm not sure your girl…" Ms. Hollister let the sentence hang out there for a brief moment. "I'd just feel better if I knew you were protected."

Addie wanted to be scared for herself, but how much worse could she feel?

"Here we go. I found some," the doctor said, holding out the pale blue scrubs. "Ms. Blake, if I can do anything else to help, please don't hesitate to call me. Grey has my number."

"Thank you." Addie looked at the pile and then at Ms. Hollister.

"Why don't I let you get changed and we can get going. Thank you, Dr. Madrigal."

Frozen, Addie glanced from woman to woman. She'd been attacked, but she hadn't lost her modesty. After she cleared her throat, Greyson looked at her, and then blushed when she held up the clothes and motioned at the curtain.

"Oh, sorry."

As the curtain was pulled, Addie could hear the women whispering. Actually, it sounded more like hens clucking, and then one said to her, "Do you need help?"

"No, I've dressed on my own for thirty-eight years now. I think I can handle this."

She flinched as she pulled the bottoms up over the bandage on her ass and tied them off. Sitting would prove problematic later, but right now she just wanted some clothes on to hide her cuts and bruises. The V-neck of the oversized scrub top she'd just slipped on practically exposed her breasts. She held it closed with one hand while she grabbed the table with the other.

She tried to stop herself from pitching forward and gasped as the room started to fade.

"Ms. Blake," someone said, scooping her up just before she crashed to the floor.

"Let's get her back on the table," Dr. Madrigal said, lifting her feet.

"I'm fine. Just a little light-headed, that's all," Addie said, pushing away the hand shining a light in her eyes. "I'm fine, really."

"Let Dr. Madrigal make sure, Ms. Blake." Ms. Hollister's low tenor surprised her. If it had been a different time, Addie might have thought it seductive. God, her life sucked.

"She looks okay. We might want to run some tests, a CAT scan maybe."

"No, no, I just want to go home, please." Addie pushed off the table and swung her legs around, slipped them into the slippers, and stabilized herself before she tumbled over again. She didn't want her boss to have to save her again. Once was embarrassing enough.

"Take a minute and get your legs under you. You've had a pretty traumatic experience, Ms. Blake," Dr. Madrigal said, steadying her.

"Thank you, I'll be fine. I'd really like to leave now, if you don't mind," she said, looking at Greyson.

"Of course. Let's find you a wheelchair and get you out of here."

"I can walk."

"Hospital policy," Dr. Madrigal said, grabbing one from the corner of the room.

"I want you to come back if your headache gets worse, you black out, or something doesn't feel right."

Addie gave her a blank stare. "Nothing feels right, Dr. Madrigal. So how would I know what to look for?"

"I know and I'm sorry, but I think you have an idea of what I'm talking about. I'll send some instructions home with Greyson. Things to watch for, instructions for wound treatment, and a date with a follow-up visit. I want you to come see me at my office in a few days so I can check those stitches."

Addie studied her boss talking to the doctor. She didn't even know her boss, only by sight, and now Ms. Hollister was her benefactor? How had her world spiraled off its axis and begun to spin in such a foreign orbit?

Chapter Nine

*H*e hovered above her, his face so close she could smell garlic. She tried to pull her arms from his grasp, but he held her down. He laughed, taunting her as she struggled to free herself. She screamed and yet nothing came out. His huge meaty hand covered her nose and mouth, smothering her.

Bolting upright, gasping for breath, Addie looked around the room. She'd been dreaming, her legs tangled in the blanket. Kicking at the massive lump, she pushed the phantom attacker to the floor. She scooted up, her back pressing into the wall as she hugged her legs. She rocked back and forth, frantic. She couldn't turn her brain off. Images crowded it, fighting for dominance. His face, the knife, her face, the blood, Drake's face. Then there was Ms. Hollister standing behind everyone reaching out to her in the emergency room, offering to take care of her. Why? Guilt?

Looking around the dark room, Addie tried to distinguish anything familiar, but nothing was recognizable. Then she remembered she was at Greyson Hollister's house. Moonlight trickled in through the light-colored sheers. Looking through them, she could see light reflecting from a pool. Trees lit up with accent lights. A swing set? Ms. Hollister had kids? Something didn't square with that thought. She couldn't see her boss with little rug rats running around. She seemed more like the cocktail-party set, first-class travel, and pressed Armani suits.

Addie ran her tongue over her lips and flinched. They hurt. Spying a glass and a pitcher on the nightstand, she suddenly realized she was dying of thirst. She couldn't remember the last time she'd eaten, let alone had something to drink. The sip in the elevator didn't count, considering it tasted more like blood than something to quench her thirst. Her stomach rolled. Hunger pangs made it cramp. Could she handle food? It was a nonissue at the moment. Her hand shook as she tipped the heavy crystal pitcher. Grabbing it with both hands to stabilize it, she filled the glass, then stood and walked around the room, sipping gingerly.

A comfortable chair was surrounded by books. Lots of books, one of them open and facedown on the side table. It looked inviting, as if it was waiting for its reader to return and pick up where they left off. Addie sat in the chair and sank into its worn leather. It wrapped itself around her. Leaning back, she studied the rest of the room. It was almost bigger than her whole apartment. She ran her toes through the plush, thick carpet, its softness caressing her soles. Pulling her legs up under her, she cradled the glass of water in her hands and closed her eyes.

She didn't hear the ding of an elevator in constant use, feet plodding up and down the hall, and doors slamming when their owner came home from a hard day's work. She'd often heard echoes of various accents throughout her building as moms yelled at their kids, couples fought, and people talked on their cell phones as if no one could hear them. She'd grown used to the noise, and it comforted her in the way she always felt someone was around. Her working-class roots were showing, and she knew she could move anytime she wanted, but why? She was comfortable in the working-class world. So being at Greyson Hollister's house now was almost too peaceful.

Addie picked up the book and studied the cover. A woman in a semi-bare state of dress graced it. Flipping it over, she noticed the dog-ear at the top of the page. She read a few lines and gave a half smile. The page was dog-eared for a reason: the sex practically leapt off it. Without notice, her stomached clenched and another hunger pang echoed in the vast emptiness. When had she eaten last? Lunch had been rushed as she shoved down a quick yogurt on her way to a client meeting, right? Or was that yesterday? God, she couldn't remember the last time she'd sat down for lunch. Everything in her life was rushed.

Looking back now, she realized she'd barely paid attention to things in her life. It was a merry-go-round that she never seemed to get off, and now, here she sat—a battered, bruised mess that couldn't remember what had happened before 10:59, when her life had changed. Another hunger pang shook her. Looking around, she hoped that something had been left for her. Venturing out of the room on her own didn't sound appealing. Unfortunately, the pitcher of water with a glass was the only thing available in the room to help her. She cocked an eyebrow, glanced at the open book, and wondered how paper tasted. She really was starving and had no other choice but to venture out.

Quietly, she pulled on the door, peeked around it, and waited for something to stir. Nothing moved; the darkness kept everything concealed. She tiptoed down the hallway, the plush carpet not giving away her presence. She had to take the stairs one at a time because her hips ached with each step. Holding the rail for support, she gingerly made her way to the entryway that opened into the house on one side and a set of doors to her left. As she ventured to the right, her view was obscured, but her curiosity piqued. Feeling around on the wall, she touched a light switch that illuminated the room. Its dark mahogany woodwork gave it a masculine feel. Surprising, she thought, considering it belonged to Ms. Hollister, a woman. She knew nothing about her boss, but she'd heard enough rumors. Ice princess, stone bitch, all seemed to conjure up images of someone who kept her life in obsessive-compulsive order, ruling with dictatorial fervor.

Her sore hand followed the curves of a soft, leather wingback chair. Huge landscapes of country settings hung on the walls. More bookshelves were stuffed to almost overflowing. Addie recognized the expensive items that filled the shelves and knew she could never afford things like these. Drake would never approve of such decadence. Drake, more often than not, complained of the excesses of the rich yet seemed more than a little jealous. Drake would be lucky to buy a house at the rate she was progressing. A mechanic's pay didn't leave much for nicer things, and Addie had provided the luxuries in their life—the travel, the clothes, nice restaurants, and their apartment.

Another hunger pang almost made her double over. Food. She'd been on a mission. Looking across to the double doors, she suspected they could lead to only one place, the kitchen. Thoughts of Drake would hold until she ate. Then she would call her and find out why she was at Ms. Hollister's house and not home with her.

Addie pushed through the doors and past a dining room, then through another door. She'd found what she was searching for, the kitchen. She looked around, shocked to see lower counters, a sink and stove on one side of the huge culinary exhibition. It looked like an industrial-type kitchen you'd see in an expensive home magazine, with the latest stainless-steel appliances, hanging pots and pans, and knives attached to a long length of metal. She instantly coveted the vast expanse, having spotted the huge double-door fridge in the corner. It had to be the size of a small liquor store.

However, Addie was still confused over the lower counters. Who could possibly work at that height? Maybe it was designed with kids in mind. Did Ms. Hollister hire child labor? Surely not. Though she'd heard a lot of stuff about Ms. Hollister, this would be the most ridiculous rumor of all.

The granite counters lacked *stuff* cluttering them. Searching around, she couldn't see a coffeemaker or teapot; everything was pristine. At her own place, she was always complaining that there was never enough room for all of Drake's stuff. Drake was a pack rat, with tools in the bathroom, tools in the closet, tools and car parts everywhere. Shoot, she couldn't walk in the apartment without bumping into an errant tool or a socket on the floor. What did Drake keep in her own apartment? She'd only been there a couple of times early in the relationship and couldn't remember what it looked like except for an engine sitting on the kitchen table. Oh, and the puzzling motor-oil stain on the floor. That alone had made Addie thankful she didn't live there.

She ran her hand along the long countertop,

tracing the vein of gray bisecting the black and white granite. The sterile feel of the room made her wonder if it was one of those kitchens the rich had to show, but no one really ever used. She imagined women and men in cocktail attire, swinging glasses of wine around as they made some wild gesture when they talked about the lower class. Hors d'oeuvres served by people in black tuxes with white gloves, bottles of alcohol scattered around the island as men poured whiskey, brandy, or some such masculine drink. Women snagging endive filled with goat cheese and fig compote drizzled with some fancy flavored balsamic vinegar, which would be the appetizer.

"Hello?"

Addie jumped, then ducked behind the island. Peeking around it, a woman in a wheelchair smiled back at her.

"Oh, my…Are you okay?" the woman dressed in a robe said, rolling only a few inches closer. Her hair was grayer, her smile lined, and her eyes crinkled, but she looked just like an older version of Greyson Hollister.

"Um, I'm sorry. I shouldn't have come down, but I was thirsty," Addie said, straightening up.

"Are you a prisoner up there?" The older woman shifted her wheelchair around her and pulled out a drawer, lifting a coffeemaker to the lower counters. Everything in the kitchen made sense now. This kitchen, or at least half of it, was designed for this woman. "Are you the new nanny?" she asked.

Addie couldn't hide her shock and was more than a little surprised by the question. Clearly, the woman had an advanced state of vision impairment, or perhaps she was senile.

"Um…"

"Probably not, huh? I mean, I couldn't help but notice you're…well, I mean you look like you've been in a fight." She moved to the sink and filled the carafe with water. "My name is Camille. Perhaps I should know yours before I call the police," she said, calmly pouring the water into the coffeemaker. "I don't know how you got in here, but I can assure you it was a huge mistake. My daughter Greyson Jane is very well-connected."

The older woman's matter-of-fact expression was almost comical. Clearly, nothing could shake her. Either that or she was the best bullshitter alive.

"I'm actually not quite sure why I'm here," Addie whispered, afraid to move.

"Really?" The woman rested her hands in her lap for a brief moment before she pulled a small walkie-talkie out of her pocket.

"Greyson, are you awake?"

"I am now," a scratchy voice piped through the speaker. "What's up, Mom? You need help out of bed?"

"No, but there's a homeless person in the kitchen. I think you need to call the police."

Was this night going to get any better? Addie wondered.

"A homeless person, Mom? Oh, God."

Within seconds Addie could hear footsteps padding down the stairs.

"Mom? Ms. Blake?" Ms. Hollister pushed through the door and stopped.

Addie shifted uncomfortably as Ms. Hollister looked from her to the woman who called herself Camille and back to her. Stepping toward her, Ms. Hollister asked, "How are you feeling? Do you need some ice for the swelling? Are you hungry? What can I get you?" She stepped to the fridge and started pulling out random items and depositing them on the island. A carton of eggs, cheese, a package of assorted meats, condiments, and stuff Addie didn't recognize.

"Mom, this is Ms. Blake. She works at Integrated Financial." Ms. Hollister motioned in Addie's direction.

"I see…" The older woman sheepishly looked at Addie, putting her hand to the side of her mouth, and whispered, "What happened to the poor girl, honey?"

Ms. Hollister looked at Addie and gazed down at the floor. She stumbled with her words, babbling something incoherent.

"What, dear? You're mumbling. Speak up."

"She was attacked at the office," Ms. Hollister said. She straightened up and grabbed the eggs without looking at Addie. "You must be hungry."

"She should be at the hospital. Poor dear," Ms. Hollister's mother said. And then she repeated herself in a louder tone. "You should be in the hospital, dear. You look dreadful."

"Mom, she's not…she's already been to the hospital."

"Well, did you call her husband? I'm sure he must be frantic."

Addie didn't like being talked about as if she wasn't in the room, but she didn't have any fight left in her for it to matter.

"I'm not married…" Addie was so uncomfortable, she just wanted to go home and pull the covers over her head, retreating from her fucked-up life. "She's right, I should be going," Addie said to no one in particular, pushing through the swinging door. She had to leave.

"Geez, Mom," Greyson hissed.

"What?"

"Ms. Blake…" Greyson wasn't sure if it was her place to explain what had happened to Addie, but her mother would continue asking questions until one of them finally broke.

"She was attacked in the elevator at Integrated Financial."

"Oh, my." Camille shuddered and covered her mouth with her hand. "Poor dear."

"Yes, and to top it all off, her girlfriend basically walked out and left her at the hospital."

"Girlfriend?"

"Yes, Mom." Greyson leaned back against the counter and gave her mom a disapproving look. "Don't even…" She wagged her finger at her mom.

"What?"

"You know what!" Greyson pushed off the counter and grabbed the door. "Can you make something for our guest to eat? I'm not sure when she ate last, and the doctor gave her some strong painkillers, so I think some food is in order."

"Of course. Eggs okay?"

"Sounds good. I'm going to check on Ms. Blake and try and talk her out of leaving."

"Please tell her how sorry I am. I didn't know, honey."

Greyson bent and kissed her mom on the cheek. "I know, Mom. I'm sure it's fine."

Addie sat on the edge of the bed. *Drake left me at the hospital?* Her heart sank. She knew things hadn't been great between them for a long time, but when she needed Drake most, she'd walked out on her. Who did that? A soft knock on the door pulled her from her thoughts.

"Ms. Blake?" Ms. Hollister whispered through the door. "May I come in?"

Addie jumped from the bed and walked over to the window. For some reason she wanted to put as much distance between her host and herself as she could. It had taken all Addie's strength to be able to stand in the same room as her earlier, though being in the kitchen with her mother was easy. Another soft knock at the door, and she heard Ms. Hollister request to come in again. Her hand shook, and a cold sweat crossed her body as she remembered why she was staying at this house. She tried to swallow, but every muscle in her throat ached as if hands were still constricting her, choking her.

"Are you okay?"

Addie looked at the small bag of clothes Paul had retrieved from her apartment. The only thing she'd taken out was a pair of sweats so she could change. Her scrubs from earlier, and what the police hadn't taken as evidence, lay in a pile at the far end of the room. She wanted to burn the mess, to exorcise the evil that had embedded itself in them. Blood, body fluids, and cologne all mixed together to create the disgusting smell she would never forget.

"Ms. Blake? Are you in there? May I come in?"

"Of course."

Addie stood at the window hiding in the shadow cast by a huge tree outside. Ms. Hollister stuck her head around the door and peered inside before entering. Addie could barely see her as the moonlight threaded through the branches, casting an airy glow and spearing through the room.

"Are you okay? I want to apologize for my mom. She didn't mean anything by what she said." Ms. Hollister kept her hands behind her.

"It's okay. I guess I should get used to it. She won't be the only one who…well…says something about the way I look." Addie was grateful for the darkness that concealed her disgusting appearance right now. She suddenly remembered Ms. Hollister's thoughtfulness earlier.

A hot bath was waiting for her before she could even ask for a shower. All she wanted was to scour the memory off her body and out of her mind. The water wasn't hot enough, so she drained some out and refilled the tub with some that was scalding hot. She couldn't stand to have any remnants of him left on her, anywhere. She let out short grunts as she lowered herself into the bath. Pulling her knees to her chest, her hands balled into fists, she wrapped her arms around her legs, lowered her forehead on her knees, and cried so uncontrollably that she could barely breathe. She instantly regretted the deep breath that expanded her bruised chest. Her neck was so swollen she could barely move her head or swallow. She'd sat in the bath as long as she could stand it.

When she finally slipped out, she started to wrap a towel around her body but stopped when she noticed the maze of scratches and bruises littering her body. Pulling her foot out of the pinkish-red water, she noticed even the tops of her feet were swollen and bluish-purple. In the tub, her blood swirled with the white soap bubbles. She cried again as she wrapped the towel under her armpits and tucked the end in between her breasts.

How had this happened?

Wiping at the steam on the mirror, she gasped at her reflection. Whoever that was revolted her. Her eyes were almost completely closed, her nose twice its size, and her lips split open. Every inch of her face was swollen and battered.

That was the person Ms. Hollister's mom had seen, a monster. No wonder Drake had left her. She was hideous.

"Ms. Blake? I hope I'm not out of line here, but I know you heard me tell my mother that your girlfriend walked out on you at the hospital. I'm sorry for that." Ms. Hollister took a step closer but still kept some distance between her and Addie.

"Why? It isn't your fault that my girlfriend's an ass. I should have known she couldn't handle this." Addie waved her hand down her body and back up to her face. "I mean, could you?"

"I hate to state the obvious, but I…I mean…"

"I know what you're trying to say, Ms. Hollister. But why did you bring me here? You don't know me from Adam."

"Adam." Ms. Hollister lifted a finger to her lips. "Does he work down in accounting? That scrawny little kid who's always making a mistake on my paycheck?"

Addie shook her head. Any other time she would have laughed at the halfhearted attempt at humor, but she didn't know Ms. Hollister, and yet here she was standing in a room in her house. She looked down at a swing set in the backyard, wondering, once again, why the head of Integrated Financial had taken it upon herself to be her benefactor.

"You know what I'm asking. Why am I here?"

Ms. Hollister entered the room farther and pointed to the bed. "Have a seat, Ms. Blake."

Without thinking, Addie sat on the edge of the bed. Though she rested her hands on her knees, little tremors kept them moving beyond Addie's control. She bounced a knee nervously as Ms. Hollister took the huge wingback chair across from her, flicked on the light, stroked the broken spine of the book on the end table, and then turned her attention to Addie.

Ms. Hollister owned the room with merely the slightest motion of sitting up straight and looking right at her. The woman who had just cracked a joke about a paycheck mistake had disappeared, replaced by one with a face void of any emotion, and Addie suddenly worried that she was going to be fired. But why did that concern her? After the night she'd had, being fired was a minus one on the scale of issues.

"Ms. Blake, I was worried about you when I heard about what happened at work tonight. I was worried for *you*." Ms. Hollister glanced down at something under her manicured fingernail, picked at it, and then looked back at her. Compassion had replaced the stoic expression. "Of course I was also concerned about Integrated Financial, but when I walked into the hallway and heard the way your girlfriend was talking to Paul…well, let's just say I was more worried about you at that point." Ms. Hollister crossed her legs and relaxed back into the chair. "I don't usually involve myself in the private lives of my employees, Ms. Blake, but may I ask you a personal question?"

"No, Ms. Hollister, you may not. I hope you'll

forgive me, but I don't think I could take another personal question tonight. I appreciate your hospitality, but I should probably go home. I wouldn't want to intrude further." Addie gripped her duffle and pulled it to her lap, hugging it tightly. She wanted to run. She felt like she needed to stay moving, because if she stopped, she would think about what had happened tonight. Sleeping wasn't an option either. Her dreams would be nightmares, and she wouldn't find relief in sleep, not right now.

"You're not imposing. Besides, you're not going back to your apartment alone. Trust me, you're much safer here and…" Ms. Hollister looked down at her hands, which she was rubbing together. "Well, you'll just be safer here. If you want to leave in the morning…" She shrugged. "You're not a prisoner here. I'll be happy to drop you off personally."

"I don't want to be a bother. I'm sure I can call Paul and he'll come and get me."

Ms. Hollister stood. "As you wish." Sniffing the air, she commented again. "I think I smell cinnamon rolls. Care to join me and my mother?" Before Addie could say anything, Ms. Hollister was motioning to the open door and had stuck her hand out to help Addie up. "It's my mother's way of apologizing. She only breaks out the cinnamon rolls when she's sorry for something."

"Me?"

"Yep. I think she feels bad for assuming you were homeless or something. Come on. Then you can crawl into bed and try to get some sleep."

Addie could smell fresh coffee; she didn't drink coffee, but for some reason the aroma made her think of her childhood and her own mother. God, how was she going to tell her parents what had happened? Without another thought, she knew she wouldn't, she couldn't. She would keep it to herself and save them the torture of not being able to help. It had already started, the altering of her life, the way she viewed herself, the world around her, and her future choices. Her life had been forever altered at 10:59 p.m.

Chapter Ten

S hall we start again? Ms. Blake, this is my mother, Camille Hollister. Mom, this is Ms. Blake." Ms. Hollister pulled a chair out for Addie and then made her way around her mother's wheelchair and poured some coffee for everyone. "Decaf, Mom?"

"Of course, sweetheart. It's late, and I suspect we'll all be up early. Ben will be up at the crack of dawn, asking to go swimming like always." Camille smiled at Addie and then patted her hand, which was resting on the table. "I'm so sorry, dear. I'm an old woman who doesn't know her place sometimes."

Addie looked at Mrs. Hollister's hand and jerked hers back. Sitting side by side, Addie could study the two women. The older one looked just like her daughter, only…softer.

"You don't have to apologize, Mrs. Hollister. You had no idea." It was all Addie could say as she choked up.

"Please call me Camille. Mrs. Hollister always sounds so fussy and formal."

"You're very kind." Addie couldn't look at Camille. She'd remembered what Camille had said earlier and just couldn't shake it. Maybe she should have stayed overnight at the hospital. What had the doctor said, severe concussion, with broken or separated ribs, all requiring bed rest?

"There, there, take a sip of coffee. Perhaps something warm will help." Camille patted Addie's hand again, then asked, "Cream?"

Addie nodded and focused on the cup shaking in her hand.

Camille placed her hand on Addie's. "Please, say when." She poured until the brown had turned to beige. "Aw, you like it like Greyson. More milk than coffee. Greyson has always drunk coffee. When she was about eight, she and her father would sit at this very table every morning, reading the paper and drinking *coffee*."

"Mom, I'm sure Ms. Blake doesn't want to hear about me and Daddy."

"It's fine, Ms. Hollister." Addie rubbed the cup between her palms and offered a thin smile.

"Please call me Greyson."

"Ms. Hollister, I—"

"Greyson. I insist."

"Cinnamon roll anyone?" Camille said before Addie could respond.

⁂

"Well, I should go back to bed," Camille said, pulling on her wheelchair and turning it deftly in a small space. "I'll leave you ladies to the dishes. Good night."

"Morning, Mom." Ms. Hollister pushed open the door and let her pass. Camille tossed a wave and left them to themselves.

"I should probably get to bed too. I can't thank you enough for opening your home to someone you don't know," Addie said, putting her half-full cup in the sink.

"How about a drink?" her boss asked. Clearly she wasn't quite ready to say good night, but Addie wasn't sure she could handle much more talking. Her jaw ached, her mouth was sore, and her headache was starting to edge its way back.

"Oh, I don't know. I'm having a hard time sleeping, so a drink might—"

"Help you sleep? You've had a rough night, and I know you can't sleep. I heard you crying earlier."

Addie flushed. She hadn't realized someone might hear her.

"I'm sorry. I didn't mean to keep you up. I just—"

"Don't apologize." Ms. Hollister reached for Addie's hands and kept them from shaking more. "Besides, I might have been walking around the house, checking the locks, stuff like that. I'm having a bit of a hard time sleeping myself. So why don't you join me for a drink, and then we'll put you to bed."

"A short one."

Ms. Hollister squeezed her fingers together and then spread them open a little. "Small drink. Come on. I keep the good stuff in the library."

Addie let herself be led to a room to the left of the entryway. Looking around, she could only imagine what the place looked like in the light of day. A light flicked on, casting a golden light around the room, and Ms. Hollister smiled, spreading her hands wide.

"The library."

"Wow."

The warm glow cast an eerie shadow down to the end of the room, where a leather wingback sat, a solitary sentinel in a room full of stories. It resembled the room she'd been in earlier, only this room was homey. Addie was reminded of those shows of the rich and famous with their opulent rooms that always looked as if no one lived in them. A stained-glass lamp hung over the shoulder of the wingback, whose companion was in Addie's room, Obviously, Ms. Hollister had an affinity for leather furniture. Matching sofas covered with fleece throws lined the wall across from the stacks, and a few toys littered the floor. The dichotomy of the rooms wasn't lost on Addie. Smiling, she ran her hand over the edge of the chair, which still had the pungent smell of leather she loved.

"Here, sit," Ms. Hollister said, urging a glass in her direction.

"Oh, a…I couldn't. I mean, I don't really drink, so…it might…" Addie muttered, pulling her hand back from the chair as she caught sight of Ms. Hollister watching her caress the wingback.

"Oh, well, I probably have something else that would help you sleep if you like?"

"No, no, that's okay." Her nightmares kept her on edge, and she'd rather forget than relive the attack.

"We'll catch him, Addie. I promise." Ms. Hollister walked to the decanters lined up perfectly on the shallow bar and poured two fingers of something into one glass and then into another. Ms. Hollister offered it again with a smile. "It's just a touch of Scotch. It'll help with your…nightmares."

"I'm not sure anything would help." Addie absently took the glass.

Ms. Hollister sat down, pulled her robe over her exposed legs, and curled up on the sofa. "I didn't know if I should wake you or—"

"I noticed you have a lot of books," Addie said. The last thing she wanted to do was talk about what had happened earlier. A clock somewhere in the house struck three a.m., signaling that the night was barely half over.

"I love books."

"So I see. Any particular kind, or are you just a collector?"

"I have bookcases scattered throughout the house. In fact, the room you're in is my 'private' library." Ms. Hollister made air quotes as she took a sip from her glass.

"I noticed that you had a book open on the side table. A few dog-eared pages." Addie turned and looked at the tall library shelves that reached all the way to the ceiling. A good twelve feet high and bursting at the seams. Impressed, she rested her hand on the ladder and gave it a soft pull. It creaked just like the ones in the library downtown. "So what's your favorite type of book to read, late at night?" Addie turned and slipped her arm through the rung and rested against the ladder.

Addie couldn't help but notice Ms. Hollister's face flush a bit and how she lifted her glass to hide it. Ms. Hollister was dodging the question, if the blush was any indication. She wouldn't push, but it was better to have the conversation pointed at Ms. Hollister than at her right now.

"I don't see any books on business in here." Running a finger along one of the leather spines, she spied one she'd always wanted to read but never had time. She slipped her finger to the top of the spine, tipped it back, hesitated, and pushed it back into its place. It wasn't her house, and she knew better than to poke around in someone else's stuff.

"I do. I have Sun Tzu's *Art of War* somewhere up there." Ms. Hollister's laugh was soft and warm.

"I didn't know *Art of War* was a business manual."

"Clearly you haven't been in the boardroom." Ms. Hollister sipped her drink.

Addie swirled the liquid in her glass, studying the amber liquid.

"No, I'm afraid I haven't spent any time in a boardroom. That's not my forte." Addie swallowed, the slow burn warming her all the way to the center of her chest. Though she didn't drink hard liquor, she suspected that after tonight a lot would change. Taking another sip, she swirled the liquid, then let out a soft moan.

"You okay?" Ms. Hollister asked.

"A cut in my mouth burns a little."

Ms. Hollister patted the sofa and smiled. "Sit." When Addie finally did, she said, "So tell me about yourself."

Chapter Eleven

*E*very muscle in Greyson's back cramped from humping over the desk all night. She'd spent the day staring at a computer screen, running the numbers on a stock acquisition that had tanked the moment it went public. Thanks to all the media hype, the tech company had not only underperformed, but its initial public offering was below the predicted price and had dropped even more by the close of business. She wished the little bastards running the tech company had just kept their ideas to themselves, but they'd leaked their intent to sell stocks, and the vultures of finance had swooped in and picked the bones clean before anyone else could buy. Now they were pissed at the twenty-dollar drop from their initial investment. So it was with the stock market: Don't gamble money you can't afford to lose.

She flicked the switch on the fluorescent desk lamp, stood, and looked around, noticing she was once again the only one left. Hell, even the cleaning crew was gone at this hour. It was a Friday night, for God's sake. The late nights were bad enough, but now she had to get on the last train of the night. If Greyson was lucky it would be on time and the platform would be empty, but at this hour there was no telling who—or what—would be on that platform. Standing at the wall of windows, Greyson looked down at the street below. The yellow *lights on top of the taxis crawled along the still-crowded street. Only a few people were darting in and out of the traffic to a bar across the street. It was Friday night, for Christ's sake. Greyson reached down and pushed her sleeve back and looked at the time. "Well, it's Friday for another twenty minutes," she noted aloud, grabbing the accoutrements of her work life. She shrugged into her Armani coat, slipped her gloves on, and stuffed a few more files into her briefcase for review over the weekend.*

Greyson stopped and had a few words with the guy at the security desk, who'd been shoving a slice of pizza in his mouth when she walked up. She waved him off, and it wasn't long before she hit the train platform. Standing under the glow of the light, she waited restlessly for her train, the last one of the night. The cold, foggy breeze blew tight little tornados on the platform, kicking up papers and discarded candy wrappers and pushing her brown hair in her face. Shoving it out of her eyes, she thought she saw someone at the other end of the platform, but looking closer she decided it was only a finger of fog wrapping around one of those round billboards.

It wasn't long before she heard the groan and squeal of the oncoming train, its brakes piercing the air as it tried to stop in front of her. She paused in front of the door as it rattled apart, welcoming her inside. Greyson squinted against the bright fluorescents. Looking around and seeing that the car was empty, she stared back at the billboard where she thought she saw someone, but no one came. She slipped onto the bench seat diagonal from the door. She'd see anyone who came in and was close enough that if she needed to make a quick exit, she could. Greyson had a forty-minute commute to the station, where she'd pick up her car and drive another twenty minutes home. Hopefully, there wouldn't be any other stops and she could be there in thirty minutes.

Greyson pulled her briefcase close and started to relax into the sway of the train. Her eyelids had closed for the briefest of seconds when she felt someone lay their head on her shoulder. Groggily, she opened her eyes to see Cate sitting next to her.

"Hey, stranger," Cate whispered. "I'm surprised to see you out this late."

Greyson jerked awake and looked at her. Taking in all of Cate, Greyson had to admit she looked amazing. Her green eyes sparkled in the fluorescent lighting, and her smile was as captivating as usual. Time had been good to her.

"I must have nodded off." Greyson cleared the sleep from her voice. "I didn't even feel the train stop."

"Same ol' Greyson. You work way too much. You know that." Cate slipped her arm through Greyson's and pulled her closer. "Do you remember the last time you and I rode the train this late? We'd stayed in the city too long and had to run for the last train of the night. We almost got stuck in the city."

"Hmm." Greyson smiled. "I remember."

How could Greyson forget the last time they'd been on the train? Cate had ditched her clothes in the office and wore only a trench coat and lace panties and bra. The fact that Greyson was a partner at Integrated Financial meant she had to keep up appearances, but Cate didn't care. Cate was like a panther—sleek, sexy, and made for speed. When she walked, it was like she was stalking her prey, the long flowing stride of a predator, and when she caught sight of her prey, she pounced. Greyson smiled to herself again. Cate had the most gorgeous body, and that night she wore a peek-a-boo bra and panties without a center. She was crazy like that, which was one of the things that drew Greyson to her.

"What's the matter, Grey? Cat got your tongue?" Cate whispered in Greyson's ear, sending a chill through her body. God, she was good, and Greyson had to admit she wanted her right now.

Cate's hand slid under Greyson's jacket and slipped between Greyson's legs.

"Oh, you're wearing those silk boxers I bought you for Christmas. Nice," she cooed. Greyson let her legs part before she could stop herself, her body reacting before her brain kicked in, which often led to interesting situations with Cate. "Let's see if we can get that kitty purring." Her hands rubbed against the seam directly on top of Greyson's clit. The silk boxers made it easier for Cate's finger to glide the material over her, arousing her even more. She flicked her tongue across the hammering pulse in Greyson's neck, trailing her tongue up and then gently biting her ear.

"Cate, we can't." Greyson looked around the train. Empty.

"It's just you and me, Grey." Cate threw her leg over Greyson's and straddled her lap. Cate's coat opened just enough that, when she pulled Greyson's briefcase from between them, Greyson could see black lace hiding underneath. This was how Cate played the game. She liked to tempt fate and always had.

"No one's here, and according to my calculations, no one got on at the last stop so we have about fifteen minutes before we reach the train station." Cate pulled Greyson's hand to her lips and poked Greyson's finger in her mouth and began to suck on it. A tingle shot right to Greyson's pussy. Squeezing her legs tight, Greyson tried to fight the urge to toss Cate down and fuck her. "You

know you want this, Grey. Open your eyes and watch me."

Cate's tongue flicked against the tip of Greyson's finger, each stroke burying Greyson deeper into the moment.

"Greyson, open your eyes," the gentle command came again, but this time Greyson felt Cate's tongue flick against her lips. "Open."

Greyson looked into riveting green pools just as Cate lowered her head and captured her lips. Her mind was swimming; she couldn't pull herself away from the intoxicating feeling that was Cate. She felt so good in Cate's arms. She craved her touch, her tongue that was begging for entrance, her body that was welcoming Greyson's touch. Opening her mouth, she dueled with Cate's tongue for dominance. They would do this until Greyson took control, and she always did just that. Cate grabbed her hands and pressed them against exposed breasts, the lace pushed down so she could rub her palms roughly against Cate's nipples. Greyson palmed the supple breasts, gently kneading and squeezing the firm, taut flesh.

Her own body ached to be touched, and as if on cue, Cate slipped a hand behind Greyson's head, pulling her tighter into the kiss, while her other hand tried to slip under Greyson's shirt. Sitting up, she let Cate pull it free from her slacks and jerk it up, giving Cate complete access to her body.

Her mind went blank, as the only instinct she had was primal. God, she was in trouble.

"Fuck me, Grey. God, I want you so bad." Cate's soft cheek smoothed against hers, and she could smell Cate's familiar scent.

Greyson glided her hand over a rounded hip and

grabbed Cate's ass, cupping it as she pulled her closer and shoving her breasts into Greyson's face. Never one to miss an opportunity, Greyson sucked in a nipple, rolled her tongue over the pebbled surface, and nipped at the tip.

"Oh fuck, Grey."

Holding Cate's ass firmly, Greyson let her other hand explore between Cate's legs. As she pushed at the panties, Greyson found the opening she'd suspected was there. Thank God, Cate was predictable, she thought, pressing into Cate's wetness. Cate gasped in her ear and then groaned as Greyson fed her fingers into Cate's hungry pussy. One, then two—

Greyson pushed off the bed with a start. Her dreams of Cate had started again. She thought she'd lost them a year ago, but they were suddenly back without warning. They had become erotic snippets of times they'd shared together. It was part of what she missed about Cate, something she'd never had with another woman, but it was unsettling as well. She couldn't wrap her mind around why Cate came to her in that way. She would take whatever she could get, though.

Cate was like a drug Greyson could never get enough of, and now in death, she was still like crack—just one more puff to get her through the day. The pictures littered around the house reminded her of their life together, the happiest of times. Her dreams, well, they contained the intimate moments of their life, and she held on to them with a vise-like grip, not quite ready to excise them.

The clock flashed six a.m. She'd find no rest today. Might as well get ready for what she was sure would be a grueling day of stomping out fires and feeding answers to a long line of questions from Detective Hill.

⁂

Greyson twirled her pen between her fingers, deep in thought. How the hell had this happened at her company? Something like this could derail her plans for expansion. But what was she thinking? An employee had been attacked, and Addie Blake deserved more respect than having her spend her energy worrying about Integrated Financial. She'd hold down the fort easily enough. That was why she'd lasted at the helm as long as she had. But her competitors would take this opportunity to smear her and I.F., so she needed to carefully consider how to get in front of this tragedy.

"Ms. Hollister, Mr. Harris is here."

Greyson pressed the intercom. "Thank you, Tara. Please send him in."

"Yes, Ms. Hollister."

Greyson stood and smoothed out a wrinkle in her slacks.

"Grey, how are things this morning?" Neil extended his hand. He always shook hands, no matter how familiar he was with anyone. It was what he did.

"Morning, Neil. Sorry about the long night last night. How's the family?"

"Good." He sat on the couch and opened his briefcase. "How did it go with Erin Green last night?"

"Bitch. Looks like Addie Blake's girlfriend, Drake, called the news station about the attack. Green was all over me like flies on—well, you get the picture. When I wouldn't talk, she jumped that Detective Hill's bones." Then Greyson remembered something else.

"There was another rape last night."

"What?"

"Yeah, I don't have any details, but Green's cameraman rushed up to her and said they had to leave because there was another rape. When the reporter confronted Hill about it, she clammed up."

"Christ. Well, maybe that will get some of the focus off you, and we can figure out a game plan before it goes crazy." Neil shook his head.

"So back to the issue at hand, Addie Blake and her sue-happy girlfriend Drake Hogan."

"I've pulled Addie Blake's personnel file. Exemplary employee, Grey. She doesn't have anything in there but some great evaluations. I got her girlfriend's name off her life insurance paperwork. Now *she* is a piece of work."

"Something we should be worried about *piece of work*?" Greyson knew she had reason to worry after hearing the way Drake had referred to Addie last night. Her meal ticket was damaged goods, and a woman like that didn't keep something she thought was less than perfect. However, if that meal ticket was a way to a bigger payday, then Drake was no dummy. She'd be knocking on Greyson's door any minute now, insisting on her big, fat paycheck.

"I got a call from a friend, who said she's making some calls, looking for an attorney. *That* kinda bad news." Neil pulled a series of folders out of his briefcase and plucked one from the middle. The label had Drake's name printed across it, and judging by the size of it, Greyson knew she had something to worry about.

"You have that much information on her already?"

"Yep," he said, passing it to her.

A tired sigh escaped Neil. She felt sorry for him because she knew he'd probably spent the night digging up all this information.

"How mad is your wife?"

"She's not. I got this while she was sleeping." He leaned back and spread his arms along the back of the couch.

His job was done. Now it was her turn to digest the report.

Greyson tossed the folder on the table, stood, and walked to the window. Pushing a blade of the verticals to the side, she looked down at the cement fountain spewing water through two swans' beaks. The arcing water formed the top of a heart and then dropped into the other stream. A few people sat on the bench around it, smoking and drinking coffee. She'd need time to go through the file, but Neil would give her a digested version in about, three...two...one.

"She wasn't hard to get dirt on, Greyson. Like you said, she's definitely sue-happy, and now you've just given her a reason for another lawsuit."

Greyson looked back at Neil, scoffing at his remark. "What do you mean I've just given her a reason? I had nothing to do with what happened."

"That's not what I meant—"

"Then you should pick your words better. You're a lawyer. You know what you say matters."

"I don't need a reminder. I just meant she's going to come after you. I suspect that the encounter you had with her at the hospital only stoked her ire. Now she's on a mission. Hence, breaking the story to Erin Green. She's going to use the media to her advantage. Get them on her side, so we need to make sure you're more sympathetic than she is.”

“This isn’t about me, Neil. This is about Addie Blake. How do we protect her?”

“Well, we make Drake the problem, her and the attacker. Who would brutalize an innocent woman trying to make a living, practically supporting her living-large girlfriend?”

“That shouldn’t be hard, Neil, since she walked out on her girlfriend and left her at the hospital.”

“She’ll just say she had a breakdown. That something so tragic made her lose her mind. Has she contacted Ms. Blake?”

Greyson shook her head. It had barely been six hours, and she doubted Drake had even so much as called, texted, or come by the house, at least not that Greyson had heard. It was doubtful that Drake would get on the grounds. She had a fence that kept even the most determined at bay.

“Well, expect a phone call from her lawyer at a minimum. I wouldn’t be surprised if she called a press conference now that she has Erin Green’s ear.”

“Speaking of the press, do we know if any of the other stations have caught wind of what’s happened?”

“They’ve already contacted Pam for a comment.”

“I’m going to call a press conference and see if we can get ahead of this story,” Greyson said.

“I’m not sure that’s a good idea.”

“Neil, we can let the narrative drive the story or we can drive the narrative. I want everyone to know that we plan to cooperate with the police and that security and safety are a major concern at I.F.”

“Greyson—”

“If the media is going to come knocking, we’re going to answer and give them our best face.”

"Can I persuade you against this?"

"Nope."

Get ahead of a problem, don't let it drive the narrative, her father had always said. In business, there was only one truth, and that was the first thing said. Anything after that was defense. She had nothing to be afraid of, and Integrated Financial had done its best to protect its employees. The memo going out to all departments encouraged anyone who knew something, had seen something, to come straight to her and let her know. She had even hired counselors to come in and deal with anyone struggling with the tragic event. She hoped Paul Winston took advantage of the service. He was a guilt bag ready to be unpacked.

She picked up the folder and sat back down at her desk. Flipping through it, she immediately saw a mug shot of Drake. *Why do women date such losers?* She flipped the page to yet another one. It seemed Drake had a small drinking problem, and the evidence was in her hands. Closing the folder in disgust, she tossed it on the desk and looked at Neil.

"So tell me more about this woman," she said, pointing to one of Drake's mug shots.

Chapter Twelve

Nancy was shuffling through the paperwork from the shopping-cart detail she'd been assigned earlier, thanks to the local merchants complaining. The chief had decided it was a top priority to wrangle carts. However, half the vendors didn't come pick them up once they impounded them. *Another brilliant idea!* The chief was definitely keeping his promise of cleaning up the downtown. Don't even get her started on the abandoned-vehicle task force he had instituted. Due to an overly observant resident with deep pockets who'd bankrolled the chief's recent reelection campaign, they now had to police abandoned cars. Shit like that wasted man-hours and was disrespectful to the training and work that police officers did. At least they could send out community officers, if the chief ever got around to hiring any for something more than parking enforcement.

"Detective Hill, I need to see you and Skippy over there," he said, pointing to Detective Cha Cha, the nickname given by his buddies when they found out he'd been a competitive dancer in his younger days.

"Yes, sir, Be right in." Nancy tapped the man still digging for gold. "Come on, Cha Cha. Clean that poker, will ya? Gross."

Sometimes being in the squad room was more like being in a men's locker room. If only the public could see all the scratching, farting, and gossip that went on in the station. Nothing like those cop shows. Well, come to think of it, one did get it right, but…*Oh, who cares?* She weaved past Cha Cha's desk, hoping nothing hopped on board.

"Hey, Detective Hill. What's for dinner?" one of the uniformed officers asked as she clipped her duty belt on.

Nancy looked at the young officer, smirked, and shook her head.

"Hey, roughing the passer there."

"Shall I call a medical?" The officer winked at Hill.

"I think I'll live. Just don't let it happen again." She spoke a little sterner than she intended.

The officer's face dropped, and Nancy felt bad. She didn't mind joking with the uniformed officers. It was pretty common among the blues, but she didn't want the wrong impression to get around. She didn't pick up strays at work or in the squad. Some officers used the squad room as their personal dating service when the new recruits came in. Others had beat wives that they visited while out on patrol, leaving their regular wives at home. That was just too much crap to keep straight, and when it went bad, it went really bad. The horror stories were real, and she'd seen with her own eyes how things could ignite if you forgot which cell phone was for which wife.

"Detectives, get your ass in here." The squall came from the other end of the squad room.

"Come on, Cha Cha."

"I'm coming, I'm coming." He jumped up behind her and stalked down the hall, the thud of his size 15s echoing throughout the warehouse room.

"Geez, Cha Cha. You sound like a fuckin' herd of elephants." He motioned to the only two pieces of furniture in the Spartan room, then stuck his hand out, but Nancy grabbed it before Cha Cha did. She wasn't about to touch anything that had touched Cha Cha's, ever.

"How are ya, Chief?"

"I'd be better if we could catch this rapist."

Cha Cha scraped the cement floor as he dragged the chair away from Hill and the desk. It set her teeth on edge, and the chief's stern look at Cha Cha wasn't helping the mood. Hey, if he wanted to be anti-social, who was she to argue?

"Cha Cha," the chief said, sticking his hand out.

Nancy had a visceral reaction when their hands touched. Taking out a little bottle of sanitizer, she discreetly popped a squirt on her palm, stuffed the travel bottle back into her pocket, and leaned forward, rolling her hands together. She wasn't usually a germaphobe, but the things she'd seen lately, both in the squad room and out at the scenes, were enough to make her careful whose DNA she subjected herself to. Resting her elbows on her knees, she rubbed her hands together, waiting for the chief to start.

"What have you got on the latest rape case? Cha Cha?"

Cha Cha snorted and then hacked, all eyes focusing on him. Then he wiped his nose on the back of his hand and snorted again.

"Same MO, chief. Elevator, girl, late night. Nothing that sticks out."

"Two in one night is what sticks out, Chief. I think he's stepping up his game. Taunting us."

Nancy jerked her head back and looked at Cha

Cha. How would he know? She'd been the one at the hospital and was planning to go over to Integrated Financial later to check out the crime scene again. She'd called him for the second rape, and when he failed to respond to the call for a detective, she went it alone. He'd been hammered at home and in no condition to be at the crime scenes, so she'd told him she'd handle it and they'd brief later. Only later hadn't come until about ten minutes ago, when he'd finally showed up still wearing the same suit he'd worn yesterday. She doubted he'd even changed, just rolled off the couch and came to the station.

"I hate to disagree with my fellow detective, but the first one seems different," Nancy said.

"Different how?"

"Just a gut feeling."

The chief looked at Cha Cha and shook his head in disgust when Cha Cha's head started to bob back.

"Tell me about this gut feeling. I reviewed the report. Looks like the same MO to me. Attacked late at night, in an elevator."

"Yeah, but he didn't rape her."

"So...maybe he didn't have time. Maybe someone stopped him. Take your pick for a reason. It's not uncommon for a perp to do something a little different. The basics are all still there, and they match all five other cases."

"I know, sir. Something just doesn't seem right. He raped the second woman, but not the first. No souvenirs either."

"What does your lead detective think?"

They both looked over at Cha Cha, who had a line of drool spreading down his chin.

The chief stood and walked around his desk and

slammed his hips against the metal drawer, sending Cha Cha sprawling to the floor.

"You're lead on this task force, Hill. I've got people breathing down my neck, and now Integrated Financial board members are calling me. Do you know who sits on the board of I.F.?"

Nancy shook her head. She didn't keep up with the social column or the business section in the newspaper. She had the paper delivered religiously out of family habit, but she was lucky if she had a chance to look at it. When she was a kid her father had read it from cover to cover. So that was as close to a family tradition she still kept. Sort of like being a Democrat 'cause your parents were, their parents were, and so on. Paper delivery was free, so her dad had got the paper. Beats hoofing down to the drugstore to get it, he'd always said. She'd been telling herself that she needed to cancel the damn thing but couldn't quite do it yet. Traditions sucked. That's why she didn't keep many of them.

"What the fuck, sir?" Cha Cha stood there wiping his mouth.

"Take a couple of days off, Cha Cha, and get a shower. You smell like you've been living in a bottle of gin."

"But—"

"I don't want to hear it. Take some vacation and get your act together. You don't think I've noticed? I sit behind this desk, but I hear everything, Cha Cha. Take the rest of the day off."

"This is bullshit." Cha Cha tried to straighten his wrinkled suit but finally relented when it wouldn't shift. He slammed the door so hard Nancy expected to see the letters slither off the window.

"Take Sergeant Martinez off the shopping-cart task force and put her on with you."

She couldn't believe he could even say *shopping cart* with a straight face. Her own expression must have given away what she was thinking because the chief continued his rant. "Don't start with me, Hill. You have no idea the pressure the mayor's office is giving me over these damn carts. Now, you need to get results. One more rape and we're going to have vigilante justice, and that won't be pretty."

"I'm looking at a couple of different angles on the case, sir. Don't ask me why, but the first victim not being raped screws with me."

"I know, you said that earlier. So find out why."

"I will, sir."

"You have a week, Hill. The feds are looking for a win at something, and I wouldn't be surprised if they step in and push this one into their column."

"How? They don't have jurisdiction."

"They're connecting the dots, too. I got a call from upstairs asking me to send over copies of the files. I can stall them, but not for long. So, unless you want company on this, get busy." He shook two antacids into his palm and then shoveled them into his mouth. The sounds of crushing chalk replaced what was left of anything he might have said.

Nodding toward him, she pushed her way past the door, careful to close it gently. It would be just her luck that the glass would break after Cha Cha's show of force.

"Hey, Hill?"

"Yeah, Chief?"

"One week," he said, holding up one finger for emphasis. "One."

"Gotcha."

Looking down at the door handle, she pulled out her sanitizer, squeezed a copious amount into her palm, and started rubbing vigorously.

"At this rate, I'm going to need to buy this by the gallon." With her pinky, she pulled the handle and shut the door. "Definitely."

Chapter Thirteen

The massive glass mausoleum that was Integrated Financial stood like a towering beacon among the old brick-and-mortar buildings from the turn of the century. Downtown San Jose had gone through a revitalization plan to keep its inner city from dying. Old mixed with new, millennials mixing with the paragons of business kept it vibrant and bustling. The sports bars were happy-hour oases for those that worked too many hours and hadn't achieved that work-life balance yet and for the more established, who sat and smoked cigars, sipping whiskey neat. How did these two cultures mix when they were at odds with each other? Easy. Money was the glue that made everything stick together. It was a life Nancy would never know, but that was fine with her. She had enough pressure in her job that she didn't need the added "clawing to the top," "step on other people" ideals that made the business world so cutthroat.

Nancy looped back around to the front of the huge Integrated Financial building. She'd already spun her cruiser up the spiral cement driveway of the parking garage searching for the ever-elusive parking spot. She could have just commandeered a spot at the front, but she hated it when patrol pulled that stunt. She was big on leading by example, so she'd take one more trip up through the garage before she resorted to that show of power.

Finally, a parking spot miraculously appeared. *Parking karma.* After wedging the big cruiser into the tight space, she shimmied out of the car. Then she pulled her coat from the backseat and shrugged it on, repositioning her Glock and tucking her pad and pen inside her jacket.

Eyeing the parking structure as she walked through it, she noted each camera and which way it was positioned. Without thinking, she tapped the down button for the elevator and stood in front of the doors, rocking on her heels. It was quiet, too quiet for her. An occasional screech of tires but nothing else. Eerie. The elevator popped open, puking a throng of people onto the floor. Talk of social media, drinking, and hot babes overtook the silence

Corporate speak?

"That one's broken," someone said, motioning toward the doors she was standing in front of.

"Oh." That was all she could muster as she still stood there, contemplating what was behind them. A crime scene. A violent crime scene, yet everyone getting off the elevators acted as if nothing had happened the night before. A couple of women in the group laughed as a guy mugged it up. Could he be the attacker? She studied him and wondered. He looked at her and stopped dead in his tracks.

"Are you okay?" he said.

"Yeah, sorry. I was just thinking."

"Hey, you're going to miss the elevator," he said, rushing back to hold the doors open.

"Right, thanks. Guess my head was somewhere else," Nancy said, stepping into the tiny box.

"No problem. Have a nice day."

She nodded at him, flashed a brief smile. "Thanks. You too."

Nancy positioned herself in front of the panel of buttons, pulled out her cell phone, and snapped a few pictures for her own use. Then she pressed the button for the lobby. She looked out of the corner of her eye, trying to visualize what Addie might have seen the night before. The highly polished brass walls reflected her own appearance. The report had echoed that very idea. Checking out her reflection, she flicked a strand of hair out of her face and turned back, facing the button panel. Looking sideways again, she could almost see the far corner of the elevator, but Addie had said she was texting. Texting accidents were the new video spoofs on social media. She'd encountered her own fair share of thoughtless people walking right into her. The endless videos of people falling into holes and fountains, and almost being run over were a nightly occurrence on the evening news. Addie had fallen victim to technology and a well-prepared attacker. It wasn't her fault.

Staring at the perimeter of the floor, she noticed there was barely enough room for her tall frame if she lay down. Had Addie hit her head when she was thrown to the floor? She faced the wall, put her hands on it, and thought about how hard Addie had been forced to fight to stay alive. Nancy looked up and spotted the camera. Did Addie see it when she was attacked? Did she think someone on the other end would come to her rescue? She'd fought for her life; her defensive wounds proved that fact. Nancy could feel the tight confines of the elevator start to close in on her. She needed to get off and out into the open. She noted the fifth floor coming up, so she hit the button and rushed out just as the doors opened.

She paused and sucked in a breath, as cold sweat lanced through her. That had never happened to her before. She was always able to detach from a crime scene or a victim. Why now? The open doors invited her to get back in and continue her downward spiral, but she wasn't about to enter that hell again to relive that experience. The stairs to her right were the only way down to the crime scene, unless she drove back down, but she didn't have time for that. She looked at her watch, noting that she was surprisingly early, even for her.

Nancy snapped on a pair of latex gloves, pulled the door handle, and stood staring at the entry to the stairs. Without thinking, she wedged her foot against the open door, pulled out her cell phone, and hit Sergeant Torres's number.

"Torres."

"Hey, Torres. Hill here. Question. Did you check the stairwell last night?"

"No, why?"

"Just wondering. Any reason why?" Hill knelt down and squinted at something on the floor. Any evidence would be contaminated and useless in a trial, but it didn't mean they shouldn't collect it if she did find something.

"I guess since the attack happened in the elevator, I didn't think to look there. I did tape down the elevator and the lobby. Crime Scene was just getting finished when they got the call on the second rape. They should still be on scene. Want me to call them to come over and check the stairwell?"

"Yeah. And why don't we get someone from Forensics down here? Thanks." Nancy poked the face of the phone, activating the camera. On her hands and knees, she snapped a few photos. Then practically lying on the floor, she scanned the cement. What was she looking for? She didn't have a clue, but sometimes that was how police work was. *The shit I do for my job.*

She noted the cameras on the door and the stairwell. Could the cameras have caught a picture of this guy? Maybe when he'd scouted the building earlier in the week? He would have had to scope out the layout before the attack. He was too cocksure of himself to not have familiarized himself with the building. She'd had the same thought when she was at the conference center last night. According to the victim, it had happened in a matter of minutes, and then he was gone. The victim vaguely remembered seeing him earlier, but only for the briefest of moments. Not one fucking witness, one piece of evidence, nothing. Were they ever going to catch a break on this bastard?

Keeping her eyes on each step, she inched her way down the staircase. Nothing. She didn't pass anyone. Where were all the health-conscious employees? The janitors? Anyone?

When she hit the lobby, she expected to see a taped-off crime scene. Instead, she found a bustling hub of people walking right through it. Who worked on a Saturday? she wondered. Clearly, the corporate culture at I.F. was one that was constantly working. Poor Bastards. The elevator had an out-of-order sign taped to it. Yanking out her phone in disgust, she dialed Torres again.

"Torres."

"Hey, I thought you said you taped off the crime scene in the lobby."

"I did."

"Well, there isn't anything here now."

"Shit. They must have taken everything down. I swear, Detective, it was taped off."

"I believe you. Damn it." Nancy had seen a lot of shit moves in her day, but to violate a crime scene was at the top of her list of stupid. "I just wanted to confirm before I ripped someone a new shit hole. Do me a favor and go by the convention center and make sure no one touches that scene. It looks like it's the only evidence we might have now."

"Yes, ma'am. Should I send a few officers down?"

"No. I'll find out what the hell happened."

Nancy poked her phone, turned it around, and snapped pictures from different angles. She couldn't avoid including a few people in the shots, but it didn't matter now. This wasn't a crime scene anymore. Looking around the lobby, she noticed a man scanning badges. Men in what appeared to be security uniforms looked like they were more adept at hassling people than securing the building. Was this Greyson Hollister's idea of security?

Someone tapped Nancy on the shoulder. "Hey, can I help you?"

Without thinking, she turned, grabbed his wrist, and put his face against the wall. She caught sight of the name of the security firm he worked for embroidered on his blazer. He looked just like the rest of the group of rent-a-cops hassling people in the building.

"Hey, let me loose or you're gonna to be sorry," he threatened her.

"I don't think so, asshole. Didn't your training teach you not to put your hands on someone?" It was a rhetorical question, but she felt the need to ask anyway.

She pointed her phone at the hunk of meat and

snapped a picture.

"Hey, you can't do that," he said, reaching for the phone with his free hand.

Reacting again, she pulled her cuffs and slapped one on his wrist, twisting him around and pushing his face against the wall, again.

"Give me your other hand," she commanded, yanking his cuffed wrist up behind his back and forcing him to bend over in compliance. Out of the corner of her eye, she caught sight of the kid who'd been wanding everyone through the lobby. He wavered between helping his coworker or continuing doing what he'd been hired to do, secure the lobby.

She looked at him and pointed to her badge and then at him. "Stand down or I'll arrest you for obstruction."

The meat in her hands tried to wrestle clear. "What the hell are you doing?"

She'd had it. She'd wasted enough time in the lobby with this bozo. Now he was about to find out what happened when you thought you were a cop.

"You've been jerking me around ever since I walked up here. I've tried to play nice, but I've had enough of your bullshit. You want to interfere with an investigation? Well, your boss is going to answer for your behavior."

"We have rules. This is private property. You can't just come in here and—"

"Look, pencil neck. I understand the rules. See this?" She tapped the tin on her belt again, just in case he hadn't seen it the first time. "I'm all about rules, but you've been yanking my chain and now you're done. You seem to think you're the alpha dog, but I'll let you in on a little secret. You're not even in the kennel, bitch. So now I'm putting you back in your cage."

"I'm under strict orders. Everyone coming in gets a visitor's badge and their picture taken. There was an incident last night, and we can't let just anyone into the building. Besides, that other cop said we could take down the tape and get back to business."

"What other cop?"

His face contorted in confusion. "I don't know. He said he was here last night and that you had all the evidence you needed. Now, can you let me go?"

"No."

"Did you get his name? Badge number?" This wasn't making any sense. No one said anything about another officer on the scene last night.

"Nope. Great. You're as sharp as a pencil, aren't you?" Nancy pulled her phone with one hand, pinning the guy to the wall with the other. "Torres, did you call I.F. and release the scene?"

"No. I would have told you earlier."

"Right. Someone was down here and told security we were done."

"Not me."

"Okay—"

"Wait, the cleaning ladies said there was another officer on the scene before me. Said the officer ran after someone. I asked dispatch if someone else was on scene."

"And?"

"I got busy and never got an answer."

"Follow up on that, Torres."

"Yes, ma'am."

Nancy released the man and turned him around. "You," she said, pointing to him. "Keep everyone," she waved her hands around the foyer, "from walking through this crime scene."

The rent-a-cop questioned her again. "But he said you were all finished here. So you're not done?"

"No shit. Why do you think I'm here? I'm the detective investigating the attack."

❧❧❧❧

Nancy had had her fill of Greyson Hollister the night before, and now here she was flashing a smug look at Nancy. She wanted to belt that smile right off this persistent woman's face for derailing her plans for the day. Of course she had a job to do, but in the bigger picture, sitting on her couch wasn't exactly getting it done. Now was it?

"Ms. Hollister, I've just run the new gauntlet you've set up downstairs. One of your new hires, however, won't be coming in to work tomorrow. Seems he was rather zealous in his duties and earned himself some silver bracelets." Nancy sat on the sofa and made herself comfortable.

"Well, I'm sure you can appreciate the predicament Integrated Financial finds itself in. I have a duty to protect my employees." The haughty woman stood at a silver service and lifted a carafe. "Coffee, Detective?"

"Black, no sugar."

"Cream?" Greyson walked toward Nancy.

She doubted Greyson Hollister served her guests, so she looked around for the little imp of a man, Jarrod Bennet.

"Yes." Nancy didn't take cream, but the damn Hollister woman had made an assumption. She hated it when people assumed things and reached their own conclusions.

"Cream and sugar are on the center table." Greyson handed the cup and saucer to Nancy and smiled. So they were playing *that* game, were they? Nancy smiled back.

"Detective, tell me you have something on the perpetrator that attacked Ms. Blake."

Nancy chided her. "Been watching crime TV, have you?"

"Well, that is what you call someone who commits a crime, isn't it? Or are those shows mistaken?"

"No, we don't have anything on the perp. I was hoping you had something promising to tell me. Something about the cameras or the security system? Maybe your cameras caught an image somewhere in this building that might help us catch this guy?"

"I wish I could help, but it seems someone disabled the cameras last night."

Nancy scratched her nose. It always itched when she was pissed. Pulling the cup to her lips, she watched Greyson over the rim. If Greyson was bothered about the attack, she didn't show it. Nancy wondered if Greyson played poker, because her face was made for it.

"So, Ms. Hollister. It seems we have a problem or two." Nancy set her cup on the saucer and cradled it on her lap.

"Do we, Detective?"

"You've tampered with a crime scene downstairs, and I'm hoping you haven't disturbed the one in the elevator."

"I have a business to run. The last thing I want is my employees or clients to see crime-scene tape all over the lobby. I'm sure you can appreciate that, Detective.

Or have you lost all sense of decorum?" Greyson sat opposite Nancy, mirroring the exact way Nancy was holding her coffee and crossing her legs.

"Actually, I can't. You see, I have a job to do that involves looking at the crime scene, studying it for patterns, and analyzing those patterns that just might—"

"And I have a business to run, clients to see, and employees who may, or may not, know what happened last night."

"I'm sure the gossip mill was working overtime this morning as well. I doubt there is an employee here who doesn't know what happened," Nancy said.

"That may be. I hate repeating myself, but for the sake of clarity, I ordered the lobby cleared. I understand that your forensics team took photographs and video. Besides, I'm sure the other crime scene will yield evidence as well."

Nancy wasn't sure how Greyson knew about the rape last night, but she wasn't going to confirm or deny it. Before she could say another word, a man pushed through the door.

"Ms. Hollister, I've taken care of—"

"Jarrod, I'm right in the middle of a meeting with Detective Hill."

Greyson didn't seem too inconvenienced by the interruption. In fact, if Nancy were guessing, she was probably grateful for it. Especially since Nancy hadn't even begun to interrogate her. She watched the silent interplay between the two. One was moonstruck, and the other had an annoyed look on her face.

"Oh. I just wanted to give you these." He bent down and whispered in Greyson's ear. "I've had the locks changed at Ms. Blake's apartment, as you asked."

That was an interesting tidbit of information. Nancy stood and offered her hand.

"Detective Hill, and you are?"

"Jarrod Bennet. I'm Ms. Hollister's personal assistant." He extended his limp hand.

Nancy probed further. "Well, Bennet, do you mind if I ask you some questions about last night?"

"I was with Ms. Hollister last night. I'm the one who took the call about Ms. Blake being attacked." He looked at Greyson and then back to Nancy.

"Yes, I can vouch for him."

"Well, I should be getting back to work. You have an eleven o'clock meeting, Ms. Hollister."

"Thank you, Jarrod. Can you move it back to eleven thirty and cancel my lunch date. I want to go home and check on Ms. Blake." Greyson dismissed her assistant without as much as a nod.

"Yes, ma'am."

Watching Bennet leave, Detective Hill wondered if Greyson had picked up on the love-struck assistant's constant mooning over her. No matter. He was her problem.

"Well, Ms. Hollister. I'd like to see the elevator if you don't mind."

"Of course. I'll have Jarrod give you access."

"Actually, I wonder if you wouldn't mind showing me, and perhaps you can lead me to the security room where the camera systems are."

"Me?"

"You aren't afraid of what you'll see, are you?"

"Afraid of what?"

"Oh, I don't know. Witnessing where your employee was brutally attacked."

Greyson's back stiffened. Nancy had hit a nerve.

Good. She wasn't about to let Hollister off the hook quite yet. She opened the door and swung her arm wide. "After you."

❧ ❧ ❧

Greyson wasn't about to let this bitch in blue intimidate her. She directed Jarrod to summon Neil to the elevator, now. She spoke to several people on the way down, purposely slowing their progress. She wanted Neil Harris to be present when Detective Hill asked questions. An exasperated sigh slipped past her ears as Hill could only stand there and watch each time she took time to address each employee. Slyly peering down at her watch, she had called a news conference for ten thirty, and with any luck, she'd have the detective right by her side when it started.

The elevator, as well as security, was in the basement. The elevator sat sealed up and waiting for the police to release it. She'd already made a trip down to security to uncover why the cameras had ceased to work and to find out if the comings and goings on the password and keycards could be checked. The staff said they'd need a day or two, but they didn't have the luxury of time.

"Shall we take the stairs or would you rather the elevator?" Greyson said, pushing the elevator button.

"I don't mind the stairs. That is, if you can handle them in those heels?" Detective Hill smirked as she looked at the designer pumps.

"Detective, seriously?"

Greyson pushed the door and willingly took the bait. Detective Hill was angling for time to question Greyson, any idiot could see that, so she bit. The workout would do her some good. Slipping her heels off, she smiled at Nancy and ushered her down the next flight.

"So tell me, Detective. You said we'd met before. For the life of me, I can't seem to remember when." Greyson took a quicker pace down the stairs, forcing Detective Hill to move faster. Perspiration was starting to bead on Detective Hill's upper lip as she opened her jacket and slipped it off.

"Still looking for my gun, Ms. Hollister?" Detective Hill quipped as she slung her jacket over her arm. A smug smile creased her face.

"You really do think highly of yourself, Detective. Yes, I was looking at your Glock."

"Aw, you know your guns too. Get that off those police shows?"

"You know, Detective, I'm not as one-dimensional as you might think. So remind me again where we know each other from?" Greyson was the master of subject change, and it would take more maneuvering for the detective to question her before her lawyer was present.

"St. Patty's Day, 2009. I was a patrol officer working downtown. Ring any bells?"

Greyson thought about where she was in 2009. "Six years ago, Detective, is ancient history for me. I'll buy a vowel for another clue," she quipped.

"You were with a cute redhead." That was all Detective Hill offered.

Cate. Now she remembered. It had been only their third date, and Greyson was sure it would be their last. Too much alcohol, a long day at work, and no dinner had been Greyson's undoing. Cate had taken on babysitting duties as Greyson purged her demons that night. She still didn't remember, but she suspected in a minute she would get a reminder.

"Not my finest night, I assure you."

"Oh, I thought you were in rare form. I think I would have been pissed if someone had sideswiped my Jag, too."

Then it hit her, the Jag incident. "Oh shit. You were the officer on duty that night." Now she remembered. Christ.

"Whatever happened to that cute redhead?"

Detective Hill was treading on sacred ground now. Greyson stopped in mid-stride, grabbed the rail, and flashed back to that night.

"Grey, it's okay. That's what insurance is for," Cate said, pulling Greyson to face her.

"It's not okay. You fucking idiot," Greyson said to the meat locker leaning against his truck. "People work hard for their shit, you asshole." Greyson pointed at the crumpled fender and door.

"Hey, we can call a tow and get a cab home, or take the train. It's fine." Cate let Greyson go and picked up their purses and jackets. "Come on, let's get you home." She lifted her lips to Greyson's ear and whispered. "Besides, I haven't seen your place yet." The innuendo was planted.

Greyson reached down and cupped Cate's face. From that moment on she was beyond smitten. Cate was exactly what she needed at that time in her life, the calming force that kept Greyson from pitching back and forth in the storms of turmoil she found herself in at the moment.

"You're right," she said, kissing Cate.

"Oh, shit. Lesbos. Great. A dude can't catch a

break anywhere, can he?" the guy said, pushing off his truck toward them.

Without thinking, Greyson pushed Cate behind her and raised her fist. "Back off."

"What are you going to do, carpet muncher?" He took another threatening step forward.

A spotlight shined in their direction and a voice boomed behind the light. "Trouble here?"

Greyson froze just as she was getting ready to hit the bloke.

A cop stepped from behind the blinding light, her hand on her baton as she looked at all of them.

"Everything okay?"

"No. This jerk hit my car. I want you to arrest him," Greyson put her hands down and around Cate.

"This bitch—"

"Stop right there," the cop said, shining her flashlight on the car. "I hope you both have insurance."

Greyson persisted. "I want you to arrest him."

"I'm sorry, ma'am. This isn't a moving violation and it's on private property."

Greyson could see the cop better then. Barely a rookie, the young woman probably didn't want to do anything more than defuse a situation that might have spiraled out of control.

Now Greyson recognized the detective. "That cute redhead was my wife."

"Was?"

"Look, if you don't mind, I'd like to get this over with. I have a lot to do today." Greyson moved quickly down the stairs. She didn't need a walk down memory lane with someone who was an intruder on her memories. They were precious treasures to her, and she didn't want to share them. Stopping at the door, she slipped her pumps back on and pulled open the door to the basement.

"The security office is here too," she said, waiting for the detective to pass.

"Good. We can kill two birds with one swipe then." Nancy slipped her coat back on and squeezed past her.

The basement was dark, humming with equipment, and the smell of damp concrete assaulted her. Greyson hated it down here. She pushed back a memory from her college days that was trying to make a pitstop, but she wouldn't let it.

"Get off me," she said, pushing against his chest.

"Come on, you tease. You know you want this. You've been flashing your tits at me all night," he said, his beer breath clouding her own alcohol-saturated brain.

"I have done no such thing." She pushed harder, unseating him from on top of her.

He grabbed her by the hair and tugged her back. "Get back here, you—"

"Hey, you okay?" Detective Hill asked.

Greyson flinched and looked down at her hand. "What? Yeah, I'm fine. Let's check out that elevator." She pushed farther into the darkness of the basement, looking for the security office.

Chapter Fourteen

Addie stood at the window watching Camille, another woman, and a young boy laughing around the swimming pool. The joy on the young man's face was clearly contagious as both women clapped when he jumped into the pool and dog-paddled to the side. Popping up sputtering, he pushed off the side for another dunk.

A sharp pain was her reward for smiling. As she touched her lip, blood seeped onto her fingertips, a reminder of the night earlier. Not that she could forget it. Nightmare after nightmare had kept sleep at bay all night. She had wrestled with a masked face, his hands choking the life out of her. Each time, just as she was about to die, she awoke, her hands still fighting off the demon.

She hadn't ventured outside yet. Looking like she did, she was sure her appearance would scare the boy enjoying a swim. Addie pulled her phone from her bag and checked the text messages that were piling up.

Drake
7:30 am—Where are you? I've been looking everywhere, and that pencil dick, Paul, won't tell me where you are.

Paul

8:05 am—How are you? Call me. Motor Girl is calling and I don't want to talk to her.

Drake
7:35—WTF, where are you?????

Paul
8:20—I'm at work and everyone is freaking out. Ms. Hollister sent a memo out. She's having a press conference to talk about what happened. Are you okay? Call me.

She quickly punched out a text to Paul.

Addie
8:45—Paul, sorry had a rough night. I'm okay. I'll call later. I'll handle Drake. Sorry about that. ☺

Paul
8:46—Addie, I'm so sorry about last night. It's all my fault. I should have waited…

Addie
8:47—Paul, it isn't your fault…

Paul
8:48—It is too. I'll never forgive myself for what happened.

Addie's finger hovered over the small virtual keyboard. She knew she couldn't say anything to make Paul feel better. If misery loved company, then poor Paul was her companion for life. She felt bad for him. He didn't deserve to carry guilt that clearly her own girlfriend didn't feel.

> *Addie*
> *8:50—TTYL. I'm tired.*

She lied. She wasn't going to be sleeping anytime soon, but she wasn't in the mood to text anyone either.

> *Paul*
> *8:51—Okay, call me later if you want to talk. Can I stop by after work?*

Addie tossed her phone into her bag. She wasn't in the mood for company. Hell, she wasn't ready to face anything at the moment. Lying on the bed, she stared at the ceiling, following the textured cracks. Suddenly she bolted up in bed. She had a meeting with a new client today, and she'd worked hard on his portfolio. He was expecting a detailed report on his investments.

"Oh shit, shit, shit, shit." She punched the bed. Pulling her hand back, she winced. Her bruised knuckles ached. God, there wasn't any part of her that wasn't torn up.

Grabbing her phone, she texted Paul.

> *Addie*
> *9:00—Paul, I was supposed to have a meeting with Mr. Cantor. You need to cancel.*

Addie waited, worried she would screw up one of the most important clients she'd been trusted with.

> *Paul*
> *9:01—I saw him on your calendar. No worries. I'll*

handle it. Again, I'm so sorry about all of this. ☹

Addie
9:01—Thanks. TTYL.

Addie lay back on the pillows and started following the textured cracks again. While she didn't have an exciting life, what she had was hers. Now, well, now she didn't have one to speak of. She couldn't imagine going back into the office. How could she? Just the thought was making her feel nauseous. Her head spun, like she'd been drinking. When she thought about getting on the elevator, *the death chamber* as she would now call it, well, that wasn't going to happen. The stairs would be the only way she'd go back to work, if she could.

She began to shake when a memory flashed in her mind. She could smell that peculiar smell again. Mothballs! Her breathing grew labored, like someone was sitting on her chest. Pulling herself back up, Addie clutched her chest. She twisted back and forth for relief, but the pressure didn't relent. Standing, she put her hands over her head and sucked in several deep breaths. The walls felt like they were closing in on her, and her need to escape the room pushed her toward the door and down the hall. She didn't know where she was going, but *out* was the only thing on her mind.

Rushing, she walked faster until she was in a full trot. Everything looked so different in the daylight. She pushed off a wall as she stumbled, almost dropping to her knees. The stairs! There they were, and the front door at the bottom would release her from her self-imposed prison.

After pulling on the heavy door, she hit her

shoulder on it as she squeezed past. Its bulk was a barrier to the outside, and she needed to be out there. Sunlight hit her in the face. Shielding her eyes, she looked around to try to get her bearings. Nothing was familiar. The large expanse of lawn rolled down toward large privacy hedges. The circular driveway led her gaze to a large metal gate. Clearly privacy was of great concern for Ms. Hollister. Addie couldn't see the street, and clearly the street couldn't see her. Plopping herself down on the edge of a front stair, she rocked back and forth, trying to calm her nerves. Fight or flight was full on, and she was having a hard time wrestling back control of her emotions.

She looked behind her at the huge mansion and then ahead at the massive gate. What was she going to do now?

Chapter Fifteen

Greyson stood in front of the bloody mess on the floor. Her stomach squeezed, ready to purge her morning coffee. The sight of all that blood, Addie's blood, brought reality crashing down on her. Until now, she'd been able to keep a healthy distance from it all. She'd placed the order to clean up the lobby shortly after returning home with Addie. So she'd never seen the crime-scene tape, the blood, or any other evidence of the crime.

"Excuse me," Detective Hill said, squeezing past her and tiptoeing around the blood spatter. "So, based on what Ms. Blake said last night..." Detective Hill stepped to the left and in front of the bank of buttons. She pulled out her cell phone and looked at it and then to the left, gazing at her reflection in the polished brass. "She could see him out of the corner of her eye." Detective Hill looked back at Greyson. "Are you okay, Ms. Hollister?"

"Fine." She was curt, too busy looking at the walls and handprints. Addie's prints. "Are those hers?" Greyson pointed to the ones that had clearly been dusted for evidence.

"Yep."

"Did you find his, too?"

"Nope."

"Did you find anything?"

Detective Hill spread her hands wide. "You're looking at it." Greyson followed the woman's gaze as it traveled up the wall and to the camera in the corner. "See, if that had been working, we might have caught a break."

Guilt purchased space in Greyson's heart. *If* it had been working, they would have something to go with.

"Any idea why your camera system went down?"

Greyson couldn't ignore the accusatory tone. As if she had something to do with it. She'd had the best system installed, upgraded to high-definition cameras, night vision outside, and keycards and punch codes that detailed every movement made in Integrated Financial.

Except last night.

"I have no idea. I have one of my tech guys on it right now. I'm sure we'll get to the bottom of this, Detective."

"Hmm." Detective Hill knelt down, pulled another latex glove from her pocket, and pulled up a few pieces of paper. She looked closely at them, flipped them over and then back again.

"What's that?"

"Paper."

Greyson rolled her eyes at the comment. The detective could make something as simple as paper sound snide.

"No kidding. That's a client prospectus," Greyson said. Paper was everywhere. "Why didn't your forensic guys pick up all of this?"

"Well, they had another case to run to, so I told them to leave it until I had a chance to see the crime scene for myself. They'll be back for it," Detective Hill said, holding up the paper by the edge. "Do you see this?"

"I told you, it's a client—"

"Yes, I know. A client prospectus. But do you see this?" She pointed to something toward the middle of the paper.

"Nope, sorry. It's just a bunch of words on paper. Guess I don't have enough training from my cop shows, yet."

"Har har. It's a heel print." Detective Hill moved it closer to Greyson's face. "See right there? The pattern of the floor is on this edge." She circled her finger around a spot. "It was lying half off the stack and he must have stepped on it." Detective Hill smiled.

"If you say so." Greyson wasn't trying to be argumentative, but she still didn't see anything.

Detective Hill swiveled on her toes and looked down at more of the paper. Picking it up piece by piece, she inspected it. They would be there all day at the rate the detective was moving, and Greyson had other plans for the cop.

"Greyson, here you are," Neil said, stepping toward the elevator. "Uh, you have a meeting upstairs, remember?" He tapped his watch.

"Right." Greyson nodded in Detective Hill's direction and shrugged. Detective Hill was part of her plan now that she was here, so she needed to get a move on before the detective figured it out.

"Detective, if you don't mind, we can come back here after my meeting. If you'll just follow me." Greyson waved toward the door.

❧❧❧❧

Addie's cell phone buzzed again. Should she tempt a look? Drake had been in rare form again this morning, and she wasn't up for another text war. Nor was she about to let Drake off so easily. She wasn't in the mood for forgiveness. She snuck a peek at the screen. Relief. It was only Paul.

Paul
10:40—Addie, turn on the TV.

Addie
10:41—What's going on?

Paul
10:42—Channel 8 news conference. Ice Queen is on.

What? Addie searched the house for a TV, spotting one downstairs in the library. Hitting the remote, she searched for the channel and didn't have to look far. All the local stations were carrying different shots of the same screen. There in the middle of the TV stood Greyson Hollister, flanked by Detective Hill and another man she didn't recognize. Questions were being fired at her boss, and with pinpoint accuracy she was shooting them down.

"Ms. Hollister, Erin Green, Channel 8 news. Is it true that an employee was attacked at I.F. and that your security system was down?"

Ms. Hollister's head swiveled around at the reporter. Addie flinched when an expression that could only be described as loathing crossed Ms. Hollister's face. Her recovery was so quick that it probably went unnoticed, but she'd seen it from Drake far too often.

She hoped she never saw that look from Ms. Hollister, ever.

"Ms. Green, I answered that question last night when you accosted me at the hospital. My answer is still the same to you, no comment." Ms. Hollister continued looking around the room and finally stared directly at the camera. "Let me say that we are working with the police to catch whoever did this to our employee. We are making every resource available, including our staff and our IT department. I will personally offer a reward of one hundred thousand dollars for information that leads to the arrest of the person who committed this heinous act."

Addie sucked in a breath. *One hundred thousand dollars. Every freak and—*

"Ms. Hollister, aren't you worried that with so much money on the table you'll draw out every quack and lunatic in the city?"

Ms. Hollister put up her hand, stopping the hum of the reporters. "Let me make this very clear. I will not stand by and watch my employees be terrorized. So…" She looked at the camera again. "Whoever did this, turn yourself in and let's dispense with this before it gets ugly."

"Detective Hill, is the department ready to call this a serial-rapist case? We hear that you've dubbed him the Elevator Rapist."

Ms. Hollister stepped back and motioned for Detective Hill to step forward. "At this time the department has no comment. We'll be releasing a statement as soon as we have more information. It wouldn't be prudent for me to give you an update."

Addie almost felt sorry for the detective. She looked more like a deer caught in a spotlight and less like one of San Jose's finest. Her phone buzzed in her hand again.

> *Paul*
> *10:50—Wow, 100,000 bucks.*

> *Addie*
> *10:50—I'm speechless.*

> *Paul*
> *10:51—You okay?*

> *Addie*
> *10:51—I'm not sure. I just want to go home.*

> *Paul*
> *10:52—Did you tell Ice Queen?*

Addie had told Ms. Hollister she wanted to go home, but that was last night.

> *Addie*
> *10:53—Kinda.*

> *Paul*
> *10:54—Maybe you should stay there. It's safer. Besides, Drake isn't...*

Addie knew where Paul was going, and she didn't blame him. Drake had been a failure as a girlfriend, and now she was proving to be a failure as a human being. How had her life become so screwed up?

> *Paul*

10:55—Sorry. I know she's your gf and everything.

Addie
10:56—It's not your fault.

Paul
10:56—I'll come by after work and take you to my place if you want. ☺

Addie
10:57—I'll call you. Okay?

Paul had seen her at her worst, and that was enough. Then there was this morning. She was certain the dead looked better than what she saw reflected back at her in the mirror. Give her a few days and maybe she'd be ready to see people, but not now. The phone vibrated in her hand, and without thinking she answered.

"Paul, I'll call you. I promise."

"Addie, I want you to come home," Drake said.

For a moment Drake almost sounded like she meant it. For a moment.

"Addie?"

Addie waited and considered hanging up. She was too nice for her own good. "Drake...I..."

"Addie, I'm sorry. I shouldn't have left you like that at the hospital. I don't know what came over me. I'm sorry."

The cynical side of Addie spoke up. "I can't believe you have the nerve to call me, Drake." Her voice vibrated. She didn't care.

"I know. I was a coward, baby. I've been sick over it. I called and texted, and I even called that shit Paul, but he wouldn't return my calls."

"Hey, baby," someone said in the background. Drake covered the phone and whispered something Addie couldn't make out.

"Where are you, Drake? Who is that?" Addie's heart seized. Drake wasn't pining over her. A lightbulb went off. Drake suddenly had a hundred thousand reasons why she wanted her home.

"I'm at the garage, baby. It's just a customer here to pick up her car. You know how it is. These chicks see the tats and they think…well, you know how it is."

"I'm not feeling well, Drake. I'll call you later and we can talk then."

"Okay, I feel ya. Oh, hey, I wanted to let you know I brought your car to the garage."

"How'd you get my car?"

"I have the other set of keys, remember?" Drake covered the mouthpiece again and mumbled something. "By the way, I tried to get into the apartment, but the locks are changed. What's up with that? I know you're scared, baby, but you got Drake. I'll protect you."

"I need to go, Drake. My head is splitting and I need to take a pain pill."

"Just call me when you need me to come get you, and I'll be there in a heartbeat. I love you, Addie."

Before Addie could tell her not to, Drake hung up. Greyson Hollister hadn't done her any favors by putting out a big reward. Now Drake was like a shark circling the chum in the water. She had no doubt Drake had called her lawyer friend, and right about now the sharks were circling Integrated Financial. Reaching for her script bottle, she popped the lid and shook one and then two pills into her hand. She needed this day to end, one way or another.

Chapter Sixteen

"What the hell was that?" Nancy said, yanking on Ms. Hollister's arm.

"Detective, two words. Police brutality?" Greyson looked at Neil and then at Nancy.

"You wish." Nancy dropped her arm. "You knew the press would be in there, and you trotted me out like I was part of all of this..." Nancy swirled her hand around her head. "This bullshit."

"Actually, Detective, I was just being cooperative. I wanted to show that Integrated Financial is cooperating fully with the police investigation."

"Bullshit. You just tossed around a hundred thousand reasons we're about to go on a wild goose chase. I can't believe you thought that offering a reward of that size was smart. Was this your idea?" She pointed to Neil. "You fucking stuffed shirts are all alike. You think you can throw enough money at something and poof, problem solved."

"Actually, Greyson didn't advise me of her plan to offer a reward. If she had, I would have discouraged her. Every lowlife from here to Salinas and back up to Frisco is going to be angling for that money." Neil pierced Greyson with a look Nancy had seen from her chief. Only problem was Greyson was calling the shots, not the suit.

"At least someone has some sense. Jesus H. Christ,

what were you thinking? I'm betting the girlfriend has called Ms. Blake angling for a way back into her good graces. If you thought you had problems before, you got a heap of them now." Nancy pulled her phone out and called the chief.

Greyson started to walk away, but Nancy pulled her arm, keeping her rooted. "You aren't going anywhere."

"What the hell was that all about, Hill?" The chief's voice boomed through the phone.

"Not my idea, Chief. I had no idea what I was walking into."

"No shit. You looked like a damn zombie standing there. The damn phones have been ringing off the hook since that Hollister woman made the reward offer. Does she have any idea what she's done?" He barely took a breath before he continued. "We don't have the manpower to handle all these loonies calling. The mayor's going to be up my ass. Handle it, Hill."

He cut her off before she could say anything. Looking at Greyson, she handed her the phone. "Want to try this again?"

"He's your problem." Greyson shrugged and walked past her. "Neil will help you with the calls."

"Wait, I still need to see the video footage." Nancy wasn't done with Greyson, not by a long shot.

"He can help you with that too. I need to get home and check on Ms. Blake. If you two will excuse me."

Nancy cocked her arm back and was ready to throw her phone at Greyson, when Neil reached up and stopped her.

He shook his head. "You don't have pockets that deep. Trust me."

Chapter Seventeen

Addie paced the hallway, frantically running from her phantom attacker. Her nightmare had become a reality. Every time she closed her eyes, the crisp edge of a knife waved back and forth in front of her face and then slashed at her. She could feel the blade shoved between her ribs to the hilt. Every time she grabbed it, he pulled it through her hands—slicing them open. Addie would stare down at her hands, blood dripping onto the floor.

She doubled over and grabbed at the pain. Pulling her hand away, she expected to see blood gushing from her stomach, but just like the first time, it never happened.

Nothing.

She brushed the sweat from her forehead with trembling fingers and dabbed at the tears that never seemed to stop. Would she ever be able to pull herself out of the depths of despair, or was it her new residence? Grabbing her prescription bottle, she popped it open. She was in pain, right? She needed to sleep. Another one or two would put her on a plane where she could close her eyes and forget. The two she'd taken earlier hadn't worked, so two more should do the trick. She gulped them down before her rational mind could take over. Swallowing them, she looked at the label. Twelve had been dispensed. Looking inside, she saw she was down to six. Hmm, she didn't remember taking the first two. No matter. At this rate she'd need another prescription before she went home.

She needed to be free from the pain. She wanted her old life back, the one with crappy fast food, a few beers at O'Malley's, and long talks about women with Paul. He was so clueless when it came to women, but he was a great girlfriend to her. She laughed at the inside joke. Paul always referred to himself as a closet lesbian. Really? Now she wondered why he called himself that. Thoughts rambled through her head, like seagulls did at the beach, dropping down and then climbing back up with the breeze. Nothing landing long enough to take purchase.

She flung herself backward onto the bed and felt…free, finally. Looking up at the ceiling that swirled above her, she tried to focus, but her eyes wouldn't cooperate. She liked the feeling of floating. That's what she was doing, right? Addie picked up her hand and then let it fall to the bed, exaggerating the bounce when it hit the bed. Things didn't make sense when she thought about the last few days. How had she gotten mixed up with someone like Drake? Oh yeah, they'd met at a bar. Drake was wearing that race jacket she liked so much. Her chick magnet, Drake called it. Why did a woman need a chick magnet?

Picking up her hand, Addie looked at the bruises, then turned her hand over and ran her finger along the severed lifeline. Funny she'd never noticed it before. Her nail rode the groove until it exited the web of her hand.

Her thoughts were fuzzy now. Then something popped into her head. She needed to go home. That would make her feel normal again. She needed to be surrounded by her things, the items that made up her small, insignificant existence on this planet. Her brain fogged as she considered all the things she'd hoped to do by now. Marriage, kids, a house—all things she would never have, ever. The sound of a child laughing somewhere in the fog of her mind made her smile. Such innocence.

A quick snap and her heart froze over. She didn't want those things. *He* had taken them away. How would she ever trust anyone? How could she love anyone again? The internal pain yanked at her heart. Reaching over, she grabbed the prescription bottle, the pain so acute she squeezed the bottle, hearing it crack with the pressure of her agony. Pulling out another pill, she chewed it, the acidic taste almost making her puke. A small price to pay if it made the pain go away. Pushing the cap back on, she grasped it tight in one hand while she covered her eyes with the other and cried. Addie welcomed the blackness eating away at her now, surrendering to its persistent calling. She greeted it with open arms and then sighed one last time. The pain was almost…

❧❧❧❧

Greyson swung the SUV wide around to the back of the house. Shading her eyes, she could see Ben swimming in the pool. He was her water dog. She would have been in there too, but work had other plans. Now with the attack at Integrated Financial, her work hours would keep her from her most treasured person, Ben. Her mother sat fanning herself. It was way too hot for her to be out, but she was a dutiful grandmother, even with a nanny in tow.

"Hey, Mom. Why aren't you in the house?"

"Mommy, Mommy."

"Ben. How's my handsome man doing? Come here and give me a big kiss and hug."

"Honey, he's wet." Camille tried to catch Ben from her wheelchair, but it was no use. He ran right past her and jumped into his mother's arms.

Greyson swung him, holding him tight. This was the best part of her day. She looked forward to coming home and listening to the childish banter. It beat the petty adult banter she was often forced to hear at work. Adulting was so hard for some people, and corporate suits weren't any different. They just did it with a better vocabulary and an adult beverage.

"How was work today, Mommy? I saw a monster today," Ben said, cupping her face and pulling it toward his.

When their noses touched, he rubbed them. She smiled, remembering when her dad used to do the same thing to her when he wanted to be affectionate. Ben looked like her dad and in many ways already reminded her of him.

"When can I come to work, Mommy?" He put his hands on his hips and gave her one of his *I'm a man* looks.

"Tell you what. If you let me know where that monster is, I'll slay it. Then maybe this weekend we can take a drive out to the beach instead."

Ben pointed up to Addie's room. Making roaring sounds, he snapped his teeth shut and then opened them again and tried to make his scariest face. "I saw the monster spying on me while I was swimming."

"That's not a monster, honey. That's a visitor. She was in a bad accident."

"Why?"

Ben had just recently started with the *why* questions. The one that stumped her was, why did he have two mommies and where was his other mommy. She slid through them by using diversions, but she wouldn't be able to do that for much longer. School was just around the corner, and they would pop up again. Only this time his playmates would ask the why questions. She wanted him to have all the answers, but sometimes they weren't that easy.

"Because a bad man made her have an accident. So when you see her, don't stare. Be *special* nice."

"Special nice like ice cream with whip cream and a cherry on top, special nice?" He pulled at a strand of her hair and wound it between his fingers. Lifting it, he smelled it and then wound it around his fingers again.

"Yep, special nice with sprinkles too." Greyson bounced him in her arms.

"Horsey, Mommy."

And just like that, his attention was diverted from Addie to playtime. Greyson shifted him to her back and galloped around the backyard. Ben had a way of bringing her world back to order and resetting her priorities in a moment. If Cate were here, the package would be complete. One more prance around the backyard, and Ben dismounted his loyal stead and Greyson was on her way to check on her guest.

Addie had been on her mind all day. Had Drake, the devoted girlfriend, called to check on Addie? More than likely she had. There were only a hundred thousand reasons for Drake's concern. Greyson knew it was none of her business, but something about Addie made her a little more inquisitive than she should be, than was proper. The guest-room door was cracked open a bit, so Greyson knocked gently.

"Ms. Blake?" Greyson didn't hear anything. Maybe Addie had gone out for some fresh air. Peeking around the door, she saw Addie sprawled across the bed. Something about the way she was lying scared Greyson.

"Ms. Blake?" Greyson ventured closer. "Ms. Blake?" Greyson spotted the prescription bottle clutched in her hand. "Oh, shit."

Yanking the bottle from her grasp, Greyson looked at the label and then counted the pills inside. "Christ."

She tossed them on the floor and felt for a pulse. Weak. Greyson climbed up on the bed and gave Addie a shake. "Ms. Blake."

Nothing.

Under any other circumstances she might have slapped her face, but Addie was already a mess. Pulling her off the bed, she carried her to the bathroom, turned on the shower to cold, and pulled Addie in with her.

"Oh, God." Greyson sucked in a breath when the cold water hit her back. "Jesus, that's frickin' cold."

Within seconds Addie was sputtering and gasping for breath. "What the…what are you doing, Ms. Hollister?" Addie pushed away from Greyson and backed out of the shower.

"Saving your life, Ms. Blake." Greyson flipped the water off, tossed a towel at Addie, and grabbed one for herself. "What were you thinking? You want to kill yourself in my house with my son downstairs?"

"What? No, no, I…what do you mean I wanted to kill myself. How dare you?" Addie wavered as she stood. "I did no such thing."

"Then why are so many pills gone? You had it

clutched in your hand."

"What was in my hand? What are you talking about?"

"I checked your prescription bottle, Ms. Blake, and seven pain pills are missing."

"I think it's best if I went home. I'm sorry. I wasn't trying to kill myself." Addie dabbed at her wet clothes. "I was just...I mean the pain and the nightmares. I guess I wasn't thinking and I...." Addie walked out of the room without finishing.

Greyson bowed her head. Perhaps she'd overreacted. She couldn't watch another person in her life die. Hell, she honestly didn't know what she was thinking. Doing the math in her head, she realized it was possible Addie had taken the prescribed amount throughout the time she'd been discharged, and then again, maybe not.

Greyson ran after Addie. "Ms. Blake. I want to apologize. How you handle your medication isn't my business. It's entirely possible that I overreacted. If you'll excuse me." Greyson tossed the towel back into the bathroom and left.

Walking down the hall, she chastised herself for letting things get personal. She was Addie's boss, not her lover. After shedding her work clothes, she grabbed her workout gear, changed, checked her watch, and headed to the gym downstairs. She needed to work out her frustrations, and punching the bag would be perfect medicine for her own ailments.

❧❧❧❧

What did she care what Ms. Hollister thought? She hadn't been attacked; she wasn't tormented in her dreams. Heck, Addie doubted she'd ever had a bad day, with the exception of having to answer for what happened to her.

Addie nervously tapped her cell phone against her thigh. It was her lifeline. If she'd only had it in her hands the night before she could have saved herself, maybe. She would never be without it, never. She could make a quick call, and Drake would be here to take her home. Was she ready to reestablish a relationship with someone who didn't care whether she lived or died?

No.

Thinking about it now, she decided she should take the opportunity to pull away and make the break. It would make sense. She could just blame it on the attack and Drake's behavior afterward. Time. That's how she'd explain it. She needed time to reassess her life, and Motor Girl wouldn't be part of the reorganization.

She needed to find Ms. Hollister and apologize. She needed her job, and if this would compromise it, she needed to talk fast. She would have to reassure Ms. Hollister she wasn't trying to kill herself. She only wanted relief from her nightmares. She'd do whatever it took to keep at least one slice of her life in order.

Moving down the hall, she knocked on Ms. Hollister's door.

"Ms. Hollister?" Knocking again, she listened at the door and whispered, "Ms. Hollister. Can I talk to you?"

"She isn't in there," someone said behind her.

"Oh, do you know if she's still in the house?"

Addie didn't recognize the woman standing there with her arms full of laundry. Ms. Hollister seemed to have quite the household staff. Nope, Ms. Hollister didn't have a clue what she was going through.

"Ms. Hollister is probably downstairs working out." Looking at the watch hanging from her sweater, the woman smiled. "Yes, it's Ms. Hollister's workout time."

"Thank you." Addie moved toward the stairs and then looked back to ask for directions, but the woman was gone.

Slipping down the stairs, she took great pains to avoid the kitchen. It seemed to be where the most action was of late. Instead, she took a right and walked down a hallway where she could hear the telltale signs of someone being hit, followed by someone panting.

Anxiety made her freeze. And then the sound of someone skipping rope?

"Good, again." A male voice gave a direction.

"Seriously?"

Addie recognized Ms. Hollister's timbre, challenging the male. Edging farther down the hall, she stopped where she could peek into the room without being seen. Ms. Hollister, decked out in skintight capris, tank top, and running shoes, stood hunched over, dripping in sweat. Suddenly, she found something sexy about this Ms. Hollister. She covered her mouth with her fingers. Hopefully she hadn't said that out loud. What was she thinking? Ms. Hollister and sexy in the same sentence, especially after what she'd been through? Her mind was truly troubled. The sooner she got home, the sooner she could pull the covers over her head and just turn everything off.

"Enough of a break. Let's go again," he said, holding up Muay Tai pads in front of him.

Ms. Hollister sprang into action. Addie couldn't take her eyes off her boss as she pounced, catlike, weaving and bobbing as she hit the target like an expert.

Addie experienced a rush as she watched the back-and-forth dance the two did, Ms. Hollister circling her trainer, landing a punch with a bang. Her hands up, she jabbed across, then alternated and jabbed across again. She repeated this pattern over and over, circling the man. A quick spin and an elbow to the pad took the stocky trainer by surprise, almost knocking him over and ending the barrage.

"Nice. Now stop holding back." He goaded her on.

"Are you kidding me?" Ms. Hollister challenged him again. Sweat rolled down her face and her back, soaking the skintight tank even more.

Ms. Hollister advanced as the man lowered the pads. She kicked the pad, rocking his bulk. Another kick with the opposite leg pushed him back farther. Raising her foot, she planted it on his chest and pushed him backward, causing him to stumble to the floor.

"Oh, shit," Addie gasped.

Ms. Hollister, seeming out of breath, sprinted to the door. "Are you okay?"

"I'm sorry. I didn't mean to intrude." Addie put her hands up and backed away, finding herself against the wall.

"You're not." Ms. Hollister reached out to touch Addie, but she shirked away. "Come in. I want you to meet someone."

"Uhm, Ms. Hollister. I just wanted to apologize for earlier. I really don't want to interrupt your workout."

"Nonsense. You don't have anything to apologize for. I made the wrong assessment. I should apologize for putting you in the shower." Ms. Hollister offered a soft smile. Wrapping her arm around Addie's shoulders, she guided her into the gym.

Addie warily walked beside her. She'd been to gyms that would kill to have this kind of training equipment. Scanning the room, she noticed a heavy bag hanging in the corner. A top-of-the-line treadmill, rower, a spin bike, and weights lined the mirrored perimeter of the room, leaving the center open for just what Ms. Hollister was doing, fighting.

"Caesar, this is Addie. Addie, this is my trainer and sparring partner, Caesar."

Caesar stuck a sweaty hand out, but Addie didn't shake it. She couldn't even make eye contact with the man.

"Nice to meet you." Her voice was almost a whisper. "I should go and let you two get back to what you were doing. Sorry again for intruding."

"Addie, stop." Ms. Hollister's voice demanded action, so Addie did as she commanded. "I think Caesar can help you out."

"Help me? In what way?" Addie wasn't exactly into kickboxing or whatever Ms. Hollister was doing. She also wasn't in any condition to train as hard as Ms. Hollister was, so how could he possibly help her?

"Caesar is a black belt in Brazilian jiu-jitsu. He teaches self-defense down at the college, and I'm sure he'd be happy to show you how to defend yourself. Right?" Ms. Hollister looked at Caesar, clearly waiting for an answer.

"Of course, Ms. Hollister. It would be my pleasure." Caesar bowed and looked at Addie. She could see that he was assessing her. His gaze lit on her bruised face, moved down her body, and rested on her hands. "I see you're a fighter already. May I?" He reached for her hands but didn't touch her.

Addie lifted them and flinched as he took them into his bulky paws. His own hands looked like they'd seen more than a fight or two in the past. Pulling hers up, he studied them and then turned them over.

"You're a fighter, no?"

"I'm not sure what you mean," Addie said.

"You hit this person who attacked you, yes?" Caesar lowered her hands and smiled brightly. She could tell he was getting some pleasure at the thought she might have laid one on her attacker. "Boyfriend did this to you? You scratch him, yes?" He raised his hands and emulated a scratching motion.

"He wasn't my boyfriend. How do you know I scratched him?" Addie was a little freaked out by this man.

"Your nails, they are gone. You had manicure, but now they are gone. Taken by the police. I see it before." His thick accent colored his language. "I can train you," he said, walking away and grabbing his bag.

"Wait. I…I don't want to be some kinda ninja or something."

"Oh, good. We don't do ninja training. Different style of martial arts." He laughed.

"It wouldn't be martial-arts training per se," Ms. Hollister said. "It's self-defense. You'd be able to protect yourself if something happens again. You'd just be more prepared."

Addie glanced down at her hands. "Look, Ms. Hollister. I don't want to impose. I'm not sure I'm ready to—"

"Look," he said. "If you want to take back your life, you be down here tomorrow, same time as Ms. Hollister. We work out and you learn how to protect yourself. You want to live scared of every bump in night, don't come. Doesn't matter to me. Ms. Hollister, I need to get to my classes." Turning toward Addie, he bowed slightly. "Nice to meet you, Ms. Addie. See you tomorrow," he said as if he knew she would be there.

"It's nice to meet you, Caesar."

Caesar was light on his feet for such a massive brick. Addie was reminded of the man who had attacked her. Taller, but he too had the same kind of scars on his hands.

"Excuse me." Something flashed in her mind. "Do you just teach martial arts?"

"It's all I do now, but I was a mechanic before. Why do you ask?"

"I was just wondering about the scars on your hand." She looked down at her own. "I won't get those if I train, will I?"

"Oh, these?" He turned his hands over, looking at his knuckles. "Dios mío, no. Not unless you bust a couple of knuckles on an engine."

"No, no. I don't think I'm changing careers. Unless, of course, Ms. Hollister fires me," Addie said quietly.

"Tomorrow then." He waved as he left.

"I'm not firing you. Why would you say that?"

Addie felt her face flush. "Ms. Hollister, I think I should probably go home. I've taken up enough of your time. I appreciate everything you've done for me, but I don't want to be a bother." Pulling on a string of her shirt, she refused to be deterred. "I think I'd be more comfortable at my place. My things are there—my bed. You know, my stuff."

Ms. Hollister couldn't hide her look of surprise fast enough. Surely she knew this was coming. Addie had to go home eventually, right?

"You can stay as long as you'd like, but I don't want to stand in the way of your recovery. If this is about earlier, I'm sorry. As I said before, I completely overreacted."

"This isn't about earlier. I just think I'd feel more comfortable there. I can get Paul to stop at the hardware store and change the locks. It's not a problem."

Ms. Hollister put her hand on Addie's arm. "I hope you don't mind, but I took the liberty of installing new locks. I also added a small security system. It's a simple press code, similar to ours at Integrated Financial."

Addie didn't know what to say. She didn't need a security system; it wasn't like her apartment was full of the latest electronics. Unless, of course, you counted Drake's prized possession, her gaming system with surround-sound and a high-definition TV. Heck, it wasn't like Addie even got to watch TV when Drake was around. It was just another reason to dump her. If she was lucky, Drake had taken her stuff out of her apartment, if she could read the writing on the wall. Now she wondered if her cheap girlfriend could even read.

"I don't really have anything worth stealing, Ms. Hollister." Addie was a little surprised at the expensive installation. "I'm surprised my super let you do that."

"I can be very convincing when I need to be, Addie. Besides, this isn't for your things. It's for you. I want you to feel safe." Ms. Hollister toweled herself off. "It's the least I can do if you insist on going home."

Without thinking, Addie said, "Well, the security system didn't work very well last night, so I'm not sure how well it will work in an old building like mine." She covered her mouth as she realized her faux pas. "I mean the fire alarm is going off all the time, and well, I just—"

"I know what you meant, Ms. Blake. I have no doubt our security system failed you, but I promise that won't happen again." Ms. Hollister tossed the towel into a basket and pulled her gloves off. "I'll shower and take you home."

"You don't have to do that. I can call Paul. I'm sure he can come get me. I don't want to be a bother." She hoisted her cell phone up and tapped the screen.

"No, I insist. I don't mind. Besides, I'd like to make sure the keys work and the system is activated."

Addie acquiesced. "Of course, Ms. Hollister. I'll grab my things and wait for you downstairs." She walked away before Ms. Hollister could say another word. She'd put her foot in her mouth, and the sooner she got away from her boss the better.

Chapter Eighteen

Nancy looked at the report from the rape at the conference center. There had been a big function with lots of mucky-mucks present. Perhaps the rapist had been attending the event. Pulling the attendee list, she moved her finger down as she read off each name. Nothing rang a bell until she hit one she recognized. Greyson Hollister.

Interesting. Hollister had been at the event, and she owned the company where the other attack took place. Once was a coincidence; twice was a pattern. Were there other coincidences? She didn't believe in them: she was more a pattern kinda gal. Patterns could predict future events, and now that they had more than a few random victims, Nancy would add the new pins to the map and study the patterns. However, she had something else to look at: Hollister's movements.

Did she think Hollister had anything to do with the rapes? Not likely, but she wasn't about to dismiss something so obvious quickly. It was their only solid lead at the moment. Pulling her phone, she called Integrated Financial.

"Greyson Hollister, please." Nancy looked at her watch. "She's gone for the day already? No, I don't want to leave a message. Do you have a number where I can reach her?" Nancy doodled on her pad. "Ma'am, my name is Detective Nancy Hill. I'm investigating the attack at Integrated Financial." Clearly, the woman felt she was helping Hollister, but she was only pissing Nancy off by interrupting her constantly. "Ma'am, I can get a warrant, but what a huge waste of time that would be for everyone. So, why don't you call Ms. Hollister and give her my number and tell her I expect a call in the next ten minutes. Yes, thank you."

Nancy, frustrated, slapped her phone to the desk. Why did civilians always think they could stonewall the cops? Did the woman think she was protecting her boss? At a minimum people like her were creating a hostile environment that made her job more difficult. Help. They just needed the public's help when it came to crimes like these. Someone had to have seen something, or someone.

Pulling the photos from last night's rape at the convention center, she thumbed through them and placed them next to the photos of Addie Blake. The attack on Blake was brutal, while the rape was somewhat less violent. Placing the head shots next to each other, Nancy stared at both women. Similar looks. Nancy studied the body shots. Again, similar looking. The only difference was that one was raped and one wasn't. Then Nancy reached the pubic areas of both women, and it hit her. No souvenir from Addie. The pubic shot of the convention-center victim clearly showed that a patch of pubic hair was missing. On Addie, nothing.

"They're not the same person," she exclaimed.

Sergeant Torres walked into the bay and over to the desk. "Whatcha got?" Torres cringed at the sight of the photos.

"Check this out." Nancy pointed at the shots. "What looks different to you?" Nancy was almost giddy with the revelation. If she was wrong, she'd take her lumps, but her gut told her she wasn't.

"Nothing. Kinda scary how similar all the victims look." Torres pushed at the photos and moved them around on the desk.

"That's a serial rapist's pattern. The victims usually have something in common. Looks, where they live, how they live, places they frequent, how they're raped. The rapist likes routine. It makes him comfortable." Nancy's pronouncement was hopefully leading Torres in the direction she'd just traveled. "Notice anything else?"

"No rape on this one, yet this one was raped." She pointed to Addie and then the other victim.

"No souvenir." Nancy tapped Addie's picture. "He always takes a souvenir, always."

"What about her purse?"

"Found it outside in the trash. Not personal enough." Nancy pulled two more folders, laid out the photos next to Addie's, and pointed out the differences. "He took the panties from this one and cut a lock of hair from that one's head—to remind him of his conquest. Why didn't he take something from Addie Blake?"

"He didn't have time? I mean, the cleaning crew has a key to start the elevator. So, maybe that spooked him?"

"It's possible, but look closer." Nancy thought about the cleaning crew and the fact that they had put that elevator into motion. Maybe the rapist hadn't planned on that, so maybe he panicked, but he still had time to take something personal. He beat the crap out of her. Why didn't he beat the others as badly? No, she was pretty sure she was on the right track.

She crossed her arms and rested against the desk,

spearing Torres with a look and raising her eyebrows in question as she waited for an answer. Torres shuffled the pictures of the torsos, and then as if a lightbulb popped, she smiled. Tapping Addie's picture, she said, "The rapist didn't do this one."

"That's what I'm thinking. A copycat." Nancy picked up Addie's face shot and looked at her. "But why her?"

"She has an enemy?" Torres asked.

"Okay, but who would want to hurt her like that? That's evil." Nancy stacked the photos, each in their own separate pile. "Now we have a problem. We're looking for two men instead of one."

"This is a big break in the case, Detective. When are you going to tell the chief?"

"Right now. If you hear screaming, send in reinforcements."

"I think you can handle him. But I'll keep an ear out for ya."

Nancy's phone went off just as she grabbed the chief's door. "Ms. Hollister. How nice of you to call me. Do you have a minute?"

Chapter Nineteen

He twirled the keys around his finger. The metal clang as the keys hit his palm was music to his ears. Twirling them again, he walked up the steps two at a time. God, he loved the anticipation. She wanted him. It was why he had her keys, wasn't it? A casual look down the hall and then back at the number on the first jagged edge sent him in to the left.

Apartment number 103.

He didn't want to ruin the surprise, so he slowly, deliberately, slid the key in quietly. Someone passed him in the hall, so he stopped and leaned against the door, hiding his face. A screaming kid followed his mom as she shouted something at him in Spanish. Twisting the handle, he pushed it with his shoulder, pocketed the keys, and slid past the barely open door.

The bright pink of a neon sign signaling to any passerby that Chinese food was available below lit the room. He waited, his eyes adjusting, his nose acquiring the smell of her perfume. The small apartment was almost how he envisioned it. Perhaps a little less floral upholstery, but it was her. The apartment contained only the kitchen to his left and a short hallway and two doors to his right. Spartan by his standards, but functional. Moving down the hall, he knew she'd be waiting for him. They always waited.

Maybe she'd be wearing something sexy, in

red preferably. The door on the right was open. A bathroom. Good to know. He'd need that later. He slipped his right hand into his pants and stroked himself. Beyond ready, he didn't need coaxing, so he reached into his pocket and fingered his other tool for the night. It had seen a lot of action lately, and tonight, well, he didn't want it feeling left out. Pulling it from his pocket, he flicked the blade out, pushed the door open with his left hand, and stared at the empty bed.

What the fuck?

❧❧❧❧

"Detective Hill, I understand you're throwing your weight around with my staff." Greyson hated it when someone tried to intimidate her employees. Clients sometimes acted as if their money gave them the right to be abusive. The badge, well, that was unacceptable and no excuse for being a bully.

"Ms. Hollister, can you tell me where you were on May 25th?"

"May 25th? I'd have to look at my calendar. Why?" Greyson's interest was piqued now.

"How about April 13th, a Friday? Any ideas where you were then?" Hill peppered her again.

"My answer is the same. I'd have to look at my calendar, Detective." Greyson's antennae went up immediately. "Detective Hill, are you implying that I'm a suspect in a crime?"

"Ms. Hollister, perhaps you and I and your calendar should meet so we can see where you were during these dates."

"I'd like to help you out, but right now I'm taking Ms. Blake home. Perhaps we can meet at I.F., and I'll have counsel there as well."

"I'm fine with that. Make sure you bring your calendar and your lawyer, and don't stonewall me this time, Ms. Hollister."

"I'll do my best, Detective."

"We'll see," Hill said. "How about we meet at I.F. in about an hour? It's still a workday, unless you'd rather meet at your home. Doesn't matter to me."

"The office is fine. I'll assume you know where to find it." Greyson ended the phone call abruptly. "Bitch."

Greyson didn't want anything or anyone, for that matter, intruding on her sanctuary, and her home was just that, her refuge.

"Are you ready Ms. Hollister?" Addie stood at the bottom of the stairs. She clutched her bag tight to her chest and looked so frail that Greyson's heart lurched.

"Gosh, Addie, how many times do I need to tell you to call me Greyson?"

"I'm sorry, Greyson. I find it really difficult since you're my boss."

"Addie, I'm not your direct boss, but regardless of that, I want you to feel comfortable coming to me if you need anything. I hope you don't mind, but I've added my cell phone number to your phone. I'm speed-dial number one."

Greyson had noticed Drake was number one. The bitch didn't deserve that honor, and maybe she didn't either, but she'd helped Addie when Drake had abandoned her.

"Oh, ah, that was Drake's number." Addie shrugged.

"I just wanted you to be able to hit me first. Of course, if you're in danger, 911 is always the best number to call. If you just need someone to talk to, I'm always available to you, no matter the time of day or night." Greyson reached for Addie's bag. "Here, let me get that for you."

"I can take it, thank you."

"Of course. Well, if you're ready." Greyson opened the door and ushered Addie to the SUV out front.

Greyson took a long, deep breath. The afternoon had a warm, summer smell, yet summer was a long way off. Her home nestled in the foothills of Morgan Hill gave her the tranquility she desired and the privacy she craved. Pulling the SUV through the gate, she admired the sprawling hillside. Soon the grapes would be harvested and another bounty of wine would be in the barrel rooms aging. A Renaissance woman, that's what the *Mercury* had called her in the exposé they'd penned. Greyson had learned early to practice what she preached—diversify, diversify, and diversify.

"Wow, the view is amazing."

"Thanks. I call it home." Greyson hoped that didn't sound like she was bragging. She'd worked hard for what she had and took pride in her ability to provide a good life for Ben and her mother.

"That must be some commute in the mornings. Why don't you take the train in? It has to be cheaper. Besides, it would give you lots of time to get work done. I like riding the train when I can." Addie's voice weakened.

"Yeah. I don't take the train anymore. It was my wife's favorite thing to do, too. Sometimes she'd surprise me and meet me at the station, and…" Greyson stopped. Another memory of Cate flashed.

"More," Cate pleaded.

The rhythmic motion of the train worked in Greyson's favor as she slowly started to pump her hand into her lover's pussy. God, she wished she were somewhere more appropriate for what she wanted to do to Cate. Splay her out on a bed, drop to her knees, and worship Cate's body. Suddenly Cate stopped, pulling Greyson out of her dream.

"What's wrong?"

Cate leaned back and let a slow smile flicker across her face as she closed her eyes and dropped her hand to her clit. "Nothing's wrong...just...keep...doing...oh... oh..." Cate brutalized her clit as she rubbed over it back and forth, mesmerizing Greyson. Cate goaded her. "Don't stop, baby."

"Jesus, you're killing me here, Cate."

"Yeah, but isn't it a great way to go?" Cate's hips rocked on Greyson's hand. "Harder."

Greyson spread her legs so her hand had more room to pound her lover.

"That's it. Oh, God, you're fucking amazing, Grey."

The lights flickered, signaling the bad connection at her train station. They were less than a couple of minutes from hitting the platform.

Just in time, Cate's body tightened, froze slightly, and then jerked back and forth as she huffed out her orgasm. Collapsing against Greyson, she rested her head on Greyson's shoulder and blew in her ear. "You haven't lost your touch."

"Good to know," Greyson said, pulling Cate's jacket around her.

"Ms. Hollister? Are you all right?" Addie squeezed

Greyson's forearm, gently rousing her.

"I'm sorry. I was just remembering why I don't take the train anymore." Greyson turned to look out the window, hoping she'd hidden the blush that had crawled up her neck and face. Cate always had that effect on her; she was a tigress. Greyson had resigned herself to the fact that this was often the only way she'd thought of Cate lately. Stress seemed to bring on those erotic dreams. Maybe she needed to see someone about her problem? No. Only if it got worse or affected her ability to do her job. Right now they were a welcome respite in a world full of crummy things.

"I doubt I'll be taking the train now," Addie said. "I guess I'll need to pick up my car at Drake's shop."

"Just out of curiosity, why is your car at Drake's? Shouldn't it be in the garage?"

Addie shrugged. "I thought it was there, but she said she came over and took it home, well, to her garage, for safekeeping."

"Hmm." Greyson looked at Addie again. Why did Drake keep mucking things up in Addie's life? It was almost like Drake did it on purpose so that Addie needed her, depended on her for stuff.

"Well, you have a beautiful drive nevertheless," Addie said, changing the subject again. "Even if it's a long one."

"It's worth it. I get to come home to this, so I'll take it. I have an apartment in town if it gets too late."

"Ben, he's your son?"

There were so many subject changes Greyson felt like she might get whiplash if this kept up.

"Yes, he's the light of my life." Greyson hoped that didn't sound corny, but it was true. Ben was the reason she got up in the morning. She wanted him to have everything he needed. Without Cate around, she supposed she overcompensated for the loss. No matter. He was the only love she would ever have now.

"He's very cute. I'm sure you and his dad must be very proud."

Greyson hesitated. Was it possible Addie was the only one at the company who didn't know about Cate and what had happened? Trying to remember when Addie was hired was impossible with the turnover of employees at I.F. While it wasn't huge, it also wasn't her job to hire and fire.

"We don't know who his father is," Greyson said casually. "Cate and I had in vitro."

"Oh, I'm sorry. I didn't know. I just assumed… well, I mean I…I'm sorry. It's none of my business." Addie blushed.

"I think it's common knowledge around I.F."

"I don't listen to water-cooler gossip, Ms. Hollister."

"Greyson," she said once again.

"Greyson."

"I lost my wife not long after Ben was born. He's the greatest gift she left me, a little part of her." Greyson's smile dimmed, more like one offered when you spoke of the dead. Reserved and conciliatory.

"I didn't mean to bring up any bad memories." Greyson watched out of the corner of her eye as Addie looked out the window at the meadow they were passing.

"Not bad memories at all." Had Addie connected the dots? They were the same, she and Addie.

Lesbians.

Maybe that's why Greyson had found herself so drawn to the woman in meetings. Her gaydar pinged every time she saw Addie. With the confirmation of Drake as her girlfriend, she had been happy to see she wasn't wrong about Addie. It was odd, but Greyson had always seemed to search her out when the teams met. She had something for auburns. Cate was a ginger through and through.

God, how she missed her. Cate was brazen, sexual, and a wild horse no one could tame, except Greyson. She was also the centering force behind Greyson. Her ability to bring Greyson down after a tough day at work was amazing. Time had lessened the yearning but not the memories. A night spent dreaming of Cate was often the only time she had with her wife. Their short visits, even if it was only in her mind, kept her from going crazy. So for that, Greyson was grateful for Cate, especially when struggling with a decision or stress, for those were the times Cate usually visited her in her dreams.

But she wasn't ready to revisit the subject of Cate, not today. "Are you sure you want to go home?"

"I need to get on with my life. I can't let this bastard win," Addie said, trying to sound convincing.

"Are you sure it's not because you're staying at the boss's house?" Greyson chuckled. "I know tongues will wag, but I've endured worse. Trust me. The Ice Queen can handle it."

Addie blushed again.

"Oh, you think I don't keep up with the water-cooler gossip? It's okay." Greyson patted Addie's hand and then squeezed it, not letting go. "I hear everything people say about me at the company."

"I've never called you that, just so you know."

"It would be okay if you had. I have a reputation that I'd like to keep intact." Greyson smiled.

"I see. Well, I won't let it slip how compassionate you are. It'll be our little secret." Addie's voice had no inflection.

Greyson wished she could change what had happened to Addie. She wished she could have taken her place and received the beating. Her heart broke seeing Addie so frail.

"Addie, I might be out of place here, but would you like to have dinner sometime?"

Greyson didn't know where that came from, but it was out before she could stop it. She squirmed, waiting for an answer.

"I'm...I mean...you're the boss and I'm an employee."

"Yes, I own the company, but technically I'm not your direct supervisor."

Greyson and Addie looked at each other, and Greyson could see the wheels whirling.

"You know what, that was completely inappropriate. I apologize. Under different circumstances, I would hope you would consider it as just a friendly gesture. I..." Now Greyson was at a loss for words. How would she spin this? "I would like to get to know you as a person, and perhaps when all of this is behind us, you'll reconsider my offer?"

God that sounded lame. Greyson suddenly felt like a schoolgirl trying to ask someone out on a date, but trying to preempt a refusal, she'd back-pedaled.

"I'd be honored to have coffee someday, Ms. Hollister."

And there it was then, a gentle letdown—*I'm sorry. I have a girlfriend, but we can be friends.*

Greyson played along. "I'd be happy to take you to coffee."

Chapter Twenty

Nancy paced Greyson Hollister's office with a menacing attitude. She'd been kept waiting long enough. Just as she reached for the door, Hollister smashed through it, threw her purse on the couch, and stopped.

"Waiting long, Detective?"

"Long enough, Ms. Hollister." Nancy wanted to punch something. The smug little look on Hollister's face infuriated her.

"You're the one that asked for this meeting, not me."

"I didn't know you'd keep me waiting for…" She looked down at her watch. "Two hours."

"Traffic was a bitch. You know, everyone going home and all." Hollister leaned against her desk, not even bothering to take off her coat. "Let's make this quick, shall we?"

"Well, I expect that will depend on you, Ms. Hollister." Nancy pulled out her pad and pen. She'd written the dates of all the rapes down and needed to compare them against Hollister's calendar.

"So, let's start with these dates. Where were you on March 16th, April 13th, and May 25th, and that's just for starters," Nancy said, her pen ready, but Hollister didn't say anything. "Ms. Hollister?"

"I'm waiting for counsel."

"Jesus H. Christ. Are you kidding me? I'm not

here to yank your chain. I just need to know where you were on these dates."

"Detective, I believe you are trying to tie me to the dates of the rape. Is that a correct assumption?"

Nancy tossed her pen on the coffee table and scrubbed her face. Why couldn't people just be more forthcoming with information? Why did they always have to have their lawyers present? Yeah, yeah, they had a right to not implicate themselves, but she was on a fact-finding mission, and Greyson Hollister's name was coming up on a lot of the dates the rapist had struck. Again, she didn't believe in coincidences, but as they always said, check the most obvious.

"I can assure you, Detective Hill, that I'm not the Elevator Rapist."

"I agree, but when I look at the dates and locations, your name is always on the guest list. I'd say that's more than a little suspicious. Wouldn't you?"

"Are you saying I have a stalker?"

Interesting. Nancy hadn't thought of it in quite those terms. Scratching her chin, she stared at Hollister.

"Have you had problems with one?"

"I'm in the public eye, Detective. I don't know. It's possible." Hollister shrugged.

"Have you noticed someone hanging around? Letters, emails, any kind of threats?"

This was a rape case, so that's why Nancy hadn't considered the stalker angle. Besides, Hollister hadn't reported any incidents of stalking, harassing phone calls, or even as much as a hangnail. Now she was trying to make it about her. Really? What a narcissist.

"No, not that I can think of."

"No threatening phone calls?"

"Integrated Financial is a business that makes

its money trading and buying shares. Sometimes it doesn't go the way a client thinks it should. They get pissed off and say things, but we haven't had anything go physical."

"Okay, so back to the dates I asked you about. Where were you?"

Hollister sat at her desk, cracked open her desk calendar, and thumbed to March. "Okay, it looks like I was at a fund-raiser for the mayor. Where was the rape?"

"Where was the fund-raiser?"

"At his private residence."

"Okay," Nancy said, thinking about the distance from the residence to the rape scene. "Did anyone else see you there? What time did you leave the event? Did you go with anyone, and can they vouch for you?"

❧❧❧❧

All Greyson wanted to do was find her bed and sleep for days. The detective's questions had taken hours. The constant lob and then volley and then lobbing back again had tired her. After coming home, she'd played with Ben in the pool again, fed him dinner, and sat with her mother while they watched her mom's favorite British series. Something here, about the room, the calm and the environment soothed her. The only thing missing was the presence of Cate, and her dad. At times like this her heart lurched in pain.

"Well, I think it's time for this little monster to head for bed," Greyson said, arching over Ben and tickling him. His explosive laughter was contagious, and she giggled as she rubbed her nose against his.

"I'm not a monster, Mommy. You're the

monster. Arrrrr," he said, arching his fingers back and making clawing motions. "I'm the superhero. I can save Gramma from you. Arrrr!"

Greyson continued her tickle-torture until Ben finally relented.

"Okay, okay, Mommy. Help me, Gramma. Help." He laughed and squeezed his arms and legs around Greyson, who stood with him firmly attached to her body.

"Check out the grip on this kid." She swung in a circle, looking at her mom.

"Reminds me of you when you were little, honey. All legs and arms." Camille swatted his bottom. "Get to bed, you. You have your first day of preschool tomorrow."

"Preschool? My baby is growing up."

"I'm not a baby anymore, Mommy." Greyson shivered. Cate would miss his first day of school. The milestones were ticking away faster and faster, putting Cate's death further and further away from her. Holding on would only worsen the pain, but she wasn't sure she could let each event pass without a memory of Cate flooding her mind.

"Yep, time for bed, big boy," she said, hearing a hint of melancholy coloring her voice.

Her mother's strong hand clutched hers and wiggled it. "It'll be okay, honey. Children remind us all of our age and our past. Hang in there. Cate's with us." She smiled at Greyson, pulling her hand to her face. Placing a kiss on it, she smiled up at Greyson and shooed her away. "Off to bed, both of you. My next show's about to start."

"Night, Mom."

Greyson kissed her mother on the forehead and

then bent down to Ben to do the same. She hoped she found peace in slumber tonight. Her nights lately had been long, arduous events, with just a smattering of sleep dropped in between.

She took Ben to his room, put him down, tucked him in, and listened to him say his prayers.

Then, finally, she found herself alone, sprawled out on her bed. Arms behind her head, she stared at the ceiling. How was Addie faring at her apartment? A quick phone call in the morning would be in order. She didn't want to seem like she was checking up on Addie, but she'd be lying if she said she wasn't just a smidge worried. Her eyes closed and then opened. She needed to remember to call Neil Harris in the morning and come up with a plan to handle Detective Hill. Why did her mind always race when it was time for bed? Her eyelids dropped again and then slammed open; she needed to remember to get Jarrod removed as her personal assistant. Her mind drifted back and forth. She was finally going to succumb to sleep as her eyes gently closed.

Pulling on her overcoat, she walked to the window and gazed down at the people below. Little ants scurrying around, weaving in and out of traffic, as the yellow cabs honked their horns at them. She shoved a bunch of files into her briefcase, then closed it and ran for the door. She just needed sleep; exhaustion was playing tricks with her mind. She'd finally overworked herself, just as her father had warned her she would. In an hour and a half she'd be home; a cocktail, a hot bath, and all would be right with the world. She'd have the weekend to relax and work on the...no, she needed to relax. Maybe she could call someone and play a round of golf. She hadn't played in months, and then she could have a couple of cocktails with her golfing partner and would be more relaxed. Oh, but he'd want to bring his wife or girlfriend. Golf was out.

Passing the security desk, she waved just as the guard was shoving a piece of pizza in his mouth.

"Good night," she said, watching as he dropped pepperoni on his shirt.

Greyson hurried to the platform, hoping no one was there. She didn't frighten easily, but she was alone and it was late. "No telling who's marauding around at this hour," she whispered to herself. Standing under the streetlight, she looked around the station.

Empty.

Suddenly it felt like cold fingers were slipping through her body. She shivered and pulled the collar of her coat up and tight against her neck. Looking down the tracks, she could see the light of the engine approaching and hear the moan of the wheels, metal on metal grinding as the brakes screeched the train to a halt. She stood waiting for the clank of the door to spread open, letting her in. Grimacing at the bright fluorescent light, she cautiously looked in and around.

No one.

She could hear the train start to gear up for its exit, so she jumped on and grabbed the rail, steadying herself as the train lurched forward to its next destination. She couldn't shake the thought that she'd been here before. Done this very thing, this very night. Sitting on the bench seat, she gripped her briefcase and held it tight against her chest. Forty minutes. Less if there weren't any other stops on the way, and then she'd get into her car, twenty minutes home, and she'd fall into bed like she did every night.

The lights inside the train car flickered, letting her know she was only a few minutes from her stop. She'd tried to doze, but her mind wouldn't let her. It raced like it did every night when she tried to go to sleep. Damndest thing, she thought. She'd taken to leaving the TV on at night for the noise. It was just enough to occupy her mind and let her sleep. Greyson figured it was a holdover from her childhood when her mother stayed up late waiting for her father to come home. The nights her mother decided to read were death for Greyson.

"Mom, turn on the TV. I can't sleep," she'd yell down the staircase.

"Grey, go to bed. Your father will be home any minute."

"Mom!"

"Greyson Jane."

Greyson bobbed back and forth as the train ground to a stop. She stood in front of the doors and waited for their final swish and her last time exiting the car for a few days. Stepping out onto the platform, Greyson looked around. She didn't know what she was searching for, but she glanced back and forth anyway. The chill seeped into her bones, and she pulled her collar tight again.

Only a few cars were parked in the rideshare lot, and the lighting was less than adequate. Why didn't she just break down and stay at her apartment in the city like everyone else did and come out to the burbs on the weekends? Her father's advice rang in her ears. "Learn from my mistakes, Grey. I can't get that time back that I missed with you growing up." But she didn't have kids so it didn't matter.

Crossing the parking lot, Greyson clicked her fob for her car and noticed someone leaning against it. A woman. *The stilettos and legs gave away her gender. Now if she could just figure out who the woman was, maybe things were looking up. Perhaps a damsel in distress with a dead battery or a flat tire. Greyson could handle any of those things, but beyond that...well, there was always the auto club. The light diffused in the thin veil of fog that seemed to wrap around the woman. Her blond hair was like a beacon as it picked up the little light that was left. She looked up at Greyson and smiled.*

Cate.

"Hello, Grey. You look good." *Cate sauntered over to Greyson.* "You also look surprised."

"What are you doing here, Cate?"

"Waiting for you, silly kitty." *Cate had a smile that had broken a million hearts, and when men found out she was a lesbian, she'd broken a few more.*

Greyson opened the back door and tossed her briefcase onto the floor. She felt Cate push herself against her back and wrap her arms around her. Sliding her hands into Greyson's jacket, Cate crossed arms and pulled Greyson back against her, then grabbed Greyson's breasts.

"I've missed you," *Cate whispered and then slid her tongue along Greyson's ear.*

Before Greyson could move, Cate slipped a hand down the front of Greyson and into her slacks.

"You're wearing those silk boxers I bought you for Christmas."

Suddenly, Cate's fingers had breached the opening of Greyson's boxers. She pushed her hips against Greyson's ass at the same time she stroked Greyson's clit. Greyson groaned at the touch. Steeling herself, she tried to ignore the contact.

"Cate...I"

Cate slipped her finger over Greyson's mouth and gently pulled her head back onto her shoulder. "Relax, no one's around. Reach back behind you." The stilettos Cate wore made her almost as tall as Greyson.

Greyson hesitated.

"Grey, slide your hand behind you and tou—"

Greyson reached between their bodies and opened the jacket. Soft, silky skin and then a patch of hair brushed against her fingertips. Cate was a drug, her drug, and no matter how hard she fought it, she couldn't fight Cate.

"I've missed you, Grey."

"I've missed you, Cate," she said as her fingers explored the silken wetness of Cate's pussy. Her mind raced. She wanted Cate; she always wanted Cate. She couldn't get Cate out of her mind half the time and spent the other half trying to figure out if she was going crazy because of Cate. Here she was the head of the country's fastest-growing brokerage house, Integrated Financial, getting felt up late at night in a dark parking lot. She must be losing her mind.

"In the car, Cate," Greyson commanded her. She wasn't about to lose it out in the open.

Sliding backward into the backseat, she pulled Cate on top of her.

"Shit."

"What's wrong, lover?" Cate asked in the sultry voice that made Greyson's knees buckle. "Got something that needs scratching?"

"The door."

Cate ever so slowly reached over and pulled the door handle, but not before she slipped out of her overcoat, exposing herself to Greyson. A red silk bra and thong that barely covered anything, and Cate had lots that needed covering. Cate let her tongue linger on the tip of her upper lip and then slid it in and out of her mouth before biting her lower lip and pouting.

"Are you mad at me, lover?"

Greyson watched as Cate moved over her body, letting Greyson's thigh part her legs. Cate rubbed herself back and forth against the long thigh, her eyelids dropping as she let out a faint moan. Greyson grabbed her hips and forced her harder against her leg, feeling the friction between them. Her hand glided up the small curve of Cate's waist and behind her. With the flick of her wrist, Cate's silky bondage was off, sliding down her arms and onto Greyson's chest. Greyson moved her hand up farther and threaded her fingers into the blond locks, forcing Cate's lips closer. She wanted to taste her, to drink her in and luxuriate in her essence, before she turned her over and fucked her crazy.

The tension in her body was so thick she doubted a quick tumble would exorcise her demonic need for Cate. Crushing her lips against Cate's, she drove her tongue and tasted her. Her blood raced through her, thrumming with electricity as Cate devoured her in return. Passion met passion, lips replaced hands as Cate peeled Greyson's slacks down to her knees. Greyson pushed herself up to her lover's lips and begged her for release. Cate's tongue spread her lips and dipped down, flicking her clit back and forth.

It never took much to make Greyson come. She was a tightly strung racket that, if hit just right, snapped instantly. Her heart raced, blood throbbed in her ears, and she felt herself pushed over the endless abyss, free-falling into something almost otherworldly. Cate kept Greyson's thighs together as she continued to bury herself in Greyson's orgasm. The more pressure she applied to

Greyson's clit with her tongue, the farther Greyson fell, and she continued to tumble.

Greyson stilled Cate's head. "Stop, please. I can't take anymore. Fuck."

Without a word, Cate moved up Greyson's body and molded herself against Greyson. Her lips buried against Greyson's neck, she started to suckle the throbbing pulse as she reached down and stroked Greyson again. Instantly, Greyson was arching against Cate's hand, pleading for release.

"Oh, Christ!"

Greyson pushed away at the hands. As hard as she tried to fight them, her body responded to the gentle urgings.

"Please," Greyson moaned. "Cate, I can't."

A buzzing sounded in the distance and pulled Greyson from her exquisite torment. Opening her eyes, she felt around for Cate, but, as usual—it was only a dream. A wonderful, erotic dream. Flushed, Greyson pushed off the bed and swung her legs to the floor.

"God, Cate. Why?"

Peeling the sweat-laden shirt over her head, she heard the persistent buzz of her cell phone again. Addie's number flashed across the face of the phone. The lateness of the hour instantly made her worry.

Swiping at the green button she asked, "Addie, are you all right?"

Chapter Twenty-one

Pound, pound, pound. "Honey, open the door."

He froze. His hand deep in lacy undergarments, he waited for the intruder to go away. He pondered the predicament for a moment. Should he open the door? His eyes shut as he fingered the silk. Oh, she would be so wanting. Glancing around the room, he assessed his options.

Let her in and take advantage of the opportunity that presented itself.

Let her keep banging on the door and wait for her to eventually leave.

Keep his little trophy and retreat for another time.

He hadn't prepared for a visitor, and from the sound of her rough voice, he doubted the piece of meat tenderizing the door would be much fun. Besides, she wasn't his type.

"Addie, I know you're in there. Open the door. I just want to talk. Why did you change the locks?"

"Why indeed," he whispered. "To keep the likes of you out of her world."

As he shut the drawer, he pocketed a pair of black panties and stroked them against his erection. Turning around, he peered out the window. That wasn't an option. Too many pedestrians meandering around. Over his shoulder, the closet. It beckoned him, promising seclusion to finger his trophy while he waited out the persistent intruder. Frustrated, he knew he'd have to stay there at least an hour until the commotion at the door left.

"Addie—" Silence. "What? I'm just trying to get into my apartment...yes, I do live here...well, no, my name isn't on the lease...Fine, I'm leaving, but I'm coming back later, Addie."

Easing back into the closet, he could smell her. He pulled a coat around himself and inhaled. They said everyone has an essence. Well, that was true, and he was bathing in Addie Blake's.

"I'll be back later, Addie," the rough voice said, "and you're going to talk to me."

"I doubt it," he whispered. "I doubt it."

❧❧❧❧❧

They embraced briefly, yet long enough for a surge to go through Addie. She was certain it was only because she was holding on to a lifeline that had been tossed to her the night before. When Ms. Hollister pulled away and looked down at her, Addie was almost certain she saw something behind those mysterious eyes, but she wasn't going there. Her boss had been gorgeous, strong, and sincere when she'd offered to help the night before. A moment of weakness, Addie was sure, but Addie was just as strong and brave, and now she needed to prove that fact to no one—not Drake, not the man who'd assaulted her—but only to herself.

"Well, I need to get going. Detective Hill is waiting for me at the office. I'm sure she has a million more questions." Ms. Hollister looked around the room.

Addie's place wasn't as opulent as Ms. Hollister's massive home, but it was functional and it was hers. She wouldn't be ashamed of her Spartan surroundings, except for the massive TV and tools that never seemed to be off it or find their way back to Drake's place. She suspected it was a way for Drake to have a reason for coming back. Drake had left pieces of herself stranded around the apartment, like their relationship that never seemed to find its way to being put back together.

"Thank you again for showing me how to work the alarm and for the new locks. I feel safer already," Addie lied.

"My number is the first number on speed dial." Ms. Hollister picked up Addie's hands and gazed at her face. "I don't care what time of night it is. You call me if you're scared or just need someone to talk to. Understand?" Ms. Hollister's voice was low and reassuring.

Addie could only nod, and then Ms. Hollister did it. She kissed Addie's forehead and left without another word. Shocked, all Addie could do was throw the deadbolt, key in the code, and lean against the door. How strange was Ms. Hollister? Taking the liberty of placing a kiss on her and without as much as an apology after. She should have slapped her. Right?

Her mind raced with thoughts that only someone who wasn't in her condition should have. Rebuilding her life was the priority, not a romantic interlude with the boss. God, she was screwed up. As she looked at her life in the confines of her apartment, she made a decision. Her relationship with Drake was over. After gathering up her tools, her gaming station, and other odds and ends, she tossed them into a garbage bag and placed them by the door. A fresh start, a new life meant getting rid of those things that brought pain into hers. Drake was more than a headache; she was the past.

Addie slapped her hands together. A few minutes and she had collected what amounted to the remnants of their life together. There was little to show for two years of a relationship. It had all fit into a small two-foot by three-foot cardboard box and pretty much summed up their relationship. A few cheap knickknacks, two photos of them together, a pair of boxers, and a few other articles of clothing. That was it.

Lying back on the couch, Addie pulled her crocheted afghan around her. It was one of the few things she had to remind her of her grandmother. It had been a gift for her sweet-sixteen birthday. Thinking about her grandmother, she remembered how every Christmas day she and her siblings would wait for Grandma to arrive. Rolling up in her old Rambler sedan, she was barely able to see over the steering wheel. She looked so tiny behind it.

Grandma was wearing her old hat that had seen better days, her gloves, and her customary patent-leather white purse hanging from her arm. Addie remembered the way the purse swung as Grandma waddled away from the car with an armload of paper bags. Those paper bags, though, held treasures. The same treasures every year, but they were one of the few Christmas gifts she could remember getting.

"Grandma, I was worried you weren't coming," *Addie said, hugging her grandmother tight. The smell of cedar hung on her sweater, and her sensible shoes squeaked as she plodded behind Addie.*

"Oh, gosh, child. I come for dinner every Sunday, and Christmas is a given. What in the world would make you think I wouldn't come this time?" She cuffed Addie's chin and planted a kiss on her forehead.

Addie didn't know why she would think her grandmother wouldn't come every Christmas, but she did worry every year. For nothing.

"I don't know, Grandma. I just think sometimes you might get tired of coming, I guess."

"Lord, child. I think you were a born worrier."

Addie sat down on the couch next to her grandmother and waited like an obedient dog did when its owner brought promises of a treat for good behavior. Handing Addie a bag, her grandmother said what she always said, "It isn't much, but it's filled with love."

Pulling the giant paper bag open, Addie inhaled deeply. It smelled the same every year. Something special from her grandmother. Addie sat on the floor in front of her grandmother and pulled out an orange and laid it on the floor. An apple, a green apple, and then a bag of nuts followed. Finally, Addie pulled out a bag of chocolate chips. Her treasures lay out in front of her.

"Thank you, Grandma."

"Well, child, like I said, it isn't much, but when I was a little girl my father gave me the same thing. Oh, with the exception of the chocolate chips. He'd give us a little bag of gumdrops, but they stick to your teeth. Chocolate's much better."

"Grandma, why did your dad give you fruit and candy?"

"Well, he'd lived through the Great Depression, and he was poor. Fresh fruit and candy were high dollar in those days. So he never forgot what it was like to be poor. Every Christmas, we kids got fruit and candy. It *was wonderful," she said, clapping her hands together. "I don't remember a lot of the Christmas gifts I got throughout the years, but I'll never forget those little paper sacks." She pulled Addie in for a hug.*

"You know, Addie, it's the smells you'll remember. They'll always take you somewhere special. Like this paper bag and the treasures inside. You'll always remember Christmas when you smell these things. I do." She smiled and pinched Addie's cheeks. "Now where's my sherry?"

Addie was jarred awake by someone pounding on the door.

"Addie, open the door. I know you're in there. I'm not leaving this time until you open the door. Now!" Drake demanded.

༄༅ ༄༅

"What's wrong?" Greyson could hear someone in the background screaming Addie's name. "Addie, what's going on?" Greyson jumped into some sweats and grabbed her keys, running down the stairs as she tried to listen. "Addie?"

"Ms. Hollister, I...I tried to call Paul but he isn't answering, and I didn't want to call the police. I mean, I—"

"I'm on my way. Stay on the line with me. Don't hang up."

"Okay, but I'm scared."

"Is it Drake?"

"Yeah. I think she's been drinking. I mean it sounds like she's drunk."

Greyson could hear the quiver in Addie's voice.

Her heart lurched. She wasn't sure she could get there soon enough, so she punched her car service and dialed.

"Addie, I'm calling Neil Harris. He's my attorney and he lives close. I want you to hang on the phone with me while I get him on the other line. Okay?"

"Okay, please hurry. I don't want her to break the door down."

Greyson couldn't mistake the battering of the door and doubted it could take much more. The neighbors would be the ones to call the police. Quite frankly, Greyson wouldn't mind if they did. It would solve one small problem for her.

"Neil Harris."

"Neil, I need you to get to Addie Blake's apartment. Her girlfriend is there pounding on the door, and she won't leave."

"Call the police, Greyson," Neil said sternly.

"I can't. I'm on the phone with her, and I have you on my car service. Besides, I don't want to make a spectacle out of this if we can avoid it."

"I'm on my way. You owe me big for this, Grey."

"I know, I know." She pushed the dash button, ending the call.

Turning her attention back to her cell phone, she could still hear Drake banging on the door.

"Persistent little bitch, isn't she?" she said.

"What?"

God, she hoped Addie hadn't heard that comment. "Nothing. Neil is on his way. Is there another room you can go into and lock yourself in?"

"Uh, let me think…"

"Addie, your bathroom. Does it have a lock?"

"Yeah, I think so…I mean, yes, it has a lock."

"Good. Go in there and wait for me. I'm about

ten minutes away." Greyson fudged on the time, but she didn't want Addie freaking out any more than she probably already was.

"Okay."

"Addie, don't hang up." Greyson could still hear Drake ranting about something, but the sound was fading. "Are you safe?"

"I'm in the bathroom. I'm so sorry, Ms. Hollister. I shouldn't have called you. I'm sorry."

"No, no, Addie. It's all right. That's why I'm on speed dial."

"Yeah, but it's late and Drake isn't your problem. She's mine, and I—"

"Addie, stop. You can't fix stupid. Okay, listen. You've been through a lot, and the last thing you need is a drunken girlfriend upending your world right now. So don't give it a second thought."

"I know, but..." Addie's voice drifted off, replaced by heavy sobs.

Oh God. Greyson worried Addie would walk out and let Drake into the apartment.

"Addie, relax. Help is on the way. Okay?"

"'Kay." The honking of Addie blowing her nose blasted in Greyson's ear. "Sorry."

"You have nothing to be sorry about."

Thankfully, traffic was nonexistent at this time of night, and Greyson was making good time.

"I hear someone outside talking to Drake. Want me to go out and see who it is?"

"No, no. I want you to stay inside where it's safe." Greyson tried to sound reassuring. Hopefully, it was Neil and he was handling the Motor Girl drama.

Punching Neil's number again, she waited for him to answer.

"Grey?"

"Neil?"

"She refuses to leave until she talks to Addie. You better get here quick. The neighbors are starting to come out," Neil barked, over the consistent pounding on the door.

"I'm almost there. Hang on." Greyson tried to reassure Neil, but she doubted he could hear her over the incessant battering Drake was giving the only thing keeping her from Addie.

Pushing down on the accelerator, she weaved past a slow bug in the fast lane.

"Asshole," she screamed as she sped past. "Addie?"

"Yeah?"

"I want you to pack a bag, okay?"

"Why?"

"It would be safer if you came back to the house with me. Just in case we can't calm Drake down."

"Oh, God, she's out of control, isn't she? She gets like that when she's been drinking."

"Addie, don't worry about Drake. She's a big girl. She can take care of herself. I'm more worried about your safety, okay?" Greyson was in charge now. She'd been in tougher situations, and this, well, this was a cakewalk in her world. A client or two had overindulged in the past and tried to be inappropriate with her, but a few well-placed pressure moves and they were begging for forgiveness. Besides, reminding them of their wives at those times was also a great bargaining chip the next morning.

"I have to go out into my room to pack my bag," Addie reminded her.

"Okay, go ahead, but keep me on speaker, okay?"

The pounding sound echoed through the phone and worried Greyson. Neil should have had the situation under control by now.

"Neil, what the hell is going on there?"

"Well, for starters, I think this woman, and I use that term loosely, has consumed a barrel of whiskey. At least she looks like she could drink that much. Second, she's like a wild animal, Greyson. Nothing but talking to Addie will calm her down. So, unless you're going to get here in the next two minutes, we're screwed."

"Hang on. I'm almost there."

"When you say almost, do you really mean it, or are you pacifying me again?" Neil knew her all too well. "Hey, keep your hands to yourself. Ouch. Why, you f…"

Chapter Twenty-two

The heavy grip of the fog offered concealment as it wrapped its long white fingers around everything it touched. The swish of the occasional wiper blade kept his view of the walk-up unobstructed. She'd been home for a few hours, if his calculations were correct. The light on in the bedroom meant she was getting ready to turn in for the night. His pulse began to race as he ran the slick panties across the front of his pressed slacks. He was going to enjoy his time punishing her for making him wait. His knuckles paled as he grasped the steering wheel. He thumped out a rhythm with his thumbs on the circular steel and started to rock forward. Energy pulsed through his body. He needed to move now. He almost squealed when he snapped on the latex gloves, pricking his skin. He was getting ready. Like a dog that hears the dinner bell alerting him to a feeding, he started to salivate.

"God, I'm ready," he whispered.

Carefully, he pulled on the door handle and eased it open. He didn't want to draw any attention to himself. Slipping out, he rested a hip against the door just hard enough for it to catch. He popped the collar of his jacket and pulled the ends around his face. The smell of a decaying city assaulted his delicate senses. Trash cartwheeled down the street, following the wafting trails of fog. The smell of urine made him gag, so he pulled out a cigarette and cradled it between his hands as he lit the tip. The smoke intertwined with the fog.

A passing SUV caught his attention. Slipping back into the shadow of the alleyway, he watched as Greyson Hollister jumped from the vehicle. He fixed his gaze on her and recorded every movement. The way she adjusted her jacket when she got out of the vehicle. The way she waved down an approaching cop car. Suddenly, he realized he was watching his well-laid-out plan for the evening disintegrate right before his eyes.

Damn Greyson. Why did she always seem to thwart him? She had turned him down recently, but he wouldn't be deterred. What would it be like when he finally possessed her? He'd show her what it was like to be with a real man. She'd let go of her arrogant ways or he'd beat them out of her. What would she feel like as she writhed under him? Greyson would be his. She would submit, screaming out his name as they consummated their sacred vows.

Just as he was about to step out of the shadows and head for his car, resolute that the evening was ruined, Greyson exited the building with Addie Blake tucked under her arm. Once again, he fixated on Greyson. He watched the way she touched the small of Addie's back, held the door open for her, and how she tucked a piece of hair behind Addie's ear as she said something to her. The familiarity sickened him.

"Well, she'll just have to pay for that little indiscretion later, won't she?" He sneered, stubbing the cigarette out. Disgusted, he threw the panties away from him. He wasn't about to sully his trophies with the silk of a slut.

Chapter Twenty-three

It had been the toughest two weeks of Nancy's life. The case was shit, her boss was climbing down her throat every time he saw her, and somewhere the Elevator Rapist was laughing at her. She knew it and had begun taking the stairs just to avoid seeing the chief. Lucky for her, a conference in Omaha had kept him out of the station recently, but not far enough away that he didn't text her several times a day for a status update. Said the mayor was climbing up his butt to catch the bastard and shit rolled downhill. Who knew a detective could be at the bottom of a shit pile?

Hell, who didn't want to catch him worse than she did?

She had to admit that she wasn't any closer to breaking the case open and all her leads had dried up. She needed something, anything, or worse—another rape. Not that she wanted to see another woman harmed, hell no, but she was starting to feel desperate.

Nancy poured another cup of sludge and popped the lid on the banker's box holding all the folders. She had to have missed something, not seen it. Two weeks didn't just pass without something happening. Had she played her hand too soon by contacting Greyson Hollister? Did she have a part to play in the rapes? An accomplice perhaps? It wasn't beyond the realm of possibility, but her gut said no.

"Hey, Detective, got a minute?" Jennifer Stoltz, Jenny for short, from the CSI unit tossed a folder on the desk and made herself comfortable sitting on the corner. "Jeez, you guys need a decorator in here."

Nancy looked at the drab gray walls, discolored from years of neglect and bad lighting. The few things on the walls were wanted posters that should have been taken down. Half the criminals were caught or dead. A bulletin board hung there, covered with postings for the squad softball team and motivational posters that sucked. Who thought of those things anyway? Nancy wanted to puke every time she read the success poster. Who followed that tripe? Losers who needed motivation to succeed. She'd give them motivation, the good old-fashioned kind her dad gave her—a boot in the butt.

"What's up?"

"Got a little something for you." Jenny flipped the folder open and smiled. "I think we caught a break. A small break, perhaps." She pushed a photo toward Nancy and pointed to a place where a piece had been cut out. "This little spot had DNA on it."

"What?" Nancy lit up. "How the—"

"Hold your horses, cowgirl. It seems that we missed it with all the grease and food on the server's uniform. If he was using a condom, at least a drop could've landed on her when he pulled it off. I mean, what are the odds that snapping that latex off his dick would be a clean yank?"

"I shudder to imagine such a thing, actually." Nancy shook her head. "Yuck."

"Yeah, well, it just didn't seem possible. Seven rapes and not one drip, not one little—"

Nancy put her hands up. "I get the picture. So?"

Nancy pulled the picture closer to her face, as if she could see the missing spot.

"It tested positive for semen."

"No shit?"

"Yep, don't know how we missed it, but we did." Jenny pushed a strand of hair behind her ear and bent over the folder. Moving the photo to the side, she pointed to another picture. "We think there might be two drops on the edge of these panties, but they're so small. We might get lucky and we might go begging."

"Shit, if it wasn't for bad luck, I just wouldn't have any luck at all."

Nancy pushed the folder away and let out a sigh.

Maybe her luck was changing. Cranking the metal chair back on two legs, Nancy teetered. Suddenly she felt like pressing her luck. Propping her feet on the desk, she smiled and then let out a loud yawn.

"Losing sleep on this case?" Jenny stood and slapped Nancy's legs.

"You have no idea how bad the brass has been on my ass about this guy."

"I gotta get back to the barn. If I'm gone too long, the techs start blowing up gloves and playing volleyball without me."

"Let me know when you get something back."

"If I get something back."

"Right, bad luck and all." Nancy smiled.

"Keep thinking positive thoughts, Detective."

"If I was thinking positive thoughts, I'd win the Powerball with the ticket I'm going to buy tonight."

"Bye, Detective."

"Later."

Nancy pored over the pictures. Pulling a magnifying glass out, she scoured each of them. If they had missed one, CSI could have missed others. She took notes on the photos and double-checked each one again. What were the odds that when he took off that condom he'd flung his DNA all over the place?

※ ※ ※ ※

Greyson sat at her desk and thought about how she had settled into an easy routine with Addie Blake over the last two weeks. They drove into work together but parted ways as soon as they reached the street before Integrated Financial. Addie had explained that she didn't want people thinking they were having a fling. Greyson agreed that it wasn't what it seemed, but tongues would wag regardless. Greyson suspected that Addie had had a hard-enough time adjusting to the stares when she'd started back last week. The bruises had healed, and only the residual purple of the black eye was barely noticeable.

Greyson had convinced Addie to start working out with her, and Addie had taken to kickboxing like she was born to it. A few bruises and bumps were Greyson's reward when they had sparred together. She'd underestimated Addie's determination to put the attack behind her, and goading her had been a bad idea from the start.

"Come on, Addie. Hit me. What if I were that attacker? What would you do then?" Greyson asked.

Her mistake had been keeping her hands down as she talked. Addie had hauled off and kicked Greyson right in her midsection, sending Greyson to her knees, clutching her stomach and coughing.

"Well, I guess that answers your question, Greyson,

doesn't it?" Caesar said, picking her up from the floor.

Addie hadn't apologized. From the look on her face, she meant business. She put her hands up in a fighting position and waited for Greyson to respond. When Greyson acquiesced and shook her head, Addie stepped back and dropped her hands and ran from the room.

"Addie, wait. I'm sorry. I shouldn't have said that. I'm sorry." Greyson decided not to reach for Addie's shoulder to stop her. She didn't need another bruise to her ego.

Addie stopped but didn't turn around. "I'm sorry, I shouldn't have done that. I mean I..."

"Look, you reacted, and that was great. That's exactly what you should do. Don't apologize for taking care of yourself. I didn't need to taunt you like that. I'm the one that should be apologizing."

Before Addie could say anything, Caesar was at their side. "Ladies, ladies, the clock is ticking and we need to finish up today's lesson." He wrapped his arm around Addie and guided her to the workout room. "That was fantastic, Addie. Your reflexes are quick like a cat. I'm sure Greyson won't be tormenting you like that anymore. Will you, Greyson?" he yelled over his shoulder.

No, Greyson would not be tormenting Addie like that anymore. Greyson was a quick learner, and she'd definitely learned her lesson. Don't poke the kitty or you'll come back with scratches. Greyson smiled. She was falling for Addie Blake in the worst way.

"Ms. Hollister?" Jarrod poked his head around the door.

"Yes, Jarrod."

"Ms. Blake called and would like to see you. I told her she doesn't have an appointment, but she insisted it was important."

"Let her know she can see me at her earliest convenience. Thank you, Jarrod."

"Of course. Oh. Don't forget you have that very important executive board meeting and dinner tonight."

Greyson sighed. Another night of hobnobbing and trying to squeeze money out of overpaid stuffed shirts didn't interest her at the moment. All she wanted to do was go home, swim with Ben, and have dinner with him and Addie. The simple things in life were a lot more pleasing at the moment.

"Any way I can get out of that?"

"You requested the meeting. Not likely. What time shall I pick you up?"

Strumming her fingers on her desk, Greyson contemplated the question. It was time to have that little conversation with Jarrod, but Addie was waiting. Decisions, decisions, decisions.

"I'll let you know, Jarrod." She rubbed the furrow between her eyebrows. He was definitely on the short list for a new job.

Chapter Twenty-four

ddie tried dodging her soon-to-be ex-girlfriend, only Drake didn't consider herself an ex. In fact, Drake had been persistent in trying to get in touch with her and trying to come by the office to see her. Now she needed to phone Drake and make arrangements to get her car back. Picking up the phone, she headed to the ladies' room to make the call.

"Hey, baby. I knew you'd see the light."

"Drake, I'm not calling to talk to you. I just need to make arrangements to get my car back."

"Are you sure that's the only reason you're calling, baby?" Drake was crooning, her voice lowered. "You just needed a little time to miss me, baby, didn't you?"

"Christ. When can I come up and pick up my car, Drake?"

"Aw, come on, baby. Why don't you let me take you to dinner? We can talk things through. You just needed a little time, and you're wanting to see your motor girl. Admit it. You miss me."

Addie tried to stay composed. Besides, when was the last time Drake had picked up the tab when they went out? Drake would say anything she thought Addie wanted to hear. They'd been down this dusty, rutted road before, and Addie wasn't about to bounce down it again.

"You're not hearing me, Drake. We're over… don't you get it? You walked out on me at the hospital. I want my car back, and I want you to lose my number."

"Who's put these bullshit ideas in your head? That little twinkie Paul?"

Addie hadn't seen much of Paul after she came back to work. He and Tara had hit it off and were spending more time together. Tragedy had a way of either bringing people together or busting them wide open. She and Drake were the latter and soon to be former.

"Are you still going forward with that lawsuit, Drake?" A long silence was punctuated by someone coughing the in the background. Most likely it was one of Drake's bed warmers. Addie didn't care. In fact, she hoped it would make it easier for Drake to take the hint and leave her alone. "Are you still there? Who are you with, Drake?"

"No one. I mean one of the guys from the shop is here, but it ain't a chick, if that's what you're asking."

Addie heard someone huff and a door slam. Well, there wasn't a woman there now.

"I was asking if you're still suing Greyson Hollister. Are you?"

"Hey, babe, I know you're in a bad spot right now, staying with her and all, but when you've had some time to think about things, you'll see I'm right. She needs to pay for what happened to you. It isn't right that she should get away with what was done to you."

Addie knew in Drake's twisted mind, she was protecting Addie. In reality, it was an opportunity Drake couldn't pass up. All the more reason to get away from her.

"You're unbelievable. You know that?" Addie took a deep breath and tried to control her temper, but Drake had played her for the last time. "I want my car. If you don't give it back, I'm going to call the police and report it stolen. Understand? I'm going to tell them exactly where to find it, and you're going to fucking jail. Have I made myself clear?" Addie yelled into the phone.

"Hey, you okay?" Paul said, cracking the bathroom door. "I can hear you out here."

Addie rolled her eyes. All she needed was for everyone on her floor to hear her screaming at Drake. The gossip about her wasn't bad enough. Now she was adding to it with her psycho rant.

"Sorry," Addie said, covering the receiver.

"Is that twinkie boy? Put him on the phone."

"I'm not doing any such thing."

"Fine. Then give him a message from me. I'm going to come down there and rip that noodle he calls a spine out of his body and beat the hell out of him with it."

"You come anywhere near my job and I'll have you arrested, Drake."

Maybe Addie needed to get a restraining order. Worse, she couldn't believe she'd let the conversation degrade into a shouting match, but she wasn't that wimpy woman anymore. She was taking back her life, and that meant taking out the trash. Drake was just white trash with neurotic tendencies.

"I've had enough of this talk, Addie. I'm coming down there, and you and I are going to discuss this like adults." Drake sounded determined, but she hadn't met the new Addie. Then Drake threw a zinger. "I love you, Addie Blake."

Christ, had Drake become desperate enough to resort to playing the *love* card? It was too late. All of that time spent wanting to hear Drake tell her she mattered, that Addie was the most important thing in her life. Addie had wasted two years on Drake, practically begged her to go to counseling, to commit to their relationship, and now Drake told her she loved her?

The old Addie would have bought it without a second thought. Now, she hated herself for falling for Drake's bullshit. She'd been at her lowest when they'd met. It was amazing what a bad breakup did to someone's self-confidence. Drake had swaggered into her life just after and said all the right things. Boom. It was a U-Haul second date.

"Don't, Drake. How many times do I have to tell you it's over? I just want my car back. Leave the keys at the garage and I'll pick it up later this week."

"When?" Drake demanded.

"Just leave my keys, Drake."

Addie knew Drake had a race up in Sears Point on Thursday. She'd been planning for it for months. No Drake, no confrontation.

"This isn't over, Addie."

"Whatever, Drake. I have to get back to work."

The line went dead. Addie slung her hand back, ready to smash the phone into a thousand pieces if it meant no more Drake. If only it were that easy. She suspected she hadn't heard the last from Drake.

"Addie?"

Slinking against the wall, Addie had lost all her bravado.

"It's okay. You can come in, Paul."

"You okay?"

Paul knelt beside her, pushed the hair out of her face, and offered her a bright smile.

"It's good to have you back. So Motor Girl is history, huh?" Paul tapped the tip of her nose. "Well, good for you. You're too good for her anyway. Wanna come out with me and Tara tonight? O'Malley's," he said with a wag of his eyebrows.

"Thanks. It's tempting, but I've got a lot of catching up to do. I've—" Paul pulled her to her feet. "I have the St. George account to present tomorrow. Besides, I don't want to be a third wheel on a date." Addie smiled and touched Paul's face. "You look happy."

"You were right. Tara's perfect for me. I thought you were kidding when you said she likes takeout right out of the box." Paul opened the door and waited for Addie.

Now why couldn't she find a female version of Paul?

Chapter Twenty-five

If Greyson's dreams were any indication, she hadn't cut her ties to Cate Hollister, yet. Her beloved Cate had been gone for almost three years. What would she say if she knew Greyson was still pining away for her? Thinking about Addie, Greyson knew she'd grieved long enough, but those interludes at night with Cate were a constant reminder of how powerful their love was. Could she walk away from Cate, even in death?

Greyson twisted the gold reminder around her finger. She hadn't taken it off in years, fearing it would snap her connection to her wife. But she needed to move forward, for her sake and for Ben's. Greyson had to come to terms with her feelings, and she recognized that she was falling for Addie, hard. Suddenly she dreaded having the conversation with Addie she needed to have. What if she shot Greyson down? What if she didn't feel the same way? All her life she'd taken risks, but now it seemed that this one could undo her neat little world. Right?

"Ms. Hollister?" Jarrod squawked through the intercom. Greyson jerked at the interruption. "Ms. Blake is here to see you. Without an appointment." He emphasized the last sentence with such disdain Greyson wondered what was going on with him.

Her heart raced. This was it. They weren't at home or in the gym being bothered or interrupted. She supposed she could have waited for the drive home or a romantic evening somewhere out on the town. But in her mind it was now or never. She wasn't one to beat a decision or situation to death, so now was as good a time as any, she hoped.

"Show her in, Jarrod."

Within seconds the door opened and Jarrod ushered Addie in with a flourish. He stood at the door waiting for a response from Greyson, but when she didn't say anything, he announced, "Ms. Hollister, you have that important meeting tonight."

"Thank you, Jarrod. I remember." She pushed away from the desk and the speech she'd been writing. She'd had trouble concentrating on the simple plea for money. Her thoughts were clouded as she thought about Addie Blake. She needed to focus. The meeting tonight was high-dollar. She was looking at bringing in some investors for a real-estate project she was working on. Setting up the meeting meant less of her cash and more of theirs. She also needed to put to rest any concerns about the attack at I.F. No one wanted to invest if they thought the company was lax in its duties, even if they involved protecting their own employees. The cash infusion would get the project off the ground, which would help a high-risk community deal with the struggling economy and provide jobs to people who needed them. A win-win for everyone.

"Ms. Blake, please sit down."

Greyson waited for Jarrod to leave, but he hadn't moved. "Is there anything else, Jarrod?"

"Shall I pick you up at seven, Greyson?"

Greyson widened her eyebrows at the familiar way Jarrod addressed her in front of Addie. She studied him before she answered. What was he up to?

For him to act so familiar in front of a fellow employee, especially Addie, surprised her.

"I'll call you if I need anything else, Jarrod," she said dismissively.

"Of course." He gave her a sickly sweet smile before edging the door shut.

Oh, it was definitely time to end this little charade. She'd let it go on far too long. He would be lucky if he wasn't bagging mail in the basement soon or, worse, jobless.

"I don't think he likes me," Addie said so softly Greyson wouldn't have been sure she'd said anything if her lips hadn't moved.

"Nonsense. Besides, at the rate he's going you may not have to worry about seeing him again."

"Oh, gosh. I didn't mean to get him in trouble or anything, Ms. Hollister."

Addie's surprised look made Greyson chuckle. If Addie knew the story behind Jarrod, she wouldn't feel so sorry for the poor bastard.

"Anyway, back to you. How are you this morning? To what do I owe the pleasure of this visit?" Greyson softened her voice. "Is everything okay?"

"I hope so," she said, not looking at Greyson.

This conversation wasn't sounding promising, at all. Greyson walked over to the tea service, poured two cups, and carried the tray to the table between them. Wanting to put some distance between them, she sat across from Addie. The close proximity of Addie Blake had nearly caused her to combust on a few occasions. Distance right now was better. Besides, Greyson was giving off so much nervous energy a blind man could feel it.

Addie tortured her phone, rubbing her fingers

across the back and then twisting it around and then back again. Suddenly it went off, and both of them stopped and looked at the buzzing intruder.

"Do you want to get that? I can step out so you can have some privacy," Greyson said, then stood to leave.

Addie looked at the number, grimaced, and then silenced the phone.

"No. She's the reason I'm here, unfortunately," Addie said, still not looking at Greyson. "Ms. Hollister—"

"Greyson."

Now Addie looked at her and gave a halfhearted smile. "Greyson," she said, ducking her head. "I spoke with Drake, and I just wanted to warn you that she's threatening to come down here. I've tried to reason with her, and I've told her that it's over…"

Did Greyson just hear that? *It's over. Sweet!* Greyson did an internal high-five and choked on her tea.

"Are you okay?"

Setting her cup down, she patted her chest. "I'm fine. Must have gone down the wrong way. Sorry, please continue."

"I'm sorry to do this, but I'm offering my resignation effective immediately."

"Wait, what?"

This wasn't what Greyson had envisioned for their conversation. Quite the opposite. She stood, trying to right her internal ship that had just listed to the side. Besides the fact that she couldn't let Addie go, to let Addie quit would play right into Drake's wicked little plan and give her more ammunition for the lawsuit Greyson was sure Neil would get thrown out. But this wouldn't help either of them.

"Addie, I—"

"That's not the only reason I'm leaving. I'm… well, I…"

Greyson switched seats and planted herself next to Addie.

"Yes."

"You've been wonderful these last few weeks. The kickboxing lessons, Ben and Camille. It's been great getting to know them, but…"

Greyson searched Addie's face, trying to get a feel for what was coming next.

"But?" Greyson steeled herself.

Addie twirled her phone repeatedly, distracting Greyson. Covering Addie's hands with her own, Greyson repeated her question. "But?"

"I have to be honest…"

Anxiety lanced through Greyson. *Just spit it out, and we can go on with our separate lives. Please, break my heart. I can handle it.*

"I'm starting to fall for you, Greyson," Addie blurted out.

"Oh, God," Greyson whispered.

"I know. I shouldn't have come. I shouldn't have said anything. It's highly unprofessional. So you see why I need to quit."

Greyson grabbed Addie and kissed her. That is what highly unprofessional looks like, Greyson thought, releasing a visibly stunned Addie.

Chapter Twenty-six

Greyson, you can just drop me off? I have the gate code. I can find my way home."

Addie caught Greyson's smile before she turned to look out the window. Had she just said home, as in their home?

"I'm not dropping you off. Color me suspicious, but I don't trust Drake."

Addie had to agree. However, this race was a big opportunity for Drake. Some of the biggest race promoters were attending, and Drake wouldn't pass up an opportunity to schmooze with the heavy hitters of racing. Drake wanted to be part of a race team, and this was her opportunity to make that happen. Whatever Addie was to Drake didn't compare to what Drake wanted with racing.

"Okay, but I'm just going in, getting my keys, and will be out in a flash."

Addie wasn't planning to make small talk with the guys at the garage. Besides, the minute she entered the garage, they'd be on the phone with Drake.

Pulling up, Addie spotted her blue Corolla sitting in the side lot next to the garage. A layer of dirt covered her old trusty steed. Drake hadn't even had the decency to clean the windshield for her. Typical.

"It's over there." Addie nodded in the direction of the lot. "I'll have to go in there and get one of the guys to open the gate. I'll just be a minute." Addie scooted out of the SUV and ran toward the open garage door.

Music blared through broken speakers. The lighting in the shop was down. It was past closing time, and Addie was surprised it was still open. Sometimes the guys would work on other people's cars for extra money, but Drake didn't care, as long as she got a cut.

Addie searched the garage. After looking under a few cars, she peered under the open hoods and still no one. She would have yelled for some help, but she doubted that anyone could hear her over the thumping bass. Didn't matter. She knew where Drake kept the keys.

Making a beeline to the office, she popped open the key caddie. After she'd pushed a few keys around, she found her little Pink Kitty key chain. Grabbing it, she turned but ran into Turk, Drake's head mechanic.

"Hey, what are you doing here?" he growled. Civility had never been his strong suit. Max, the yard dog, had more going for him than Turk.

"Hey." Addie put up her hands, the Pink Kitty hanging from her thumb. "Look, I don't want any trouble. I'm just here to pick up my car."

"Ain't you Drake's girl?"

She could debate the nuances of whether she was Drake's girl, especially since Drake still considered Addie hers. It was more like ownership with Drake, but she didn't feel like an honest answer would be conducive to her leaving with her car. So she lied.

"Yep. She knows I'm here," Addie said. Glancing at the door to the garage, she knew if she could just get to it, she'd be out of his hair. She considered bolting for the other door from the office, but Max was chained just outside.

"I better call the boss."

Addie saw her opening and shuffled past him, but not before he stuck out a greasy hand, wedging her between a car and the exit. He jerked the sleeve of her jacket, forcing her to face him.

"Turk, right?" Drake had taken Addie to one of the few dinners with the guys from the shop, and Turk and his girlfriend had been there. She remembered Turk's girlfriend. Hell, who could forget her? She'd looked barely over eighteen and was draped all over Turk's arm. Addie had caught sight of Drake ogling the young thing, and before the night was over, Drake had cornered the girl, practically fucking her in the bathroom.

Caught in the act, all Drake could say was, "She likes my tats." Drake had slid the girl off her thigh and winked at her. "I'll catch you later. Come on, let's go," she'd said, grabbing Addie's hand. God, she was so glad that part of her life was over.

"Look, I'm sure Drake has told you things are… well, you know…so I thought I'd go up and surprise her at the race track tonight. But my car is here and, well…" Addie smiled, hoping her lie sounded convincing.

"I don't know. She'll be pissed if I screw up and let a car out of the garage."

"Aw, come on. Wouldn't you be thrilled if your girl showed up in something sexy?" Addie winked at Turk.

On cue, Turk blushed and threw Addie a face-splitting grin.

"Well."

"Hey, dude. Boss told me she had my money," someone boomed behind Addie. She froze. She'd heard that voice before. In fact, she'd heard it in every nightmare for the past few weeks.

It was *him*.

"Hey, Carl. How you doing, buddy. I thought Drake told you to make like a ghost and be invisible for a while?"

"Yeah, yeah. I was down in L.A. hanging with my sister. I can only take so many days with those little rug rats running around and climbing all over me. You know what I mean?"

Addie felt him move nearer. His looming body was so close, she could take one step back and be right in his lap. "So, I called Drake and she said she'd tucked some cash away for that job I did for her a few weeks back. I didn't have time to pick it up then, so I'm here now."

"Yeah. I think I saw an envelope with your name on it in the desk drawer. Let me go get it. And you," Turk said, pointing to Addie, "you stay right here till I get back."

"So you here to pick up your wheels?" Carl said to the back of Addie's head. Clearly he didn't know who he was trying to make small talk with.

A chill sliced through Addie. She could smell mothballs, again. Her stomach lurched. Her fight-or-flight response had kicked into high gear. The adrenaline push was like mainlining heroin. Her muscles tightened and her head spun. She spied a torque wrench lying on the fender. Without thinking, Addie snatched it up, turned, and in one fluid motion clocked Carl upside his head. The look of surprise lasted only a moment as shock and then a loud crack echoed through the garage. Carl clutched his head and fell to his knees.

Addie raised the wrench above her head and

brought it down with such force that as she hit Carl with a glancing blow the wrench skittered across the cement floor and lodged under a toolbox.

"What the fuck?" Carl screamed. "Jesus Christ."

Addie jumped on Carl, straddling him. Her own attack played out in her mind as she rained blows on Carl's curled-up form.

"Think you're too good to talk to me?" He was close enough that she smelled stale nicotine on his breath. Without warning, he bashed her against the wall, instantly splitting her lip. Blood seeped into her mouth. "You should've been nicer."

"You wanna fuck with me?" she screamed. Her once-violated body responded with the kickboxing she'd been training in since the attack. She landed punch after punch to the side of his ribs. She was determined to prove she would never be a victim again. Another memory flashed from that night, spurring her on.

She tried to push off the wall, but he forced his body against hers. If she could get turned around, maybe she had a fighting chance. She felt him pulling her back by the strap of her briefcase. With one motion, he threw her to the ground. The pain from her face making contact with the floor almost made her black out.

"You bastard," she screamed. She pummeled him, like he was the punching bag she trained on every day. Her body was on autopilot, her mind a frenzy of images she'd been trying to forget. She was trapped in the elevator again, a knife in his hands, a blow to her face, and finally she saw herself lying in a pool of blood.

Her blood.

All because of him.

Carl.

She wanted revenge on the man who had taken away her freedom. Who'd changed her life forever. For what? A couple hundred dollars? Then the reality of his words struck her. Drake had orchestrated the whole thing. She'd paid Carl to hurt her. Her own girlfriend had...

Addie felt someone pulling her off the now-unconscious man.

"What the fuck did you do, you crazy bitch? I'm calling the cops."

"Please do," Addie said, shaking with rage. "Please do, before I kill him."

Chapter Twenty-seven

Greyson sat in stunned silence, watching the first squad car arrive, followed by a second and then an unmarked sedan. Officers jumped out, guns drawn and in a tactical position. Without thinking, Greyson called Neil Harris. He needed to get down here ASAP because something was wrong. A woman stepped from the unmarked car.

"Hill," Greyson said as she jumped out of her SUV. "Detective Hill, what's happening?"

"Seems some crazy lady is trying to kill someone inside, so back off, Hollister. This doesn't concern you, unless you know what's going on."

"Addie." Greyson sprinted past the officers, who had their weapons drawn and aimed at the door of the garage.

"Ms. Hollister, stop," Detective Hill ordered her.

Greyson made it to the garage door and could hear Addie's voice.

"Let me go, you bastard."

"You aren't going anywhere until the cops get here. You crazy bitch."

"Addie?" Greyson called out, edging closer to the voices.

"Over here, Greyson. Let me go," Addie said. Judging by all the grunting going on, it was clear that Addie was wrestling with someone. "Let me go, damn it."

"Let her go." Greyson finally stood in front of the pair, with Addie standing over a bleeding man on the floor. "What the hell happened in here?"

"It's him, Greyson. It's the guy who attacked me in the elevator."

"Oh, Christ, are you sure?"

"I don't know anything about an attack in an elevator," the man holding Addie's arms said. "All I know is Carl there worked for my boss up until about three weeks ago, and then he was gone."

"Let her go," Greyson ordered him.

"I'm not letting her go until the cops get here."

"Well, then you're in luck," Detective Hill said over Greyson's shoulder. "The cops are here." She flashed her badge. "What the hell happened?"

Greyson, Addie, and the mechanic all started talking at the same time.

"Stop." She had to yell to be heard. "You." She pointed to Addie. "What the hell happened?"

Greyson stepped in front of Addie. "Don't say anything, Ms. Blake, until counsel gets here."

"Hollister, get out of the way, or I'll have you arrested for interfering in a police investigation." The detective looked at the uniform standing next to her. "Get Medical in here and let's get this guy to the hospital. Cuff him until we know what's going on."

Greyson still stood in front of Addie, and she wasn't moving. She'd be damned if she would let Detective Hill traumatize Addie anymore.

"Step aside, Greyson," the cop demanded. When Greyson didn't comply, she said, "Arrest her and put her in a squad car."

"You can't do that." Addie ran to Greyson and

put her arms around her.

"Ms. Blake, please back away, or you'll end up in new jewelry, courtesy of the SJPD, too."

"I'm fine, Addie. Don't say anything. Wait until Neil gets here."

The cold metal against her wrists made her straighten. As they tightened the cuffs, she shot Detective Hill a dirty look. Just as she was about to say something, the detective beat her to it.

"Don't forget to read her Miranda rights, just in case she decides to get mouthy."

"Come along, Ms. Hollister," an officer said, pulling her away from the scene.

"Don't say anything, Addie. Nothing." Greyson jerked her arm out of the officer's grasp.

❧❧❧❧

"Hog-tie her if she gives you any more trouble. I mean any trouble."

"Yes, ma'am."

"Oh, you'd love that, wouldn't you?" Hollister snarled.

"I would get a certain amount of satisfaction seeing you hog-tied." Nancy was being honest. Seeing the haughty bitch facedown in a patrol car, her feet and hands tied up like a Christmas goose, had an appeal to it. Nancy doubted Hollister was foolish enough to screw up that bad, but one could hope.

"Ms. Blake, want to tell me what happened here?"

"I'll wait for my lawyer," Addie Blake said in a monotone that lacked emotion. This reaction worried Nancy. She'd seen victims barely able to talk. But Blake had been the aggressor this time. The blood on her hands was a dead giveaway.

"Look, I don't want to traumatize you any more by putting you in handcuffs and doing a perp walk to the station. So why don't you just tell me what happened?"

"Traumatize her? What about Carl? The bitch practically kills my buddy, and you're worrying about her. This is some bullshit."

Nancy directed a uniformed officer to grab Blake. "Tell me what you saw, sir." Nancy wasn't in the mood for a hostile witness, so she walked over and pulled him into the office.

"That crazy bitch is the boss's girlfriend. Said she was here to pick up her car." He pointed to Blake and then to the victim being loaded on a stretcher. "He comes in and asks for some money the boss left him for doing a job. I come in to get it. I go outside to give it to him, and the first thing I know, that crazy bitch is on top of him, beating his ass. End of story." He took a breath. "You gonna arrest her or what?"

Nancy scribbled what he was telling her on a pad. "He looks like a pretty big guy. Did you see how she got him down on the ground? I mean she's pretty tiny and all." She pointed her pen in Blake's direction.

"It's the small ones that take you by surprise," he said, shaking his head. "I didn't see what she did. I only saw her after he was on the ground. She was pounding on Carl. The guy didn't even look like he was defending himself. I think she must have knocked him out."

"Really?"

"Did you see him? He's bleeding all over the place. Look at that big puddle of blood on the floor." He walked over to the office window and pointed.

"How about you let us do our job? What's the owner's name and where is she?"

Nancy scribbled some more and waited for the information. Her mind was snapping pieces of the puzzle together quickly. She hoped what she was thinking was wrong. If not, Drake Hogan had hired someone to attack her girlfriend. For what? Money? Nancy suspected that, but she wouldn't know for sure until she questioned Hogan.

"You wanna help? I need you to go down to the station and officially give your statement." Nancy smiled. She didn't want him clamming up when what he'd just said about Drake Hogan paying this guy was crucial to her investigation.

"No problem. I want that bitch locked up."

"Well, your statement could help do that, so go with this officer..." Nancy waved a cop over. "Make sure you write down exactly what you just told me."

"Okay," he said, his chest puffing up. "I just need to lock up the garage."

"I can't let you do that. A crime was committed here, so our officers will need to photograph and run the scene. We'll make sure it's all locked up tight. We don't want anyone taking anything until we get all the facts. Now do we?"

"Okay, but if anything goes missing, it's on your head," he said, walking away.

"Take this guy down to the station and get his statement." Nancy motioned the policeman over. "Pull his cell phone and don't let him talk to anyone, not even his boss. I don't want him giving her a heads-up."

"You got it."

"Thanks."

Nancy walked out to the bustle of activity around

the scene. Markers were being laid out at every blood spatter. The flash from a camera lit up the dingy garage bay, and Addie Blake just stood there, surprisingly calm, watching everything happening around her. Nancy studied her, wondering what had happened.

Gazing at the pool of blood, she knew Addie didn't have the strength to hit the big guy hard enough to draw that kind of blood. As she turned, she noticed the tight confines of the cars, toolboxes, and a drop-down bay that allowed a mechanic to gain access to the underbelly of a car. A car with its hood open sat next to the blood pool. Tools were laid out on the fender, but she spotted a hole in the neat lineup of tools. One was missing. Looking back at Blake, she sized up the petite woman. It was possible.

"Ms. Blake, mind telling me what you hit him with?"

Addie glanced over at the floor under the stack of toolboxes lining the wall and then quickly away.

Nancy's instincts fired off. When questioned, those who didn't practice deception usually led with the eyes.

"Hey, under that toolbox." Nancy pointed out a red stack. A CSI tech ran over, looked under it, and nodded at her.

"Don't touch it. Get someone to help you move those boxes."

He stood and started to move a few.

"Be sure to get some photos before and after you move anything. Shoot some with the toolboxes in place, too. Oh, and run it for prints."

Nancy looked back at Addie. "Have anything to say?"

Addie shook her head.

"Okay, let me tell you what I think happened, off the record. You came here…" Nancy pointed around her. "To your girlfriend's garage to pick up your car—"

Addie corrected her. "Ex-girlfriend."

"Ex-girlfriend. While you were arguing with the guy running the garage, the guy who attacked you at Integrated Financial came in. He said he was here to pick up some money for a job he did a few weeks ago for Drake, and you recognized his voice. You put two and two together and went postal on his ass. How am I doing so far?"

Addie only offered a blank stare. She didn't nod, blink an eye, or flinch as Nancy laid out what she was almost certain had happened in the garage.

"You know what else I'm thinking? I'm thinking his DNA is going to match the DNA we scraped from under your nails the night of the attack."

Still no response from Addie.

Nancy didn't know whether the woman was traumatized for a second time or following Greyson's instructions, so she continued. "I wouldn't be surprised if he recognized you, and put his hands on you, and you were defending yourself, again."

Nancy had never planted a seed, just in case, but this case was so disgusting on so many levels. She couldn't see Addie Blake doing time for assault because of a dirt bag like him. Drake Hogan, on the other hand—well, she wanted to personally arrest that bitch. How despicable to use your girlfriend for monetary gain. She needed to get her hands on Hogan before Greyson Hollister did. When Hollister found out…she could just imagine the uproar aimed at the department for not figuring out Drake's participation in all this. Christ, the chief was going to hit the ceiling when she briefed him.

She scratched her head. Was Carl their elevator rapist? Doubtful, but one could wish for a nice, tight-wrapped package, right?

"Ms. Blake, I'm afraid I'm going to have to take you down to the station for further questioning. Cuff her."

Blake had seen too many cop shows. Without asking, she put her hands behind her back, ready to be cuffed, but Nancy stopped her.

"Put her hands in front. I don't see her as violent."

"But, ma'am, procedure says—"

"I know what procedure says, but you have no idea what this woman's been through. Just cuff her in the front and pull a car up to the garage door. I don't want to perp-walk her out and give her ex a chance to run." Nancy offered Blake a half smile. "I'm sorry."

The poor woman shrugged and looked down at the cuffs being sprung on her wrists. Even being arrested didn't seem to ruffle her feathers. Nancy had no doubt she wasn't about to incriminate herself.

Nancy followed them out and put her into the cruiser. Bending down to talk to her, Nancy spoke softly. "Ms. Blake, things are going to get crazy in the next few hours. That reporter from Channel 8 is over there past the chain-link. I'd duck down across the backseat if I were you. It's bad enough that I've got Greyson Hollister over in that unmarked, and I'm sure the news media knows her car. So, the spin has already started, considering this is your ex's garage. I'm sorry for all of this. I truly am."

When she didn't get a reaction from Addie, she stood, shut the door, and tapped the top of the cruiser. She could only hope Addie would take her advice and lie down. If not, the shit storm waiting for her back at the station would be a blizzard. Intake would be through the underground entrance, so if Blake followed directions, her exposure to the media would be limited. If not, well, neither she nor Hollister could protect her from the speculation of the crackling police scanners. As they drove away, Nancy smiled. Blake had taken her advice. She wasn't visible.

"Detective, who've you arrested?" someone yelled from across the yard. The yard dog went crazy, diluting anything Nancy might have said. So she raised her hand to her ear and motioned she couldn't hear the reporter. As if that was their cue, all the reporters started to shout questions at her. Perfect. Like sharks smelling chum in the water, they walked closer to where Nancy was standing and yelled questions at her again. This time the dog was practically off his chain running back and forth in front of the fence. If someone wasn't careful, the dog might get lucky and get a snack.

Nancy made her way to the other squad car. Lucky for Hollister, it was hidden from the prying eyes of the reporters. She was the picture of controlled rage. Nancy called it that when someone in a power position was pissed. They didn't lose control like the average Joe. They simmered, plotted, and used their mouth to exact a response, and when that didn't work, they resorted to their basest level of rage, striking out via a lawyer or someone who could make Nancy's life miserable for a few days. That was okay. She'd dealt with lots of power players in her day, and Greyson Hollister wouldn't be the last.

The window was cracked just enough for ventilation, so Nancy didn't need to open the door to talk to her.

"Ms. Hollister?"

She was laser-focused on the car taking Addie out of the yard.

"Ms. Hollister. I'm going to explain to you what's going to happen next."

"Am I under arrest?"

"You're being detained for your own protection—"

"Protection, from whom? You? Ms. Blake? That's laughable, Detective."

"Perhaps, but I think when you hear what I suspect has happened, you won't think it's so funny."

Hollister snapped her head around and glared at her. Nope, they weren't going to release Hollister until they had Drake Hogan in custody. She had murder in her eyes. Nancy had seen it before in domestic-violence cases. Hollister would stay in custody. Period.

"I'll see you down at the station, Ms. Hollister."

Nancy didn't offer the same advice she'd given Blake. She didn't really care if the reporters drew their own conclusions this time. Part of her secretly hoped they would tear Hollister limb from limb with their accusations. Bad attitude on her part, she knew, but the woman had earned her scorn. Her high-priced lifestyle, her smug attitude, and her stonewalling had kept Nancy from doing her job, and now a man could be dead because of it. Well, maybe it wasn't all Hollister's fault, but damn it all, she loathed Greyson Hollister.

After tapping the roof, she watched the squad car travel the gauntlet of reporters. "Lights, cameras, and action," she whispered.

Erin Green from Channel 8 stuffed the mic by the window and yelled, "Ms. Hollister, why are you under arrest?"

"Sometimes people get what they get," Nancy said, shaking her head. Pulling her phone, she dialed Sergeant Torres.

"Torres."

"Sergeant, keep those women separated. Don't even let them be in the same holding cell."

"You got it."

"I have to make a trip to northern California and should be back in a few hours. Don't book them until then."

"Okay. Any reason why?"

"Yeah, and it doesn't look good."

She hung up and pulled her keys. If her suspicions were right, arresting Drake Hogan would be the only way to keep Hollister from killing her when she found out what had really happened that night at Integrated Financial.

Chapter Twenty-eight

Greyson kept her eyes forward and her mouth shut as reporters peppered her with questions. She didn't know why she was cuffed like a common criminal, but, worse, she'd seen Addie stuffed into a squad car. She kept her eyes on the cop car ahead of them, but lost sight of it as the reporters slowed her progress out of the gate. Why didn't the cop just floor it and mow them down, doing all of them a favor?

Neil stood on the opposite side of the street. They locked eyes, and she watched as he nodded at her, then jumped into his car and waited to fall in line behind her. At least she was sure Addie would have counsel when they arrived at the station.

A huge cement building loomed before the squad car. The giant letters spelled out their destination, Santa Clara County Department of Correction. The monolith was a testament to the rising crime in San Jose. Over ten stories tall, it housed an assorted three thousand misdemeanors and felons, plus the personnel needed to control them. How did she know? She was a huge supporter of those in uniform, but she might have to rethink her support of the police benevolent society if this went south.

Greyson expected to see throngs of reporters as she entered the facility, but obviously she wasn't being taken through the front. Her eyes had to adjust to the sudden darkness of the underground intake area. The sound of the huge rolling door being lowered startled her.

"Thank God. Now I can get these damn things off," she said, shifting again so the cuffs quit cutting into her wrists.

The car door opened and the officer motioned her out. "This way, Ms. Hollister," she said.

Greyson recognized the officer as one of those who was at Integrated Financial the day after the attack.

"When do I get to make my phone call?"

"In due time, Ms. Hollister. In due time."

"Perhaps you can tell me what I'm being arrested for?"

"I'm sorry. I don't have that information."

"Really? So you're basically ignoring my civil rights and arresting me for no reason." Greyson knew how to get someone's goat. "Are you just a lackey, Sergeant Torres?"

The sergeant yanked Greyson's arm and pulled her toward the intake door. The gray cement box of the underground garage was cold and smelled of exhaust and something else she couldn't put her finger on. She noticed a chair sat next to the door. Straps crisscrossed the chair, and leg and wrist restraints lay open, signaling it was ready to envelop its next out-of-control prisoner. A window, with a deputy behind it, looked to be about two inches thick. A few scratches littered the window. Between the restraint chair and the window, it was clear Greyson was in a place where civility was often lacking. Now she had to wonder what kind of people she'd see inside.

Sergeant Torres hit her fist against the buzzer and pulled Greyson closer to her. The heavy metal door creaked open, and Torres pushed her into a small room with boxes lining the wall, where a man almost the size of the door stood waiting.

"How you doin', Torres?" he said as he snapped on a pair of black latex gloves.

"Good. How's the wife and kids?" Torres took her gun and locked it into one of the boxes.

Greyson was surprised at how casual the conversation was in the jail. What did she expect? Honestly, she expected aggressive, angry people ready to manhandle her into submission.

"Good." The huge man slipped another set of handcuffs on Greyson and handed Torres hers. "So what do we have here?"

"Detective Hill said to bring her down. Possible accessory charges."

"What? Are you fucking kidding me?" Greyson tried to twist around to look at Torres, but before she could move she was pressed against the wall, a shoulder in her back and the deputy controlling her hands and head.

"Calm down," he directed her. His voice lowered to a command timbre that shook Greyson to her core. "You're not going to act out here. I don't care who you are. Do you understand me?"

"Get off me," Greyson demanded.

"Do you understand me?"

"Hill said if you need to hog-tie her, do what you have to do to keep her controlled."

"So she's one of those."

Greyson answered for Torres. "No, she isn't one of those."

"Then you're going to behave in my jail, right?" He eased up a tad. "Are you going to behave?"

"I'll behave." Greyson wasn't in any position to lose her temper, and he knew it.

"Process her?" he asked Torres.

Torres shrugged.

"Wait, you're not booking me? Then release me," Greyson demanded. Suddenly the pressure was reapplied to her back.

"Calm down."

"I'm good. I'm good." She tried to relax, but the pressure was making it hard to breathe.

"Seems she drove the attacker to the garage where the attack took place."

"Look, I can explain. I just drove Ms. Blake to the garage." Greyson didn't want to say more. She'd have to let Neil Harris do the talking. She suddenly remembered the advice she'd given Addie and shut her mouth.

"She's been read her Miranda rights, so if she says anything, just document it," Torres said, looking directly at her.

"No problem. We'll get her out of her civies and into a jumpsuit." The man pulled the defiant Greyson along.

"Oh." Torres turned back around. "Don't put her with the other woman brought in for the attack. Detective's orders. She doesn't want them talking."

"You got it. Can she go into general pop?"

Torres was silent for a moment. "Sure. I don't see why not."

Greyson piped up. "When do I get my phone call?"

"After we process your paperwork and find out what you're being charged with. Come on. Your friend should be done by now," the guard said, pulling

Greyson again.

Addie stood at the desk. Her fingers flattened as a light hit them, and then each finger was pressed against the glass.

"Addie," Greyson yelled.

Shock crossed Addie's face when she looked at Greyson in handcuffs. "Sorry," she mouthed.

"It's okay, don't worry. Neil is on his way."

"Hey, no yelling," the guard said, then jerked Greyson in the opposite direction. "Let's go get you changed."

Greyson and Addie stared at each other until Greyson couldn't see her any longer.

"Christ." Greyson let her head drop. *What the hell happened in that garage?*

⁕⁕⁕⁕

Greyson sat on a bench in a large room of women. The stench of the room made it clear that some needed a bath, while others needed a change of clothes. A woman sat in the corner muttering to herself about God and being chosen for some higher order. Urine stained her jumpsuit, so obviously that's where some of the smell was coming from, while another woman puked into the steel toilet in view of everyone.

"Christ," Greyson whispered again.

Nobody played favorites here. Greyson pulled at her orange jumpsuit, two sizes too big, and looked down at the worn-out slippers she was wearing. Nope, she was just one of the twenty or so women who littered the cell.

"Hey, can I bum a cigarette?" a young woman across from her asked.

Without thinking, she answered, "I don't think you can smoke in here."

"Oh, okay. I'll save it for later," the woman said, sticking a dirty hand out. The only clean spots were the bottoms of her hands where they'd taken her fingerprints.

"I don't smoke."

"Ah, shoot. Thanks anyway," she said with a toothless grin.

Without thinking, Greyson asked, "How old are you?"

"Twenty-four."

Greyson felt an "I have shirts older than you" comment coming on but bit her tongue.

"Hollister, you have a visitor."

Greyson jumped when her name was called.

"You must have some pretty important friends. You haven't even been officially booked, and you get to have a visitor," the deputy said, motioning for her to turn around and be cuffed.

Again, Greyson bit her tongue. She wasn't about to mouth off and be sent back to sit with women who… well, she knew when to keep her mouth shut.

The deputy escorted her past a series of cells with a series of tables where two people sat opposite each other. At least one of those in the cell looked like a legal representative, while the other looked like her—a criminal. The deputy opened the door to a room and released one cuff, hooked it to the table—for her protection, he said—and then stood near the door. She sat in a seat that squeaked as she swiveled toward the table. Both seats were mounted to the floor, and they'd clearly seen lots of use because the paint had worn off long ago. Greyson surveyed the room. There was no window, a flickering fluorescent light that probably doubled as a torture device hung overhead, and her chair squeaked each time she moved. The scene looked like it had come right out of a movie set.

A minute later she heard a buzz at the door, and another beefcake of a deputy ushered Neil through the door. Suddenly she felt as if she might cry. The onslaught of emotion overwhelmed her, and she fought back the tears that threatened to fall.

"You okay?" Neil asked. He looked worried, which only made Greyson more anxious.

Turning away, she wiped back her tears, then faced Neil. "Have you seen Addie?"

He nodded. He wasn't good at hiding his emotions, and a myriad of them played over his face in a matter of seconds. He put his briefcase on the table and then pointed toward the cuff on Greyson's wrist. "Is this necessary?" he asked.

"It is for now," the deputy said, hooking his thumbs in his belt.

"Neil, what the hell is going on?"

"You're not going to like this, Grey." Neil sat and motioned her closer.

"What is it?"

He popped his briefcase open and took out a pad and pen. Looking over at the deputy he whispered, "They've booked Addie."

"What?" Greyson jumped up.

"Sit down, prisoner, or the visit is over. Understand?" The deputy nodded at Neil. "Counselor."

Neil motioned to the seat. "Greyson, sit down. Please."

Greyson looked at her cuffed wrist and then at the guard, who shook his bald head, and then back at

Neil. Sliding back into the seat, she squeaked around and faced him.

"That's not all, Greyson."

"Okay," she said calmly. "What else is going on?"

"The guy she attacked…"

"Yes." She gritted her teeth, forcing the word through them.

"She says he's the guy who attacked her at I.F. and—"

"So that's what she meant. Shit. I wasn't sure what she was saying because she was shaking so badly."

"Please remain calm as I finish telling you the rest." Neil looked over at the guard and then peered back at her. "Promise me you will not act out."

"I'll try, Neil. Just tell me."

"Promise me, Grey. If you have another outburst, our visit is over."

Her heart raced. She wasn't good with bad news. The night Cate died, she'd crumpled to the floor when she was told. She tried to steel herself once more for what was coming, but nothing could be as bad as losing your wife. Nothing.

"I'm fine. Just spit it out."

"Drake hired him." Neil sat back as if waiting for the impending explosion. When Greyson didn't move, he inched closer. "Did you hear me? Drake hired him to attack Addie Blake."

Greyson's stomach lurched. Maybe she hadn't heard Neil correctly. No one was that evil. Not even a simple gear-head like Drake Hogan.

"Say that again. Surely you're mistaken."

Her knuckles cracked as she clenched her fists. Her knees started to bounce with nervous energy, and her mind was spinning. There was something else Neil wasn't telling her, but at the moment all she could think about was getting her hands on Drake Hogan. She rocked forward and whispered to Neil, "Where is that fucking bitch?"

"Greyson, they're talking about booking you as an accessory."

She didn't say anything. Rage was blinding her, and all she could think about was killing Drake. She closed her eyes and envisioned putting her hands around Drake's throat, choking the life out of her. No, that wasn't good enough, she'd pull her—

"Greyson, did you hear me? This guy is in pretty bad shape. Did you know she was going there to do this?"

"What? Are you serious? We went there to pick up her car. She wouldn't even let me go in with her. He better hope he dies, 'cause if he doesn't, I'm gonna kill him and that bitch Drake for doing this to Addie." She leaned farther in and whispered, "Who does that, Neil? Who pays someone to attack their own girlfriend and then sues me for it?"

Neil shook his head. "Don't say another word."

"Where's Drake?"

"Addie said she was up at Sears Point for a race or something. I suspect they're picking her up right now."

"Get me out of here, Neil."

He scribbled something on a piece of paper and then said, "I'm trying to get them to either charge you or cut you loose."

"But you said they wanted to book me as an accessory."

"Look, it's all bullshit. They haven't fingerprinted you, taken your mug shot, or charged you with anything.

They keep telling me they're doing the paperwork. I asked about bail, and they told me they're working on it."

"How did you get in to see me?"

"I called in a favor. You're having dinner with Judge Stewart next week."

"What?"

"She's a very nice woman. Besides, you need a few strings pulled, so don't burn that bridge in case we have to go to court."

"Christ. You're pimping me out."

"I'm helping you out. Besides, she's the one who got me in to see Addie."

Greyson rested her chin on her folded hands. "I think they're keeping me in here and out of the way so they can pick up Hogan," Greyson said.

"My thoughts exactly."

"Why?"

Neil showed Greyson his note pad. In big letters it said, ELEVATOR RAPIST.

"No shit. You think so?" Greyson questioned Neil's logic. She didn't do it often, but this time something didn't feel right. She pushed her bottom lip out, perplexed at the suggestion. "You think they figure him for that?"

Neil shrugged. "Maybe." He closed his briefcase and looked at the deputy and then back at her. "I'll keep you posted. Expect to get out in the next couple of hours."

"Make it one."

"I'll try." He stood, gave her a quick hug, and whispered, "Be good in here."

She hugged him tight. He was her lifeline to the outside world, and she felt it slipping from her grasp as he motioned to the deputy.

"We're done."

Patting Neil on the back, she asked, "Hey, can you call Jarrod and tell him to reschedule my meeting tonight?"

"Already done."

"Thanks, buddy." She rarely used terms of endearment with Neil, but he'd stuck his neck out—well, pimped her out at least—and she was grateful for his expertise.

He made a zipping signal across his lips and then smiled.

She did the same just before her hand was cuffed behind her back. Her mind tried to reason with what her heart told her was true. How could one human being be so evil?

Chapter Twenty-nine

Nancy weaved her way through the thick crowd at the raceway. She'd been directed to the pits where Hogan and her team were prepping for the race. A cloud of exhaust hung low in the air, and Nancy wondered how anyone could breathe. She had a warrant, two officers, and determination on her side. If Drake Hogan gave her any shit, which she hoped the woman was stupid enough to do, she'd shoot her.

Nancy had made up her mind on the way up to Sears Point. She'd seen all kinds of depravity in her career, but the kind that Drake Hogan had still astounded her. She'd witnessed the worst kind of domestic violence—men beating their wives to the point of death, only to have the wife return for a second and third time. Women who beat their kids after being so drunk they could barely hold their heads up at the station. But Drake Hogan, she was a special kind of depraved soul.

Nancy spotted Hogan, snuggled up to some sweetheart, nuzzling the woman's neck. Disgusting, she thought, watching the scene play out. Hogan reached around and groped the young girl, and then she squeezed the girl's ass, making her giggle. Nancy motioned to each of the officers, one to the left and one to the right, and she threaded herself between two of Hogan's pit crew and latched on to her arm.

"Drake Hogan, you're under arrest."

Hogan swung around and cocked her arm back, ready to launch her fist right at Nancy. The sound of a handcuff being sprung made Hogan turn toward the officer on her right as he twisted her arm behind her and bent her over. Two men in her pit crew lunged at the cops, knocking one down and hitting the one with the cuff on Hogan. She made a move to sprint out of the pits but stopped when the sound of a gun being cocked echoed near her ear.

"Do it, Ms. Hogan. Give me a reason." Nancy smiled as Hogan froze. Nancy looked at the two men from the pit crew, who stood frozen too. "You're all under arrest."

"Fuck you," Hogan spit out between clenched teeth.

The officers cuffed the two men and left them lying on the ground. As one of the officers moved to cuff Hogan, Nancy stopped him.

"I'll do it."

Nancy slapped one cuff on Drake's wrist and then snarled, "Your other hand."

"You can't do this. I haven't done anything wrong, you bitch."

"Does the name Carl Fletcher ring a bell?"

One of the officers jerked Hogan to face Nancy. If Hogan recognized the name, she didn't let it register.

"Nope."

"Hmm. Your guy at the shop says different. Says you paid him to beat up Addie Blake."

"I want my lawyer."

"You have the right to remain silent..." Nancy smiled. Hogan had lawyered up, so the conversation was over. She finished Mirandizing Hogan and pulled her along toward the parking lot. She'd toss the two pit-crew guys to the local P.D. She'd got what she'd come for, and two more didn't make it a party. Only another pain in the ass if she took them too. Besides, it was going to be a long drive back to San Jose.

Hogan struggled with the officer, who threatened to put her on her ass again. Nancy only watched as she worked herself into a fit.

"You got the wrong person, Detective. You want Greyson Hollister. She's the one responsible for Addie's attack. I didn't have anything to do with it." Hogan wrestled against her cuffs. "You're barking up the wrong tree. You're also out of your jurisdiction."

"Ms. Hogan, are you going to school me in police procedure?"

"I know my rights. You can't arrest me here."

"I have this little piece of paper that says I can." Nancy waved the warrant in front of Hogan's face. "Did you forget your get-out-of-jail-free card?" Nancy taunted her. "Otherwise, you're going to prison."

"I'm going to sue you for wrongful arrest."

"You might intimidate Addie Blake, but you don't scare me. Where you're going, you're going to find out what it means to be someone's bitch."

Nancy wanted only three things right now—the guy in the hospital to live, the DNA to match, and that they had the elevator rapist cuffed to that hospital bed.

But she had a sinking feeling that, with her luck, she'd be lucky to get one out of three.

Chapter Thirty

A hot shower had never felt so good, Greyson thought, hanging out under the spray. Neil had sprung her within the hour. Addie, on the other hand, was still being held without bail. Greyson had requested to see her, but her request was denied. Only her legal counsel could see her, and Neil had said he'd pass on Greyson's message to Addie.

She had written a quick note telling Addie not to worry, that she would do whatever it took to get her home as soon as possible. She also stopped by the hospital and touched base with Dr. Madrigal, searching for any information she could get on the attacker's condition.

Nothing. All Millicent could tell her was that he was in ICU and stable. She had her fingers crossed that he'd make it through the night, and then the odds would be better. Greyson had never wanted anyone to live as badly as she did right now. She'd never even been given a chance to make such a wish with Cate, and she hated thinking she would waste something as valuable as a second chance on such a lowlife as Carl. It would be the only way Addie wouldn't face murder charges, so she'd sacrifice it this one time.

Greyson had briefly told her mom what had happened, but she needn't have bothered. Her picture, coupled with Addie's, had been all over the news, and

Erin Green from Channel 8 was hanging around out front with a few other satellite vans, trying to catch a glimpse of her as she arrived home. She'd flipped them the bird as she was driving through the gate. Lucky for her, the blacked-out windows of the sedan left it her little secret.

Now, all she could do was wait for Neil to do his job. Pulling the sheets up to her chin, she flipped through the news channels. Within minutes, the TV controller slipped from her hand and she was out.

The sound of a vacuum running pierced Greyson's consciousness. "What the fuck?"

"Argh, oh, Jesus. I didn't see you there, Miss Hollister. I thought the office was empty. I'm sorry. I'll come back later."

"No, no, that's fine, Norma," Greyson said, taking her feet off the window ledge and turning the chair back around toward her desk. "I must have dozed off. I'm sorry. I didn't mean to scare you."

"Oh, you made me see Jesus, Miss Hollister," Norma said, crossing herself.

"Seriously," Greyson deadpanned.

"You don't look so good, Miss Hollister. You should go home and get some sleep."

"Yes, well, I would sleep if I could, but I haven't been able to lately." She pulled her jacket from its resting place on the back of the couch and stretched it across her shoulders.

"Oh my God, what's that on your neck, Miss Hollister?" Norma grabbed her own neck and flinched. "Did you burn your neck with a curling iron? Oh, that looks bad. You should get that looked at, and soon."

Greyson reached up and touched her neck. She

didn't feel anything, so she stepped into her bathroom and checked her reflection in the mirror. "Christ, where did that come from," she said, fingering the purple bruise.

"Yeah. See. It's even worse in the light, huh?" Norma said, looking over her shoulder. She grimaced again. "Yeah, that's a nasty one. If I didn't know better, I'd say it was one of those hickeys my daughter used to come home with. But you ain't dating anyone, so it ain't that…Yeah, you better get that checked out. Might be ringworm or something."

Greyson clapped her hand over her neck. "It isn't ringworm." Glaring at the cleaning woman, she turned and surveyed her appearance. Dark circles were forming from lack of sleep, and she had a splitting headache, but other than that she'd never felt better.

"I'll see you tomorrow, Norma." Greyson waved at the woman.

"Oh, no, you won't. Tomorrow is Saturday, and you may not take a day off, but I still get one, right?"

"What? Did you say tomorrow is Saturday?"

"Yep, today is Friday." Norma looked down at her watch pinned to her uniform. "At least for the next twenty minutes. You better hurry if you're gonna catch the last train out."

"Huh?" Greyson turned from the window and stared at her.

"The train. It's gonna leave without you?"

"Oh, right." Greyson pulled her gloves from her coat pocket and slipped them on.

"Hey, you dropped something, Miss Hollister."

Greyson looked down at the floor and froze. Black-and-red fabric lay at her feet.

"Here, let me get that for you." Before Greyson

could stop her, Norma had picked up the pile and had them separated and held them up. "Woo-hoo, these are nice. Now, if you wear stuff like this you're gonna catch a man, Miss Hollister." Suddenly, Norma was holding them out by the tips of her fingers. "I hope you haven't already worn these...I mean..."

Greyson snatched the bra and panties and shoved them back into her pocket. Her head was spinning and something wasn't right.

"You better hurry. The train's gonna be here soon." Norma was pushing her out the door, slamming it behind her.

Walking in a daze, she hit the platform just as the train was rounding the bend. The brakes squealed, the doors swished open, and she got in and sat down, gripping her briefcase to her chest. She pulled the silk and lace from her pocket and fingered them. Then she reached up and touched her neck. Her mind drifted, but she couldn't nest on anything in particular. She needed to go home and sleep the weekend away. That's what she needed to do, sleep.

Maybe she'd call her parents and go over and spend the weekend with them. She hadn't seen them in a while. Perhaps she needed some sage advice from her father, the captain of industry. He dispensed it without even asking, so he'd be flattered she asked. The lights flickered, signaling that her stop was coming up. Grabbing the rail, she hoisted herself up and waited for the lurching stop she'd become accustomed to, then stepped to the doors and let the cold, wet night hit her in the face.

There were only a few cars in the parking lot. Pressing her fob, she found hers lit up like a Christmas tree. The drive home was quiet. No music tonight. She didn't feel like it. The trees passed like sentinels watching and making sure she made it home. In the winter their limbs bowed heavy with snow reflected her mood. She hated winter, the shorter days. In the spring they were filled with birds, squirrels, and things that scurried. And in the fall…well, it didn't matter. She didn't know why she was suddenly waxing philosophical. Sleep, she needed to sleep and get this damn day over. After driving through the gates, she watched them close behind her as she pulled up to the front of the house. Out of the corner of her eye, she caught someone leaning against the column.

Cate.

"Hey, Grey."

"Cate, what are you doing out here?"

"Waiting for you, sexy." Cate grabbed Greyson's hand and pulled her toward the front door. "It was so beautiful out here, I thought I'd sit and look at the stars and wait for you. Remember when we would do that— sit and look at the stars?"

Greyson pulled Cate back and stopped. Cate fell against her and smiled. Reaching up, she threaded her fingers through Greyson's hair and ran her tongue along Greyson's jaw.

"Have I told you how hot you look in that Armani? I get tingly just thinking about how good it's going to look on the floor."

"That's an old line."

"If it ain't broke, why fix it? Sometimes old-school is better." Cate ran her nails down Greyson's ribs and reached around and pinched her ass. "Besides, you have too many clothes on for what I have planned."

"Really." Greyson cast Cate a dubious look.

Cate took her hand and put it under her coat.

Greyson never tired of touching Cate, and Cate knew it. Pulling the coat open, Greyson saw that Cate had on a pair of blue silk panties, a matching bra, and a garter belt and stockings.

"I see you thought of everything for a cold night."

"Is it cold out here? I hadn't noticed." Cate giggled and pulled her into the house. Before she could say anything, Cate had jerked her belt from her slacks and was pushing her arms behind her back.

"What are you doing?"

"Shh, tonight's my night. Remember? Fridays are my night to do what I want."

"Oh, right. I forgot."

Cate cinched the belt around Greyson's wrists, then pushed her into the wingback chair. Stepping back, she let the coat fall to the floor. After she kicked it to the side, Cate swung her hips seductively, running her hands down her body. She walked toward Greyson, turned around, and shook her ass in Greyson's face, then slowly lowered herself and rubbed her ass against Greyson's lap. Standing, she freed herself of her bra and wrapped it around Greyson's neck like an ornament.

"Oh, did I do that?" Cate ran her fingertips over the hickey on Greyson's neck. "Did I leave any others strategically placed on your body? Maybe we should check?"

"Maybe we should." Greyson twisted her arms. "If you let me out I'll help you find them."

Cate wiggled her finger in front of Greyson's face and shook her head. "Uh-uh. I got this."

Greyson could only sit and watch as Cate played with herself in front of her. This was Cate's version of torture, and she played it out exquisitely. Greyson followed Cate's finger as she dipped it into her panties and stroked herself and then pulled it out and moved it in front of Greyson's lips. Before she could snake her tongue out and catch it, Cate withdrew it and admonished Greyson for being too eager.

"Patience, kitty," Cate said as she sat on the coffee table. Slipping out of her high heels, she pointed her toes and swung her legs open and closed, tempting Greyson with a view of her wet panties. Clearly, Cate was as excited as Greyson. Now, if Greyson could just get the belt off her wrists, she'd dominate Cate in all the right ways.

"Uh, uh, uh. If you get loose the party's over. So be patient. Your time is coming, lover."

Suddenly Cate morphed into Addie, and Greyson sat up straighter. What the hell was going on? A wicked smile lit up Addie's face, and Greyson melted.

"What's wrong, lover?"

"Nothing. I'm just—"

Addie smothered Greyson's mouth with her own, parting Greyson's lips with her tongue. Greyson returned the kiss and let her tongue duel with Addie's for control, only Addie was winning this battle.

Addie pulled back from Greyson, unclipped the snaps from her garter belt, and slowly rolled a stocking down her leg, flicking it at her. The stocking landed in her lap, and Greyson growled at the temptation and wrestled with the belt again.

"Yoo-hoo," Addie said, catching Greyson's attention again. She wagged her finger one more time before moving on to the other stocking. Rolling it down, she fell to her knees and slowly crawled like a sleek cat over to Greyson. Addie's breasts swayed with each twitch of her hips, and languidly she rubbed her face the length of Greyson's thigh, stopping at the apex. Greyson grew

wetter as Addie rubbed her face back and forth over her crotch. She stopped and blew hot air on Greyson's pussy. God, she's good at torture, Greyson thought. Moving up and onto Greyson, Addie straddled Greyson and started to tie the stocking around Greyson's mouth but stopped. "If I do that, you can't use your mouth, can you?"

"And I'm very good with my mouth." Greyson leaned down and plucked a nipple between her lips and sucked. Addie's ass tightened on Greyson's lap, and Greyson knew she had her. She let her tongue glide up to Addie's neck and started to suck at the spot that always gave Addie goose bumps. Addie threaded her fingers in Greyson's hair and jerked her head back.

"Uh, uh, uh, lover. My night, remember?"

Without warning, Addie ripped Greyson's shirt open, buttons flying everywhere. She pushed her bra up and dropped back down on her knees between Greyson's legs and worked her lips across Greyson's chest. Greyson lay somewhere between sweet torture and frustration, her body screaming for release, and her mind, well, her mind was a wasteland of emotions. Addie rose above her, slipped her panties off, stroked herself in front of Greyson, and slipped a wet finger between Greyson's lips. Sweet torture.

The buzz of a phone broke through the fog of Greyson's mind. She tossed and turned, her legs tangled in the sheets as she tried to push them away. Throwing an arm over her eyes, she tried to shut out the life around her. The dreams she'd been having with Cate as the centerpiece now featured Addie. Was she finally letting go of Cate? Or was Cate finally leaving her now that Greyson was falling for Addie?

Threading her fingers behind her head, she

stared into the darkness. Seeing nothing, she hoped for even less. She felt like she'd been to battle and barely survived. Swinging her legs over the side of the bed, she sat for a moment and stretched her shoulders. They ached. Looking down at her wrists, she rubbed the thin, red welts. After she stood, she looked around the room for Cate, but she wasn't there. She slipped her feet into her slippers, walked over her clothes from the night before, and flipped on the bathroom light. The mirror said it all—*I'll love you forever!* C. Finishing her business, she washed her hands and then ran her finger over the edge of the ruby-red-lipstick C. Her eyes watered, her throat clenched, and she couldn't swallow the pain. It strangled her as she tried to choke it back.

The darkened bedroom mirrored her mood. She searched out the small altar to Cate. A framed picture of them at their wedding, a candid shot of Cate at the beach, and a small handwritten note, the edges frayed from being stored in Greyson's pocket.

Greyson flipped her phone over and read the text.

"Shit."

Chapter Thirty-one

Realization dawned on Addie as she rubbed at the black ink smudges on the sides of her fingertips. After they'd done a live scan and put her fingerprints into the computer database, they'd insisted on rolling her fingers with ink and across the grids of fingerprint paper. Addie had asked why, but the deputy had only provided a curt answer, telling her that they kept them on file at the jail and used them for comparison, or something or other. She was a bona fide criminal. She didn't feel like one, but her bright-orange jumpsuit with SCDC on the back said it for her.

She couldn't get warm sitting on the cold cement bed. It seeped into her bones. The room was in horrible shape. Others who'd stayed at the jail had carved their initials into the wall. How had they done it, considering the deputies had taken everything she had, including her underwear? She should feel contrite for what she'd done, but she couldn't muster any compassion for the man she'd beaned with a wrench. Part of her hoped he died. He'd taken so much from her. She'd never feel safe around men again. Poor Paul. He was now looped into that category, which had been evident when he'd come to visit her at Greyson's. Addie had made him sit across from her, positioning herself closest to the door just in case.

In case of what? She thought about it. In case

he touched her. She'd cringed and stiffened when he'd given her his customary hug and a peck on the cheek. Her reaction was so bad, she'd apologized at the outward disdain she'd shown him. He hadn't done anything to her, but what was between his legs kept her from returning his comfort.

As for women, she wasn't sure they were much different now, with one exception—

Greyson Hollister. However, now she wasn't sure how she could face Greyson after what Drake had done. God, people were screwed up. She could almost hear her mother now.

"I told you Drake was bad news."
"Mom, really? Can't you give her a chance?"
"Honey, there's just something about her. Call it mother's intuition, but she's bad news."
"Mom." Addie wanted to stomp her foot like a child and throw a tantrum. "You never like any of my girlfriends. It's because they're girls, isn't it?"
"Nonsense. I like that girl from the swim team, Missy. She was polite and very sweet."
"She wasn't my girlfriend. Besides, she's straight."
"Oh."

Her mother's intuition was right. Drake had been trouble. Only Addie had excused it all away, trying to prove her mother wrong. Looking back now, Addie realized that all her friends had avoided her and Drake. Stubbornly, Addie had defended her actions with Drake. She hated being wrong and had defended Drake when there was no defense for her behavior. Love was deaf, blind, and stupid, and now she was paying for that stupidity. Then a thought hit her between the eyes. Was Drake the elevator rapist? Addie hadn't paid attention to the case, but she did know there wasn't much in the way of evidence. Was it possible? Could Drake and this guy be working together? Christ, her life was so screwed up.

The screams of a woman down the hall pulled Addie back to her present situation. The jail wasn't quiet, as prisoners yelled at the guards, banged on the walls for attention, and those with mental conditions screamed profanities nonstop. She shook her head. She had no one to blame for her predicament. She'd put herself here. If only she'd—She could play *that* game all she wanted, but she had only herself to blame. Still, she had to admit, she wasn't sorry for what she'd done.

Addie had been promised one phone call hours ago. Would she get it, or had they forgotten all about her? It didn't matter. Who would she call?

Greyson sprang to the top of the list, though Addie knew she wasn't going to call her. Addie was sure Greyson wouldn't want anything to do with her when she found out Drake was responsible for all the trouble at Integrated Financial.

Would she call her mother and father? They didn't have the kind of ready cash it would take to bail out an attempted murderer.

Paul? He definitely lived hand-to-mouth. He was out.

No one. She'd take her punishment and live with the consequences of her actions. She wouldn't play the victim card either. A split second had changed her life a few weeks ago, just as it had today. Only today, she'd meted out punishment for a crime committed against her. In the time it took to toss a coin in the air, she'd made an irrevocable decision. It sounded clichéd, but she didn't have any other way to think about what she'd done. Her toss had come up tails and she'd lost.

Her attacker's face flashed in her mind. She could hear him asking for the money Drake owed him as if he were standing in front of her. His deep rumble made her tense. Even now her reaction was visceral. Addie shuddered at the memory. Carl, that's what the mechanic had called him, stood only a few feet behind her, but she was back in that tiny elevator the moment she heard his voice.

"Carl." Even saying his name made her gag, but she did it to exorcise the demon that had lived in her head. Now she could put a name to the face that had tormented her every waking moment on this earth and every nightmare she'd had for the past three weeks.

His looming bulk over her at the garage had made her pause, but then her hatred had taken over. Spying the giant wrench on the car fender was a stroke of luck, literally. She'd reacted before her mind could engage. Addie still couldn't believe she'd clocked him like that. She stared down at her open hands and marveled at the damage her small, frail fingers had exacted.

"Blake." Someone on the other side of the door yelled out as the food port dropped. "Hands."

What he was referring to? She held up her hands for inspection.

"Now, get over here and put your hands through here to cuff up. You have a visitor."

How could she have a visitor? She hadn't made her one phone call, yet. Slowly, she made her way to the door.

"Come on. We don't have all night," he commanded her.

Was it night already? How long had she been

here? She would have guessed a few hours at most. It was true what the prisoners on the lock-up shows said. You did lose all track of time locked in these tiny rooms.

"Face the port."

Confused, she turned back around and faced the door, shoving her hands through the opening. The cold metal of the cuffs bit into her wrists. She would have said something, but why? They didn't care. They heard it all the time, and besides, they were just doing their job.

Another command came as the door was opened. "Back up."

Stepping back and pulling her hands toward her, she noticed the chain attached to the cuffs. What the hell? The door opened farther, and the deputy reached around the door and grabbed the length of chain, wound it around her waist, and padlocked it. The chain kept the cuffs secure to her body. She noticed the set of shackles in his other hand, and suddenly a pang of panic hit her. Wasn't this type of treatment reserved for those who were violent?

"Is this really necessary?" she asked, her voice quivering.

"You're considered dangerous. So yes, it's necessary," the female deputy said, grabbing her elbow. The pressure on her elbow kept her compliant as the male deputy shackled her ankles. The weight of the iron on her ankles hurt. Another chain was locked from the waist restraints to her shackles, limiting her gait. God, she was glad her mother couldn't see her. She would be so ashamed of how far she had fallen.

"Let's go." The deputy pulled on her elbow, guiding her down the loud cement chasm.

She couldn't guess who her visitor was, but suddenly she didn't want to see them. Her embarrassment was profound as the catcalls from the other female prisoners echoed with the jangle of her chains as she hobbled down the hall. Addie scurried as fast as she could shuffle. Her curiosity about her visitor would be eased when the deputy stopped her in front of one of many unopened doors. The deputy keyed the next-to-the-last door and swung it wide, ushering her in, then cuffed her to the table and left.

On the other side of the table sat Neil Harris. A little disheveled, but a welcome sight for her weary eyes. Greyson had kept her word.

Neil stood as she sat.

"Is this really necessary?" Neil's voice was pitched with anger.

"Counselor, that's the second time you've questioned jail policy." The deputy's voice contained a warning.

"Well, this just seems a little over the top." Neil pointed to the waist chain and then the shackles.

"She's been booked for attempted murder, not check fraud."

"It was self-defense," he reminded the deputy.

"Save it for the judge and jury. I'm just doin' my job. Now, if you don't mind." He motioned to Addie. "You've got half an hour."

He stood at the door like a sentinel. Clearly he wasn't leaving, so Addie assumed they would have to keep their voices low, just in case she said something incriminating. Neil tossed his briefcase onto the table, obviously disgusted, but Addie couldn't do much about it.

"I'm sorry, Mr. Harris," she said.

"For what? This isn't your fault, Ms. Blake."

Addie shot him a look of surprise.

"Well, I mean…this is all Drake Hogan's fault. She's responsible for your attack."

Addie hunched her shoulders over and hung her head in despair. Drake was responsible for her attack, and by default she felt responsible since Drake was her girlfriend—ex-girlfriend.

"Ms. Blake, I've arranged your bail, but it's going to take until morning to get you in front of a judge. Can you hang in there that long?"

Addie grimaced. Of course she'd still be here in the morning. "Do I have a choice?"

"No, I don't suppose you do. It was a rhetorical question, designed to give you hope and put your mind at ease."

Addie studied Neil. Who talked like that? At least he was brutally honest with his answer. She wanted to see how he did with her next question.

"Who put up the money to bail me out?"

Neil didn't miss a beat. "Greyson, of course."

"What are the terms?" She needed to know what she was getting herself into financially. Odd that would be her most pressing concern. She should be thankful she wasn't going to spend another day in this piss-ridden, cold jail.

"Terms?" Neil didn't even glance at Addie while he scribbled notes on his pad. "Ms. Blake, Ms. Hollister doesn't work like that. She's very worried about you and what happened. Now, if you could please tell me everything that occurred from the time Ms. Hogan was banging on your apartment door last week, up to and including the events in the garage."

Addie began describing what had happened at

the apartment, the phone calls from Drake, and then the attack at the garage. She spilled her guts about every detail of their relationship, or lack of one. Once the words had passed her lips, she felt unburdened. She almost made the sign of the cross like she did in the confessional, but she resisted, happy to be free of the weight of her association with Drake.

Neil didn't say anything. He peered at her, squinted, then pursed his lips and rested his busy hands. Clearly he wasn't a man to be trifled with, and she wondered if she had said something she should have kept secret. She started to say something, but Neil raised his hand, stopping her.

"Do you think Ms. Hogan is unbalanced?"

"Unbalanced? You mean crazy?"

"Yes."

"No. I think she's a cold, calculating bitch. However, up until yesterday, I didn't know that side of her." Addie smarted from the realization that she had slept in the same bed with someone who'd professed her love but thought nothing of having someone almost beat her to death to line her pockets. No, until yesterday, Addie had just thought Drake was a heartless bitch.

"Ms. Blake, do you think Ms. Hogan could be the elevator rapist? Before you answer, remember she was able to get someone into the building, cut the camera feed, and attack you. It was well thought out and the work of someone who lacks a conscience."

Addie had seen Drake take apart an engine on the living-room floor, then rebuild it without instructions, drop it back into a car, and rewire the whole electrical system, again without instructions. So could Drake break into the camera system? Sure. But would she risk being found out? Not a chance. Addie searched Neil's face, looking for an answer. He must know something if he was asking her. This Drake was someone she didn't know, didn't want to know.

"Mr. Harris, I thought I knew Drake. Clearly, she isn't who I thought she was." Addie looked beyond Neil, staring at something insignificant on the wall. Anything that helped her avoid Neil's persistent, prying gaze. "Drake's a cheater, a liar, a deviant who I'd classify as wicked. So, I have a hard time imagining Drake doing something so evil, but I'm finding that I never really knew Drake."

Addie was sure Neil's pen tapping against the table reflected his frustration. She faced him and wanted to confirm both their fears, but she couldn't. "I'm sorry. I wish I had more for you, Mr. Harris."

"Me too." Neil gave a tight smile, tossed his pen and pad into his briefcase, and rested his clasped hands on top of it. "May I give you some advice, Ms. Blake?"

"Of course."

Who was she to turn down any advice her lawyer might give her? She wasn't exactly in a position to negotiate a plea deal, and if Neil thought she should throw herself on the mercy of the court to get out of jail, she would do it in a heartbeat.

"I've known Greyson since college, and she's had only one woman in her life who could get through her well-constructed wall. Cate, Ben's mother, was a remarkable woman. She set Greyson back on her heels. She was beautiful, talented, and smart. I never thought I would see Greyson happy again." Neil brushed his hands toward her in case Addie was thinking of making a remark. "Now it seems that another woman has gotten under her skin."

Their eyes met, and Addie noticed that his gaze softened. Clearly he cared for Greyson.

"Me?"

He nodded. "Don't break her heart. I had to…" He surprisingly stumbled over his words. "She's very dear to me, and I don't want to see her hurt."

She hadn't expected his declaration. She was prepared for a well-thought-out speech about conduct in the courtroom, or his strategy for getting her released tomorrow. However, a softhearted speech about Greyson caught her off guard.

"Truthfully, Mr. Harris, I don't know where I stand with Ms. Hollister. I'm getting ready to go to prison for attempted murder. I doubt Greyson will be keeping me around, and I'd be a fool to expect her to."

"You don't know Greyson. Besides, you aren't going to prison. Greyson won't let that happen. Even if you're right and she's not in love with you, which she is, Greyson will do the honorable thing and get you out to make sure you're safe until all of this blows over." Neil patted her hand. "Trust me. I'm your lawyer and I'm that good."

"But—"

"I'll see you at the arraignment tomorrow. Do you need something to wear when you leave?"

"I suppose I will. They've taken my clothes."

"It's evidence now, so I'll make sure Greyson brings you something appropriate. Have you called your parents yet?"

"No, I haven't. I don't know when I'll get my phone call, and I don't want to worry them."

"You've been all over the news. Your face and name have been on every channel in the tri-county region. So call them. I'm sure they're worried and just want to hear your voice. It will bring them some comfort if you tell them that we're working to get you released tomorrow."

"But…I don't know what to say to them." Addie started to cry. The realization of her situation hit her like a bulldozer. She was being arraigned tomorrow, going to court and actually facing a judge for attempted murder. Oh, how she had disgraced the family name, her Aunt Vera would rant and rave to her mother. Addie was sure Vera was on the phone right now with her mother, chastising her for the terrible child they had raised. Nothing like her corporate-raider son, Michael, the salt of the earth who'd practically bankrupted his former company. No, she would officially be the black sheep of the family now.

"Ms. Blake, I don't mean to sound callous, but what's done is done. No need for tears now. Why don't you concentrate on what you're going to say when Drake Hogan is arraigned. We'll ask for a victim-impact statement to be read, and I want you to be ready. I want your statement to focus on how the attack has wrecked your life."

"But—"

"You want out? Then just tell the truth in your statement. Drake Hogan did this to you, and you shouldn't be held responsible for defending yourself."

Neil was so casual about the court date tomorrow. Didn't he know what she might be facing? What if Carl died? She'd be a murderer. It wouldn't matter that he'd attacked her. It wouldn't matter that Drake had set the whole thing up just to grab a few bucks from Greyson. Nothing would matter.

"But isn't that usually done when someone's been convicted?

"If Drake Hogan doesn't take a plea deal, she's a fool."

"You don't know Drake, Mr. Harris. If she smells money, she's like a shark. She'll bite at anything."

"No, you're right. I don't know Drake, but I've met lots of people just like her. Event opportunists, I like to call them. They can't pass up a bad situation to make a buck, but I've seen and heard the evidence. I've looked at her bank records, and she doesn't have the kind of money it's going to take to keep her out of jail, let alone prison. The public defender will recommend she plead it out."

Addie thought about how prideful Drake was, and while she didn't have a lot of cash, she had a set of brass ones that would override her common sense.

"You could be right," Addie admitted. No, she hoped Neil was right. Otherwise, they were all in it for the long haul.

"Ms. Blake, I'm paid to be right, so please don't worry. Tomorrow is just a formality. We'll have you out and back to work by Thursday." Neil tapped the door, put his face in front of the window, and told the deputy they were done. Looking back at Addie, he smiled briefly. "Think about what you're going to say in your victim-impact statement. I want it to be powerful, but not over the top."

"I'll try."

"I'll see you in the morning, Ms. Blake."

"Thank you for all your help."

"Don't thank me. Thank Grey. She's the big gun here."

"Of course." Addie stood but couldn't move. She was still cuffed to the table, keeping her on a short leash. She wanted to hug him for some reason, but he didn't seem to be the type for physical displays of affection.

"Don't forget to call your parents. Keep it short and simple. Everything is recorded."

Addie nodded at the fatherly advice and slid back into the squeaky seat. What would she tell her parents? Her mom would say, "I told you so. I knew that Drake Hogan was bad news." Her father, he was probably a mess. She was his princess, and he still called her that name every time Addie called home.

"Oh, God, what do they think of me now?" she murmured, wiping her nose on the sleeve of her jumpsuit.

Chapter Thirty-two

Nancy had the pleasure of walking Drake Hogan into booking. Dragging the struggling woman through the front of the jail was a choice Nancy made the minute Hogan spit at her. She'd intended to take the underground access, but the cussing woman had earned herself a perp walk right in front of the waiting reporters and cameras outside the jail. Vindictive? Maybe. However, Hogan was some kind of evil that needed to be outed for what she'd done to an innocent woman like Addie Blake.

Nancy would never forget the look in Addie's eyes when they'd met the first time. The hollowed-out expression, the torment that she wore like a gown as she'd asked Nancy, why her? It was the same with all victims, but Hogan was the perpetrator of this little vignette. She'd put all the players in motion, and everyone had acted out his part with practiced precision. For what?

Money.

Pulling Hogan from the sedan was like waving raw meat to starving animals. The reporters bunched around them just as Hogan landed on her feet. The peppering of questions started, and Erin Green was at the front of the pack. If Nancy didn't know better, she would have sworn Erin was licking the drops of saliva from the corners of her mouth.

"Detective, why is Drake Hogan being arrested?"

"Ms. Hogan is a person of interest in the brutal attack of Addie Blake."

A hum sliced through the gaggle of reporters as they digested the first morsel of the story.

"Is Hogan the elevator rapist then?" Someone thrust a mic in Nancy's face, waiting for the answer. Before she could respond, Hogan replied for her.

"Hell, no, I'm not the elevator rapist. This is just a misunderstanding between me and my girlfriend."

"Ms. Hogan, why did you attack your girlfriend?"

"Ms. Hogan, do you have any comment about the man Addie Blake attacked in your garage today?"

Nancy and Hogan looked at each other, and then Nancy held up her hand, trying to stop them. "No further questions."

"I didn't hurt anyone," Hogan said defiantly, yanking her arm out of Nancy's grasp. "They've got the wrong person on this. They should be out there looking for whoever hurt my girlfriend. Instead…" She shot Nancy a dark look and said, "Instead, this bitch decided to waste time and taxpayer money and drag me down here without cause."

"Ms. Hogan, what about the man attacked in your garage?"

"I'm sure Addie is just suffering from PTSD. Once I talk to her, we'll clear all of this up and get on with our lives together."

Cameramen and reporters kept Nancy from moving very far, which was fine with her. The more Hogan talked, the more likely it would be that someone would punch her well-honed buttons. Nancy searched out Erin Green and then raised her eyebrows, cocked her head, and gave her one of her looks that said, "Is that all you've got?" Baited, Erin stuck the mic in Hogan's face and said, "I have it from a reliable source that you paid someone to beat the crap out of your girlfriend so you could sue Greyson Hollister, Ms. Hogan. Is that true?"

"What the fuck? Of course I'm denying that. Did that Hollister bitch put you up to this?" Hogan leaned toward Erin Green and leered at her.

Instantly, Green took a step back but kept the mic and the pressure on Hogan. "Is it true?"

"All right, enough questions. We'll be holding a news conference after the arraignment in the morning," Nancy said, yanking Hogan back.

It would be a long night of questions and denials, so she wanted to get the dance started. She still needed to brief the chief and check on the status of their number-one witness slash co-defendant, Carl. If she was lucky he would be awake and ready to save his own neck, throwing Hogan under the proverbial bus.

"Let's go, cupcake," she said, jerking Hogan toward the doors. It took several minutes to cut a path through the thick cloud of reporters. Even inside, she could still hear them yelling questions through the glass. Glancing over her shoulder, she could see Erin Green had already gone to a live shot, attempting to scoop her fellow reporters, who were still trying to get answers. Nancy groaned as she realized she was still in the picture. Moving Hogan farther back and toward the doors to the jail, she elbowed the buzzer and waited.

"You fucking did that on purpose," Hogan screamed. "You know there's another entrance in the underground garage, but you wanted a perp walk."

"Is there another entrance to this place? How would you know that? You seem like such a fine, upstanding citizen, Ms. Hogan."

"Fuck you."

"I just have to know, do you kiss your mother with that mouth?"

"Don't talk about my mom. She's twice the woman you are and the salt of the earth."

"Then how did she raise such an evil, soulless bitch like you?"

Nancy knew she was pushing Hogan's buttons, but she didn't care. People like Hogan were the reason she'd become a cop. The scourge of society, they were the underbelly of a city awash in crime, which made Nancy sick, but someone had to clean it up so nice people would stay. So they could walk their kids to school without the fear of being mugged or shot.

Pushing Hogan forward, she wished she could push her through the window and feed her to the news media. Hogan didn't deserve any respect after what she'd done to Addie Blake, but right now Nancy was merely a glorified enforcer. It was her job to make sure people followed the law, and when they broke it, she bent it into order again. She'd bent it slightly in Addie's case, and hopefully Addie had read between the lines earlier and Hogan would go away for a long time. If this had been Hollister, Nancy was sure Hollister wouldn't be surprised, but Addie, well, Nancy saw goodness and honesty written all over her. Sometimes, the nice people got the screw. She just hoped Hogan wasn't the nut on the other end.

"Hey, when do I get to make my phone call?" Drake yelled as she was taken down the hall to processing.

"Hopefully when hell freezes over," Nancy mumbled.

Addie pulled at the chain connecting the shackles to the waist chain. The pain was like a knife against her anklebones. Each step jarred the shackles and cut against her skin. The catcalls started again as she passed the cells. Trying to ignore them, she looked out the window toward the intake room and stopped.

Drake stood just on the other side of the glass being fingerprinted. Detective Hill stood next to her, her arms crossed. The detective shot Drake a look that Addie recognized. She was pissed. Knowing Drake, she was probably mouthing off about the mistreatment she was receiving.

"What's the problem, Blake?" the deputy said, pulling on her upper arm.

He followed her gaze. "Someone you know?"

"You could say that," she said. Her face heated with rage. Without thinking, Addie stepped toward the window and hit it with her forehead. Detective Hill and Drake both turned at the sound.

"You…"

It was all Addie could get out before the deputy pulled her away from the window and pushed her against the wall. "What the hell's wrong with you?"

She never took her eyes off Drake, who was mouthing, "Sorry." Addie spit at Drake.

"I need a restraint chair and a spit mask," said the deputy into his walkie on his shoulder.

"I'm fine," Addie said, still staring at Drake.

"Ms. Blake?" Both Addie and the deputy turned at the sound of Detective Hill's voice. "Deputy, can I have a word with Ms. Blake?"

"What? No. She's being put in a restraint chair and spit mask until she can calm down." He kept Addie pinned to the wall.

"I don't want to go over your head, Deputy, but that woman right there had your prisoner brutally beaten and she almost died, so I think her reaction is pretty mild, considering the circumstances."

"I don't care. No prisoner of mine is going to beat her head against the window and hurt herself or spit while I'm around."

Another deputy walked up to the group. Addie still hadn't taken her eyes off Drake. If she could just get in that room, she'd show Drake she wasn't a victim anymore. Just a few minutes alone was all she needed, and she'd do to Drake what she'd done to Carl. Addie seethed with anger; it colored her vision and gave her a sick feeling.

"Deputy, may I speak to you for a moment?"

"Detective—"

"Deputy, you're impeding my investigation of a case at the moment, and I have a few more questions for this witness."

"Witness?"

"You heard me. She's a witness in a major rape case. I'm sure you've heard of the elevator rapist."

He looked at her dubiously and then back at Addie. Releasing Addie, he gave the female deputy strict instructions not to let Addie move.

"Detective, this had better not be some ploy to get this prisoner alone. I've had about all the bullshit I'm going to take today. Understand?"

"Are you accusing me of something, Deputy? I'd advise you to watch what you say, or you might find yourself with a worse duty than this."

"Are you threatening me, Detective?"

"Let's everyone just take a breath. You see that woman over there? I don't want her housed anywhere near Ms. Blake. That woman was just arrested for the assault on Ms. Blake. Do I make myself clear?"

"That's all you had to say, Detective." The deputy stepped back and turned Addie around.

Addie flinched away as he raised his hand to brush it through his hair. If the look he shot Addie was any indication of his mood, she was more than a little frightened.

"Ms. Blake, may I speak to you for a moment?" Detective Hill gestured to a spot just down the hall, out of earshot of the two deputies. "Don't do that again, will you?"

"What?"

"Don't go around hitting your head against the glass, don't spit, and don't bring any more attention to yourself. You see Hogan? She's all spun up now, and I haven't had a chance to question her, yet."

"But..." The muscles in Addie's jaw bunched as she clenched her teeth. "Detective, that woman is the reason I'm trussed up like this," she said, rattling the chain and holding her cuffs up as high as she could. "Do you see this? I'm being treated like a murderer."

"Ms. Blake. I can only hope that you understand this is for your own protection."

"My protection. Are you fucking kidding me?"

"I wish I didn't have to do this, but if you were free, what would you be doing right now?" The detective stared her in the eyes and then looked at Drake, who was still trying to get Addie's attention.

"Knowing what I know now? I'd have hunted Drake down like the dog she is and beat the living hell out of her."

"Exactly."

Addie was glad she was far enough from Drake that she could only hear her yelling. It would serve Drake right to be put in a restraint chair or, even better, hog-tied and put on her belly. Before Addie could say anything, a commotion broke out in the intake room, and the two deputies waiting for Addie went jetting through the door. Detective Hill pulled her closer, and they watched as Drake was dropped to the floor and restrained.

A deputy walked out of the room, snapped off a pair of rubber gloves, and tossed them into the trash before walking over to the women.

"There's more than one way to get a DNA sample," he said, standing next to Addie. "We done here?"

"Yeah, we're done," the detective said. "Ms. Blake, remember what I said. Patience isn't a virtue many have, as you can see." She nodded in Drake's direction. "So I suggest you exercise some, and you'll be out of here sooner rather than later. I'll see you at the arraignment tomorrow."

Addie was about to say something but stopped. Detective Hill was right. She didn't need any more trouble. Looking at the deputy she said, "I'm ready to go back to my cell."

She just needed to wait out the night, and hopefully she'd be out by morning. Hopefully.

Chapter Thirty-three

"D NA isn't a match," Jenny, from the CSI unit, informed Nancy.

Kicking her feet off the desk, Nancy stood and grabbed the file from Jenny.

"Are you sure?"

Jenny quirked her eyebrows at Nancy and crossed her arms.

"Of course you're sure." Nancy looked at the file and then back at Jenny. "Anything else?"

"Yeah. Your rapist is Hep C positive, and Carl isn't."

"What? Shit." That's all they needed. Now Nancy had the shitty job of informing all of the victims of this new development. Not only had they been brutalized, but now they could contract Hep C. It meant another added charge once they found the bastard, but the idea that they would need to be constantly tested for Hep C added another element of fear to the attack.

"He wore a condom, but that doesn't mean they're safe. Any leakage, any exchange of body fluids still puts them at risk for contracting the disease."

"Jesus, this just gets better and better, doesn't it?" Nancy raised her hand. "Don't answer that. I know. This shouldn't be a surprise."

"Not really. I wish I could say it's uncommon, but remember the Ranch case? That bastard was infecting women with Hep C on purpose and was having consensual sex.”

Nancy sighed. It wasn’t like it didn’t happen, but this was a different kind of vicious.

“Thanks. Well, we can eliminate a ton of suspects with this new information. I’ll go over and break the news to Ms. Blake. Can’t we catch a damn break on this?”

“Catch him.”

“No shit.” Nancy tossed the folder to the desk and looked at the clock. It’d been a week since Hogan’s arrest, and she’d done exactly what Nancy had thought she’d do. Hogan had refused a plea deal, and now they were going to have to go to trial. It didn’t really matter to her, but the arraignment had been a shit show. Both Addie and Hogan were in the same courtroom, in the same prisoner line, cuffed only a few people apart. Someone had disregarded her orders to keep them separated. The blowup in the courtroom had been monumental.

When Addie had stood up to be arraigned, Hogan had made it a point to yell that she wasn’t responsible for Addie’s attack. The judge had ordered the courtroom cleared, and only Addie, lawyers, and cops were present during the arraignment. Nancy was able to give her statement and why she thought Addie had reacted. Lucky for Addie, Greyson Hollister’s lawyer had a game plan and the bail money to spring Addie that moment. Hogan’s outburst had only helped Addie.

Nancy had spoken with the DA and the public defender, and both agreed that Hogan didn’t stand a chance once the case went to court. Carl had survived the night and improved quickly. His thick skull had saved his life. It turned out that he had just received a glancing blow that had knocked him out. Once awake and facing attempted rape charges, he was a proverbial songbird, but not before the arraignment.

Then again, criminals always claimed they were innocent, but now Nancy had the truth in her hand. She was glad they had convinced the asshole to take the plea. Didn't hurt that he was facing a lengthy sentence if he didn't take it and they went to court. Nancy had told him that Hogan was claiming it was all his idea. The wheels were greased and he cooperated.

Carl wasn't Hep C positive, so that eliminated him from the list of possibles in the elevator-rape cases. Now she had to go and tell Addie that he wasn't the rapist. It should be a relief, but it was just another indicator of how deviant society could be, and was. A quick trip out to Greyson Hollister's and then home for what promised to be another sleepless night working on the case were in Nancy's future.

"You going to tell Ms. Blake?"

Nancy picked up her car keys and jangled them. "On my way now. At least this is some good news for Addie."

❧ ❧ ❧ ❧

"Watch me, Addie."

Addie took a mouthful of water as Ben cannonballed into the pool. His water wings popped him right to the surface giggling. He wasn't afraid of anything. The innocence of youth, she thought as she grabbed him up and pulled him to the side of the pool. She'd grown to care about the little tyke and wondered what her life would be like when she didn't see him every day. She'd been putting off having the conversation with Greyson, but she needed to get back to her own life, soon. After she put him on the edge of the pool, he stood, took a few steps back, and plunged again into the pool. Addie was sorry Greyson had to miss tonight's fun, but she was a decent surrogate, if she did have to say so herself.

"Ms. Blake, there is a Detective Hill here to see you," Carmen said, pointing to the door.

The detective walked past Carmen, thanking her, and stood above Addie in the failing sun. Shading her eyes to see the officer, Addie felt a spike of anxiety slice right through her.

"Detective, why don't you join us? Do you have your swim suit?" Addie knew she didn't, but being polite wasn't something Addie dispensed with just because she didn't want to see the detective.

"Thank you. If I'd known there was a pool party going on, I would have packed it. I'm actually here to give you and Hollister some news."

Addie hadn't been kept up to date on the case against Drake and Carl. Not because she didn't ask, but because Neil wanted her to focus on her case and not be burdened by side issues. Drake was a side issue, a problem that Addie just wanted to disappear.

"Is she here?" Nancy looked around.

Addie had hoped Greyson would be here to enjoy the last few crisp days of fall, especially on a Friday. They'd begun having dinner after work and then a swim with Ben every night. Addie would miss the routine they'd established, but she did have to get back to work. Addie had thought she would measure her life in terms of B.A. and A.A. Before the attack and after the attack, but it was looking more and more that it would be measured by the court case against her. She was confident in Neil's ability to minimize the damage to her career and life.

"Ms. Blake?"

"Sorry. Greyson's at one of those societal functions she has to attend."

Before the detective could say anything, Addie noticed her expression shift to one of concern.

"When was the last time she had one?"

Addie shrugged. It's been awhile, she thought. "Weeks, I guess. She's put them off until things calmed down. She didn't want the memory of it all being so fresh when she met with potential clients and board members."

"I see." Detective Hill pulled out her pad and pen. "Do you know where this meeting is and who's going to be there?"

"No, but I'm sure Neil Harris does. Would you like me to call him?"

"If it wouldn't be too much of a bother, yes." She helped Addie out of the pool.

"No bother. Is something wrong? You seem concerned." Addie grabbed her cell phone and dialed Neil's number. Waiting, she watched the detective pace back and forth around the pool.

"Addie, we gonna swim?"

Addie smiled down at Ben. Holding up a finger, she said, "Give me a second, honey. This nice lady needs to talk to your mommy, and then we can swim some more." Addie sat on the pool's edge and let her legs dangle in the pool. "Hi, Mr. Harris. Do you know where Ms. Hollister's meeting is tonight?"

"Addie, how are you? Is everything okay?"

"Detective Hill is here and needs to speak with

her."

"Can I talk with Detective Hill?"

"Sure." Addie called her over and passed her the phone.

The detective grabbed the phone and sighed.

"Is this really necessary that you get in touch with Greyson, Detective?" Neil sounded agitated.

"Mr. Harris, I was fine until I found out that Ms. Hollister is at another dinner. I'm a little concerned now."

"What are you implying?"

"Mr. Harris, I have a theory, but it's just a theory—"

"Aw, yes. Is this the one where you think that a rape happens every time Greyson is at an event?"

"Mr. Harris, the address?"

"She's at the Event Center attending the Chamber of Commerce business mixer. Perhaps I should meet you there just in case she needs some advice?"

"I'll give her a call, and if she thinks she needs you, I'm sure she'll let you know. Thank you, Mr. Harris." The detective ended the call abruptly.

She handed the phone back to Addie and smiled down at Ben. "So what's your name, big guy?"

"Ben," he said, sticking his hand out to her.

"Well, you must be the man of the house. Right?" Detective Hill shook his hand, her smile widening.

"Yep," he said, pushing off the wall and seeming embarrassed.

"So, did you get the address?" Addie asked.

"I did, but can you do me a favor and give Hollister a call?"

"Sure. Is something wrong?"

"I hope not, but if she sees it's from you, she's

more likely to take it than if it was from me, and I need her to pick up that phone."

Detective Hills's voice was edgy, and her body language, while soft with Ben, had tightened up. Tension oozed off her, and Addie was concerned for Greyson.

"Okay, let's get her on the line and maybe we can all relax." Addie pushed speed dial for Greyson and passed the phone to the detective. Addie could hear Greyson's voice message signaling that she wasn't picking up. "Want me to text her?" Addie held out her hand.

"Please. Could you tell her to call you now?"

4:45—*Greyson, can you give me a call ASAP? Thanks, A*

"Is this an emergency? I thought you were here to give me an update?" Addie was worried now that the detective was pushing to talk to Greyson.

"I do have news, but I'm a little worried about something else."

"What?"

"Ms. Blake, I just need to talk to Hollister, but we're wasting time, so I'm just going to jet over to the hotel and see if I can find her. Does she have a date?"

"No, just her usual. Jarrod Bennet, her office assistant. He goes with her so he can keep notes, so to speak."

"Okay. Well, if she calls you, can you please ask her to contact me? It's very important that I speak with her tonight," she said, walking back the way she came in.

"What were you going to tell me?"

Detective Hill stopped in mid-stride, turned, and bit the inside of her mouth. "Carl isn't the elevator rapist. DNA doesn't match. He's taken a plea deal and will testify against Hogan, so this should wrap up nicely. I'm sorry, Ms. Blake, but I need to get going. If you have any more questions, just give me a ring." With that, the detective broke into a dead run toward the front of the house.

Addie did have questions, lots of them, but clearly she wasn't going to get them answered right now.

"Addie, swim," Ben said, patting the water.

"You bet, big guy," Addie sat back down on the pool edge. "Let me text your mom and then we can swim some more before dinner."

4:55—Greyson, Detective Hill was here. She needs to talk to you. She wants you to call her.

"Ooookkkaaaayyyy," Ben said, launching himself into the pool.

Addie sent another text. Her first went unanswered, which was odd for Greyson. Her phone was usually glued to her hand, even at formal events. She was always on call for I.F. except when at home with Ben. That was the only off-limits time she made for herself.

Something wasn't right. Sending another text, this time to Neil, she alerted him to the fact that Greyson wasn't answering. His reply was swift and to the point.

"I know. I'm worried too. She hasn't responded to any of my texts either. I'm going down to the hotel. I'll keep you posted."

Addie's mind went in a dozen directions. Surely

there was a logical explanation for Greyson being off-line. It wasn't like her. She needed to get to the hotel and find out what was going on. No, she needed to mind her own business. Greyson was a big girl and could take care of herself. Besides, she was sure there was a logical reason for Greyson not answering her phone.

I'm just being paranoid, she told herself.

"You okay, Addie?" Ben swam up and hugged her knees.

Not wanting to worry Ben, she smiled and patted his head. "You know what, I think we need to eat dinner. What do you say?"

"Hot dogs?"

"Hot dogs it is."

"Yeah."

Addie would pass Ben off to Camille and drive down to the hotel. She needed to quell her own fears. She'd just explain to Greyson that she was concerned, especially after what had happened to her. In reality she was scared for Greyson and wanted to make sure she was okay.

God, she hoped Greyson didn't think she was a stalker or butting into her business, but better to ask for forgiveness than permission. Wasn't that what Drake always said? Great, now she was quoting a psychopath.

Life has really turned, hasn't it?

Chapter Thirty-four

He casually looked down the corridor and punched the elevator button. His libido in overdrive, he caressed himself through his pocket. He had been down too long. His last little escapade was weeks ago, and he had needs. Deciding to hold off until the heat eased had brought him both pleasure and pain, only to find out some stupid bitch had tried to copycat his unique style. He was pissed. He'd been so close to having that Blake woman, but now he was glad he hadn't moved on her.

As for tonight, he'd tortured himself exquisitely watching Greyson Hollister from afar. She was close enough a few times that he'd caught a whiff of her perfume and almost reached out to touch her. Like a dog in heat, he wanted to pull her into the bathroom and dry-hump her tight ass. Women shouldn't wear tight-fitting, low-cut dresses. They just invited trouble by tempting men that way. She didn't even know he existed, but it didn't matter. If he was patient, he'd stake his claim on her too, eventually. However, he'd have to work his magic on the cute hostess first. What he had in store for her would slake his unquenchable thirst for Greyson Hollister.

He wrung his hands as he peered up at the elevator floor lights and noticed that the elevator had almost reached his floor. Ten more minutes and he'd have his mouth full of a writhing little nubile woman and then collect one last little trophy. It was a good thing he was moving on. New city, new life, new energy, and new prospects. It was like being reborn. The ping of the elevator landing at his floor pulled him back to the present. The door spread wide, and he had to stop as he realized the elevator had delivered an unexpected surprise.

Greyson Hollister.

She stood semi-crouched, leaning against the wall, barely able to hold herself up.

"Oh, thank God it's you," she said, clutching her stomach.

"Are you all right?" he said, offering her a gloved hand. "Here, let me help you."

He stepped into the elevator, hit the close-door button and then the stop button, and smiled with satisfaction as the doors closed. Karma had finally delivered Greyson to him.

❧❧❧❧

Nancy slid her cruiser into the nearly vacant parking lot and assessed the area. A few stragglers stood outside talking. A limo waited, the driver leaning against it having a smoke.

"Hey, who are you driving tonight?" she asked.

When the guy stone-faced her, she pulled her shield and repeated the question with a little more force. "I asked, who are you driving tonight?"

"Greyson Hollister and some guy. I think the little smug bastard said his name was Jarrod Bennet."

"Thanks."

Nancy took the steps two at a time and stopped

at a gaggle of men.

"Excuse me, have you seen Greyson Hollister?"

A couple of guys shrugged, but one said, "I think I heard her say she was going to the bar to get a drink with some guy."

"Thanks." Nancy ran and then stopped. "Where's the bar?"

"Top floor."

"Of course," she said, hustling into the glass menagerie of the lobby. She palmed her badge and flashed it before the security guard could say anything.

"Is there a problem?" he asked, following her.

"I hope not. There's going to be a uniformed officer following me. Tell her top floor."

"But that's a private club."

"And here's my special membership card." Nancy showed him her badge again.

"But—"

"Tell Officer Torres to meet me up there. If you give her any grief, I'll cuff you myself. Understand?"

"Yes, ma'am."

She tapped the button for the top floor, but nothing happened. Looking at the panel, she realized it took a special key card to activate the top-floor button.

"Hey."

The guard peeked around the corner. "Yes."

She wiggled her fingers and stretched her hand out, pointing to the slot with her other.

"Gimme your card."

"But I'm assigned this card and—"

"Gimme the fucking card," she said, pulling her cuffs. "Or I'll—"

"Here." He ran over and slid the card in and was about to pull it out when, tired of his crap, she stopped his hand and took the card.

"Do you have another one of these?"

He nodded.

"Give it to the officer when she gets here and tell her to hurry."

"Yes, ma'am."

Nancy watched the floors tick off as one elevator traveled down. The other one hadn't moved since she'd tried to select the top floor. That didn't make sense.

"Hey, are both of these working?" she yelled.

"Yes, ma'am."

"Do you take them out of service for cleaning?"

She was getting a bad feeling.

"Every fourth Sunday night, the elevator company sends someone to do maintenance."

"Do you have an override key?"

"Ma'am?"

"The key you give firefighters when there's an emergency."

"They have their own, but we keep a spare at the desk."

Nancy kept her eyes on the display. "Get it." Something was wrong, and she didn't need some rent-a-cop to keep her from finding out what the problem was on the top floor.

"Why?"

"Just get the fucking key!"

She hoped she was wrong. No, she prayed she was wrong, but her gut told her something was happening in that elevator stalled out at the top of the hotel. Torres and Neil Harris walked through the lobby at the same time. Even if Harris was Hollister's talking head, he could help with the situation.

"Fuck, I'm so glad to see you two."

Harris looked a little more than surprised at the proclamation. Pointing to his chest, he said, "Me too? Well, that's a change, Detective."

"Look." Nancy pointed to the stalled elevator. "I think something's going on in there. The dinner's been over for an hour, and Hollister was supposed to be meeting someone in the bar for drinks."

"Jarrod Bennet. She's meeting him for a drink. At least that's what she texted me earlier." He showed her his phone. "He told her he got a job with another company, so she's having a drink with him to celebrate."

3:55—Jarrod is leaving I.F. Got a new job with that prick from Global. Can you get the separation paperwork ready? I'm having a drink with him later to congratulate him dodging a bullet.

Neither the pronouncement nor the text comforted her. Drake Hogan's evil behavior had surprised her, sort of. Her gut still told her that Hollister was linked to the elevator rapist, and conveniently she was staring at an elevator that wasn't moving.

"Okay, this is what we're going to do. You." She pointed to Torres. "Start up the stairs. I don't want us missing this guy if he decides to bolt."

"You think the elevator rapist is here?" Harris sounded surprised.

"I do, and I think he's up there," she said, pointing to the still-unmoving elevator. "I want you to go with me," she told him. "Hey, come here," she called to the security guard.

"Yes?"

"Go lock the lobby doors and any other exits so no one can get out of this building from here. Then stay here." Nancy pointed to the floor. "Don't let anyone leave the hotel. I've got a call in for backup so they should be here in a minute or two. Once they get here you can return to your station."

"Okay, but there are only a few people," he said hesitantly.

"All right, Torres, get started up the stairs. Keep your eyes open for anything out of the ordinary. Someone comes out into the stairs, assume they're trying to get away. Otherwise, they'd use the one good elevator. Harris, we're going up," she said, holding up the key. With this we can skip all the floors and get to the top in about..." She turned and looked at the security guard.

"Two minutes."

"Two minutes. We're going to open that elevator and see what the holdup is. If it's nothing, we're going to go looking for Hollister. Ready?"

Harris's pale face told her he wasn't ready. But it didn't matter. He needed to be or sit this one out.

"Would you rather stay here?"

"No, no. I'm good. Let's do this." He didn't sound very convincing. Oh well, shit happened, and they were in the middle of it. If her gut was right, the rapist was in that stalled elevator, raping someone. They needed to hurry.

"Let's go," she said, stepping into the elevator and pushing the override key into place. She took a deep breath, pulled her gun, and hoped she was wrong about Hollister.

Chapter Thirty-five

Greyson fell to her knees, barely able to keep her eyes open. Who would have guessed Jarrod would be her knight in shining armor to save her. If she could just get to her car she could drive home and slip into bed and wait it out. Jarrod would have to take a rain check on that drink.

"Greyson, are you all right?" Jarrod leaned down and watched as Greyson slipped farther to the floor.

"Jarrod, I need you to get me to my car," she said, her eyes closed when the pain in her gut intensified. "Please."

"Well, isn't this a predicament." Jarrod raised Greyson's chin and stared at her.

"What are you talking about?" Greyson jerked her head from his grasp.

"Karma, Lady Karma has delivered you to me, finally." He smiled and pulled out his knife. "You've been waiting for me, haven't you, Greyson?"

"What? Put that thing away." She clutched her stomach as another pain shot through her. "I need to get home. I'm feeling sick and I—"

"It will pass, Greyson. It's just a little something I slipped into your drink. You see, I didn't think you'd want to have a drink with me later, so I took matters into my own hands."

"You did this? You fucking little prick. What the

hell's wrong with you?"

"Is that any way to talk to your future lover?" He flicked his thumb across the knife.

Greyson looked at it, then at the elevator panel, and realized they were stopped. She was trapped with Jarrod. Things started to click into place. The elevator, the way he referred to her as his future lover, the knife, the way he was wielding it around her face, and his demented smile.

Shit!

Before she could finish her thoughts, Jarrod interrupted her. "Greyson," he whispered next to her ear. "We can do this the hard way or…" He pulled back and looked her in the face. "The easy way. I prefer—"

"Fuck you," she yelled, pushing him back and lunging for the button panel.

Jarrod caught her before she could touch it. Rolling her to the floor, he pinned her down, his face just inches above hers. Greyson heard the knife clatter to the floor somewhere to her right. If she could reach…A slap brought her around, ending the thought.

"With you, I think I'm going to enjoy the hard way, Greyson." He raised himself above her and smiled. "I know you want this as bad as I do. I've seen the way you look at me when we're together. I've wanted you the same way for a long, long time, Greyson."

"Get off me, you crazy bastard," she yelled. Squirming underneath his weight, she tried to toss him off. She just needed to get her hands free, and then she'd pummel his ass.

"You need to calm down, honey. We've got a long life ahead of us." He smiled and then licked the side of her face.

"You sick fuck."

Greyson bucked her hips, but Jarrod just straightened his legs out, putting all his body weight on her. For such a little wimp, he was proving to be tough to dismount. Her stomach cramped. He trapped her hands above her head and tightened his grasp, pinning them to the floor.

"Arrgh, get the hell off me. It hurts." Greyson screamed in agony. "Oh, God."

The more she struggled, the more the stabbing in her stomach intensified, so she stopped moving.

Jarrod lowered his face again and took a deep breath. "You always smell so good, honey."

Greyson jerked her head to the side. His breath reeked of alcohol. She spotted the knife. If she could get it, she could make this bastard squeal. She needed to keep her wits about her. Jarrod grasped her chin and jerked her head around to face him.

"Look at me when I'm talking to you, Greyson. I'm not your little whipping boy anymore. You're going to give me the respect I deserve."

Greyson tried to twist her head out of his tight grasp, but he only dug his fingers deeper into her face.

Before she could think, she sneered. "Get the fuck off me, you piece of shit."

Jarrod repositioned himself on her, pinning her arms under his knees. Then he raised his fist and landed a solid punch to her cheek.

"You should be nicer, Greyson."

"Fuck you," she said, spitting blood all over his face. "You're going to pay for this, you son of a bitch."

"Wow, you're really gutsy. I gotta give you that, Greyson."

"Let me up and I'll show you how gutsy I am."

Another punch landed on Greyson's face. A

crunch echoed through her head, and she struggled to stay focused on Jarrod's face as the edges of her vision started to go black. She wasn't about to let him beat her unconscious. She bucked her hips again, almost dislodging him, but he managed to stay on top of her.

Jarrod shifted his hips and let his hand wander down Greyson's body.

"If you just relax, I guarantee you'll like it. Women have told me I'm pretty talented in that department."

"You touch me with that hand and I'll break it," Greyson said through clenched teeth.

Another blow landed on her mouth, and she could taste blood. It was taking all she had to stay conscious. One more punch to her face and she was sure she'd be out.

"Shut up. You never knew when to stop, Greyson."

Jarrod fondled her breasts and then roamed down, pulling her dress up past her hips. He pushed a knee between her legs and forced them apart. Greyson felt his hard cock against her hip as he rubbed himself against her. His hand slipped up and under her dress. His finger slipped under her panties and groped her, looking for her opening. He huffed in her ear as he pushed his fingers inside her and then slipped them out, licking them. She wanted to gag at the display. He smiled as she groaned internally.

Christ! He was going to rape her in this elevator.

Shit! He was...no, he couldn't be. She would know, right? She needed to think quickly or she'd be his next victim. Peering up at Jarrod, she offered a slight smile, closed her eyes, and tried to center herself. He would be suspicious if she was sickly sweet, so she'd need to be Greyson.

"You know, Jarrod, you just might be right?" she said in a voice he was used to hearing.

He cocked his head and smiled. "I'm listening."

"I've been avoiding my feelings for a very long time. You're my assistant, and you know my policy about personal relationships amongst the employees. Sets a bad example, but now that you're leaving the company—"

"Don't fucking play me, Greyson. I've seen the way you look at..." Jarrod contorted his neck, stretching it as if his tie was choking him. He mumbled something to himself, snapped his head around, and focused back on Greyson. "Mr. Harris, your 'legal advisor,' and those business lunches and late nights because of that bitch, Ms. Blake."

Greyson lay stunned by Jarrod's accusations. Surely, he knew she liked women, but this didn't sound like a man dealing with a full deck.

"But Jarrod, Neil's married—"

He cast a wicked smile toward her, narrowed his eyes, and lowered his head close to her face. "I know, but I thought I'd go along with the game you were going to play. I know you've got a thing for Addie Blake. I've known for quite some time. I saw you two together at Addie's apartment, the night she decided to go home. If it hadn't been for that bitch, Drake Hogan, I would have savored that little dish, too."

"What?"

Greyson mentally kicked herself. She'd left Jarrod in charge of changing the locks to Addie's apartment. Now he was stalking Addie and her. She was trying to string together the things he was saying, but she could barely stay coherent.

"Jarrod, are you telling me that you were there,

in Addie's apartment?"

"Wouldn't you like to know?"

He looked like a cat who'd licked the butter dish as he offered her a smug smile. God, how she wanted to slap that look right off his arrogant face.

Bastard.

Greyson bucked her hips again and tried to dislodge him. His face just above hers, she slammed her forehead against his nose. She didn't have enough room to generate the force needed to break it, but when he yelped in pain, she knew it stung. He grabbed his face, blood trickling out of his nostrils. They wrestled on the floor as she squirmed to the side. Even wounded, Jarrod was quick as he pushed the weight of his body against her. Adrenaline rushed through her body. She needed to think, quick.

Relaxing her body under his, she started convulsing as his weight began to smother her. Her eyes rolled back and her gag reflex started as she tried to throw up. Her arms and legs shook violently. Jarrod jumped off her in an instant and tried to make her sit upright.

"Greyson, Greyson." He slapped her across the face.

She kept gagging, trying to expel the contents of her stomach. Apparently frightened, Jarrod leaned her over so she wouldn't puke on herself.

In an instant, Greyson grabbed the knife, the blade pointed backward and twisted toward Jarrod, stabbing him in the torso as many times as she could. He fell back away from her, and as he did, he kicked at the knife, missing it and hitting Greyson in the face. She felt the elevator jerk before she blacked out.

Chapter Thirty-six

Nancy twisted the key into the elevator and pushed the button. Nothing happened. She could hear Jarrod Bennet on the inside, screaming Hollister's name over and over again. Desperate to get inside, she twisted the key again and tapped ferociously at the button. Still nothing.

"Help me," she ordered Neil Harris as she slipped her fingers into the doors. She grunted and strained, and he tried to position himself under her, but it wasn't working.

"Move to the side. You get on one side of the doors and I'll get on the other, and let's see if we can open these," he told her.

She worried as it suddenly went silent in the elevator. Frustrated, she punched the button panel. "Open, you bastard."

As if on command, the doors burst open. Hollister lay on her back, not moving, her face resembling a well-used punching bag. Bennet held a bloody knife and was looming over her. In an instant, Nancy pulled her gun. "Drop it."

As if someone had pushed the slow-motion button, she watched as he turned toward them, his knife at the ready, then fell back clutching his stomach. Blood covered his shirt and his hands, and oozed down onto the floor of the elevator.

"Oh Christ, Greyson," Harris shouted.

Nancy stopped him from entering the elevator. "Stop, this is a crime scene. Call 911 and get an ambulance up here."

"Are you kidding me? Greyson's hurt."

"Call 911," she ordered him. Focusing on Bennet again, she commanded him, "Drop the knife."

She needn't have bothered, because he lay motionless on the elevator floor, his eyes closed. Cautiously, she kicked the knife away from his grasp and studied him for a few moments before she reached down and felt for a pulse.

Slow and erratic.

He needed medical attention, but she needed answers. Which one would win?

"Detective?" Sergeant Torres said, huffing.

"Did you run up the steps?" she asked, and without waiting for an answer she barked, "We need Medical up here. Two victims. One with visible stab wounds. The other unresponsive. Make the call."

"Yes, ma'am."

She holstered her gun, bent down, and pulled Bennet's hand away from his stomach.

"How did this happen?"

"That crazy bitch stabbed me," he rasped.

"Really?"

Harris fell to his knees next to Hollister and cradled her head in his lap. "Grey," he said before he looked over at Bennet. "What the hell have you done?" A swift movement and Harris was on him, punching him.

Nancy pulled him back and off Bennet. "Do you want me to arrest you?

"She's my best friend, Detective, and this maggot

did something to her."

"This situation is already fucked up. The last thing I need for you to do is compromise my investigation. Now get the hell back. Torres, get him out of here."

"Yes, ma'am." Torres jerked him up and out of the elevator. "Don't move. If you do, I'll arrest you for obstruction. Do you understand?"

"My best friend is in there unconscious."

"I get that, but you're going to become part of this case if you don't settle down. We've got Medical on the way. Just relax." Torres kept her hand on Harris's chest as Nancy looked around the elevator. Bennet wore a pair of latex gloves, had a knife, and was alone in an elevator with a woman. All the hallmarks of the elevator rapist.

Nancy put her knee on Harris's hand as he tried to reach for the knife.

"Argh, get the fuck off me." Bennet pushed at her, wiping blood all over her leg. Pulling her cuffs, she slapped one on his pinned wrist and then tossed him onto his stomach. Her knee in his back, she yelled, "Give me your other hand, now."

Jerking his shoulder, Nancy pulled his hand toward her and finished cuffing him. As she tossed him onto his back, she was able to assess his wounds and realized they didn't look to be too deep. Nothing was gushing, but she wasn't a doctor.

"Torres, how far out is that ambulance?"

"Downstairs at the doors. They should be here in a few."

"Good." She kneeled over Bennet. "You have the right to remain silent, if you give up—"

"I know my rights. Now go fuck yourself. I'm not saying anything. I want a lawyer," he whispered.

"Not a problem, but you don't actually think you're going to beat this, do you? I mean the gloves, the knife. I bet if I look in your pocket you've got a condom on you."

"Of course I have a condom. I'm a single man and I like the ladies. They like me, and I don't pass up a piece of ass when they offer it to me."

"Is that your story?"

"And I'm sticking to it."

His face was pale and sweat beaded his top lip. He was going into shock. She wasn't about to let this bastard die on her, not when she was sure she was looking at the elevator rapist. She took her jacket off and stuffed it under his legs, pushing the blood back toward his heart.

"We'll see." She pulled out a pair of latex gloves and picked up the knife, holding it by the end. Torres, I need some evidence bags."

"You got it."

She could hear a gurney rattle out of the elevator. Two men filled the doorway. One went to Hollister and the other to Bennet.

"This guy has a couple of stab wounds. Get him stable. I need to talk to him. And help her. She's had the shit beat out of her." Nancy pointed to Greyson Hollister, who hadn't stirred even with all the excitement breaking around her. Probably just as well, because Neil Harris was barely controllable. The last thing Nancy needed was another irrational woman mucking up her evidence scene. "Can you call for another ambulance? She's going to need to be transported, too."

"Jesus, what happened to her?"

"Him." Nancy jutted her chin toward Bennet.

"Can you uncuff him? We need to start a line, and we can't do that if his hands are behind his back." The EMT cut off Bennet's shirt and started pulling IV line.

"I can, but I need to cuff him to the gurney. He's under arrest and should be considered dangerous." She slipped one cuff off, leaving it open for later when they transported him.

"We've done this before, Detective," he said, seeming rather perturbed.

"I know you have, but this guy could be the elevator rapist, and I don't want anything happening to him before I get a chance to question him. Got it?"

"Got it."

Greyson moaned as the EMT started to treat the wounds he could see. As he applied a bandage to the cut on her forehead, Hollister tried to push his hand away. Nancy kneeled down and pulled her hand away.

"You've been attacked. You need to lie still and let the EMTs do their job," she said, finally able to study Hollister, who looked horrible. Her eyes were swollen, her jaw looked like it was broken, and blood oozed out of her mouth. "Can you hear me?"

Hollister barely nodded. "Jarrod…"

"Relax, he's being looked at right now," she reassured Hollister. Was she actually worried about Jarrod Bennet? How was she linked to all this? Obviously she'd been beaten, but was it a cover, or was she the last victim of the elevator rapist?

"He's the rapist," Hollister forced out between swollen lips.

"Did he rape you?"

She barely shook her head, then looked at Nancy. She wasn't the strong paragon of business right now, but rather a defeated, victimized woman who'd probably just realized her own personal assistant was possibly the elevator rapist.

Nancy patted her hand. "It'll be okay. We're going to get you to the hospital. Would you like me to call your mother?"

"Neil."

"Greyson, I'm right here." Harris stepped forward and knelt next to her. "Hang in there. We got the bastard. He's not going anywhere, buddy."

Hollister nodded. Tears started streaming down her face, and Nancy felt embarrassed for her. She was sure it took a lot to make this strong woman cry, but after what she'd been through, Nancy couldn't blame her for being emotional.

"Grey, would you like me to call your mom?" Harris asked.

"Addie…is she okay?"

"I think so, why?" Nancy said. Why would she be asking about Addie? "Why?"

"I think he said he was in her apartment."

"I just left her at your house, so she's fine."

"Thank God." Hollister's eyes rolled back in her head and she was out again.

"Where's that elevator?" Nancy yelled at no one in particular.

"Just pulled up."

"Good. Let's get her out of here. Torres, I want the forensics team in here, now."

"Yes, ma'am."

"Have every inch photographed, and tell the team to look for anything and everything. I want to see results, and let's get this place closed down. Bag his hands." Nancy pointed at Jarrod Bennet. Picking up her jacket, she slipped it on and turned to watch him being put on the gurney. In an instant, she was next to him, making sure she personally cuffed him to the frame.

Nancy looked at Bennet. Her gut told her she'd caught the elevator rapist, but she wouldn't relax until the DNA results confirmed what she knew.

Chapter Thirty-seven

Nancy slapped the warrant against her legs. She was getting frustrated. It had taken the better part of the night to get the warrant and find Bennet's landlord to serve it. Now she stood in front of the idiot, listening to him give her some bullshit story about not knowing Jarrod Bennet and raving about police brutality.

"Look, we know you own the home. So, you can either accompany us to the residence and open the place, or we take a battering ram to the front door. Your choice." Nancy shrugged.

"I need to call my lawyer."

Nancy put her hand on the door as he tried to slam it in her face. "Officer, arrest this man for obstruction."

The clink of the metal cuffs being pulled brought him to a stop. "Hey, now wait just a minute."

He held up his hands and stepped back into the house. Nancy recognized the fight-or-flight response that was plastered all over his face. He was going to bolt on them. She knew it.

"Stop," she said, still standing on the stoop.

A small crowd had started to gather around the yard. This wasn't going to end well if she didn't get this guy on board quick. Peering over her shoulder, she watched as a few men started to advance on them.

"I suggest you step back through that gate and go home, or you're going to be arrested too. Call for backup," she directed the officer who'd pulled the cuffs.

"Yes, ma'am."

As he talked into his mic, Nancy looked at the unshaven mess still trying to pull her chain.

"Now, you can call your attorney on the way to the house, or I arrest you, he takes you downtown, and books you. Meanwhile, I'll be knocking that door off its hinges, and who knows what else might get broken in the process. It is a potential crime scene. Your choice."

He scratched at something in his scraggly beard and then looked at the crowd beyond the rickety fence. If he was assessing his options, Nancy wanted to cut them down quick, so she put her hand on her gun and snapped open the retention guard with her thumb.

"Another unit is in the vicinity. They're two minutes out," the officer said.

"Thanks." Nancy checked the crowd one last time and then looked back at the man. "Well?"

"Fuck. I'll get my jacket."

"And your pants?" she said, pointing to his knobby knees sticking out of his boxers. "You need to put some clothes on."

Nancy snatched the key from the landlord's hand and slipped it into the lock. She'd had enough of his hateful rhetoric slamming cops. His incessant droning on about police brutality, which didn't mesh with his bitching about how slow the police were to react to his calls when there was an emergency, just mirrored many people's opinion—love 'em when you need them.

Slowly, she turned the handle and pushed the door open. Standing behind the doorframe, she peered into the black room. The shades were drawn, so there was nothing to light up the small space. The room had a musty smell, like dirty gym socks and wet towels. She reached around the corner searching for a light switch.

Nothing.

She jumped when the landlord yelled. "What are you waiting for? I don't have all day to be standing around here. I got shit to do."

"Shut. Up," she yelled back at him, leaning into her voice.

Shaking off the jitters she suddenly felt, she snapped on a pair of latex gloves and paper booties, and held out her hand. "Gimme your flashlight."

She didn't know what to expect with Jarrod Bennet. He'd proved to be a twisted son of a bitch when he raped women, so nothing in his house should surprise her. Flicking the light around the room, she made out the usual couch, coffee table, and chair. Spotting a lamp, she lit her path to the light and switched it on.

"Holy shit," someone behind her said.

Turning, she echoed the sentiment in her head. *Holy shit!*

"No one comes in until forensics gets here."

"Yes, ma'am."

A homage to Greyson Hollister covered the wall across from the couch. Candid pictures mixed with magazine and newspaper articles littered every inch of the expanse. Nancy couldn't see even a free inch of wall as she looked at the photos. Off to one side hung a wedding dress, still in the plastic storage bag, a price tag dangling from the hanger.

"Five hundred, seventy-five dollars, and ninety-five cents. Jesus Christ," she said, placing the tag the way she'd found it. "Call in Forensics, Corporal."

"Yes, ma'am."

"And get this guy out of here. Find a unit to take him home."

"Hey, what about my key?"

Nancy shot him a look that would wither a flower. He raised his hands, his lips pinched in disapproval.

"Whatever. I'm sure I'll get it back at some point."

"If you're lucky," she whispered.

Nancy moved back down the wall and looked at the photos. Some had definitely been taken at the office and what looked to be a coffee shop, and a few even had Addie Blake in them. Pulling her cell phone, she snapped pictures of every inch of the wall. She'd want to look at these later, before CSI got theirs done, catalogued, and sent over to her.

God, camera phones would be the death of her. They popped up on arrests and at car accidents. Hell, she'd even gone to an accident where everyone had their phones out taking pictures, but no one had offered assistance. What was this world coming to when even the basic necessity of offering help to someone who needed it went unanswered? Now she was looking at proof of how pervasive they could be in stalking someone.

Greyson Hollister had been the intended target all along. Each victim had features similar to hers. The same hair color and body type. They could all be sisters. Now they were sisters, in a twisted sort of way. Victims of the same nut job.

Making her way to the bedroom, she was in for more surprises as she turned on the wall light. Pinned up were hundreds of pairs of panties that made up a tapestry of sorts on the wall facing the bed. Souvenirs from his victims, she suspected. But there were more panties than vics. Jarrod had probably started as a peeping Tom and graduated to stealing panties from women and then moved on to raping them when he couldn't sustain the same adrenaline rush in his earlier days, but she was only guessing at this point. A forensic psych exam would be in order for this deviant. Searching around the room, she was shocked by its condition. It was immaculate. Steadying her phone, she snapped more pictures. It wouldn't be the last ones she'd take here, she was sure.

The bed was made with not a wrinkle in the duvet. The pillowcases matched and looked as if they'd been ironed as well. Crisp, clean, and white. The forensic team was going to have a field day in this apartment.

Moving toward the bathroom, Nancy tried to make sure she searched every nook and cranny. Few items littered the nightstands. No other pictures graced the walls, except a few more of Greyson. One in particular drew her attention. Two heart-shaped frames joined together. One had a picture of Greyson facing left, and the left heart had a picture of Jarrod Bennet facing right.

"Christ, this guy's a nutter."

Nancy knelt to look at the others and snapped more photos. Only glossy pictures of Greyson, clipped from various magazines, sat in the frames. As she searched the bathroom, she found it to be in pristine condition as well.

All white. At least a hundred-watt bulb lit the room. It was so intense that she had to almost close her eyes as she took everything in. The guy had a thing for white. She was sure the docs would tell them something about what the color represented to him, but she knew it probably had to do with purity and how he saw himself. Nothing out of the ordinary stuck out, until she opened the medicine cabinet.

❧ ❧ ❧ ❧

Addie had been watching Greyson sleep for hours. She'd had been warned that Greyson had been beaten, but nothing could prepare someone for the way she looked. Her jaw had to be wired shut, her eyes were almost closed, and Addie could only imagine what lay under the blankets. She was still in shock at the revelation that Jarrod Bennet was the elevator rapist. She'd never liked the guy. He'd always given her the creeps, but a rapist?

Detective Hill had told her that perhaps she should see Greyson first, but Camille had been adamant about going to the hospital. It had practically destroyed Camille to see her daughter so badly beaten. Camille's MS was flaring up due to the stress of the situation, and Dr. Madrigal had prescribed a sedative to calm her. Neil's offer of a ride home and some coaxing from the doctor had convinced her to go home and rest.

Addie had assured her that she would call her the minute Greyson woke. Unfortunately, Greyson hadn't woken up yet from the beating she'd sustained. The doctors said she would eventually, that she just needed time. Rubbing her cheek against Greyson's hand, Addie couldn't stop her tears from falling and wetting the back of it. Wiping them away, Addie kissed Greyson's knuckles and rested her forehead against them.

"Please wake up, Greyson, please."

"How's she doing?"

Addie jerked upright. Dr. Madrigal stood beside the bed and placed a reassuring hand on Addie's shoulder.

"I don't know. She's still the same, I guess."

"It's going to take time, Ms. Blake. She'd suffered a traumatic head injury. The force it took to break her jaw easily gave her a concussion. Be patient. I know it's hard, but she's strong."

"Thank you, Dr. Madrigal. I'd give anything to trade places with her."

"If I know Greyson, and I do, she wouldn't let you do that. Besides, you've been in this exact place, so you'll know what she's feeling when she comes to."

Dr. Madrigal busied herself looking at Greyson's chart and checking her vital signs. Addie had no illusions about the road ahead for Greyson. She only wondered if she should move out now. She would be a constant reminder of what had happened to both of them, though their perpetrators were different people with different goals for each of them.

"Well, I'll leave you two alone. Please call for the nurses when she wakes up."

"Thank you, Dr. Madrigal, for everything. Greyson's lucky to have a friend who cares about her so much."

"Greyson's an extraordinary woman. Take care."

Addie turned her attention back to Greyson. Even in this condition, she had an underlying beauty that shone through. Addie just wanted to touch her face, soothe her wounds, and make everything better. Standing, she tucked a few strands of hair behind her ear and then gently caressed Greyson's face. She was breathtaking.

Addie thought about the torment she had suffered through after her attack. Sleepless nights, and when she could sleep, the nightmare of what had happened haunted her. Greyson would be faced with the same, and she'd need time and space to process, just like she had. She wanted, no, needed, to be there for Greyson. Besides, she was falling for her boss.

Chapter Thirty-eight

Nancy froze in front of the medicine cabinet. Before her lay stacks of boxes just a little bigger than matchboxes, each with a date lettered on it in black block letters. Her hand trembled as it reached for a small box labeled **6/18/2018.** Pushing the box open, she gasped. A piece of fabric, stained with blood, lay on top, and below, poking out, were strands of hair. She pulled her pen and gently lifted an edge of the fabric, looking at the dark-brown hair. Short and curly, clearly it was pubic hair, but there were no roots. They'd been cut from their owner. They wouldn't be able to trace her from the root follicle, but the blood and any other fluids on the panties might help them match her to a crime. Turning the box around, she studied the date again and wracked her brain. That was only a few days ago. There hadn't been a report of a rape.

Shit.

Closing the box, she put it back on top and ran her finger down the rows of boxes. She counted fifteen boxes total.

Christ.

This was worse than she thought. He'd been raping women for a while. The earliest date was back in 2010. Eight years. For eight long years he'd been terrorizing women. She would have to find out how long Bennet had worked for Greyson and then see if she could correlate those dates to events and travel. Though they didn't have a reported rape, there could be one in the surrounding counties.

Just then something struck her. Pulling the top box out again, she opened it, noted the color, and walked back out into the bedroom. She held the box up against the wall of panties and matched it with one particular set. Then she lifted the front of the panties and noticed a hole in the inner fabric.

"Sick fuck," she said as she picked up other sets and noticed the same pattern. There were so many sets on the wall and so few boxes in the medicine cabinet. Some of these were probably from his early, nonviolent days. Snapping more pictures of the boxes, she suddenly felt sick to her stomach.

"Hey, Detective. Whatcha got?" Jenny said, setting her cases on the floor. "You haven't contaminated my crime scene, have you?"

"Funny." Nancy handed her the box. "Check this out."

Nancy gingerly walked back into the bathroom and stood waiting for Jenny to say something, and as if on cue she did.

"Okay, I have to be honest with you. I don't see anything. It is pretty bright in here, and it's all white. How am I doing?" Jenny shielded her eyes. "Boy, I'm going to need my sunglasses if we stay here any longer."

Nancy pulled the tip of the door open and, like a practiced magician, motioned to the stacks of boxes.

"Holy shit. Is that what I think it is?" She hesitated and then moved closer to the medicine cabinet.

"His trophies. I've looked at only one box, but if all of those boxes contain the same stuff, you've got your work cut out for you."

"What stuff is inside?"

"Fabric with DNA on it. Pubic hair. God only knows what the rest of the boxes have in them." Nancy turned away from the collection and suddenly felt like she wanted to throw up.

"There are a lot of dates here," Jenny observed.

"Yep, and we don't have that many reported rape cases."

Jenny pulled a box, pulled a pair of tweezers, and lifted a strip of fabric. "Oh shit." Her voice rose several pitches.

"What?" Nancy walked back to Jenny

"Oh, shit." Nancy closed her eyes, wishing she could unsee what lay in the box.

A circle of skin lay in the bottom.

"Why doesn't it smell?" Nancy arched her head away from the box.

Jenny tweezed it, lifting it from the box and putting it in her latex-covered palm.

"Gross. Jesus, what a sick fuck."

"It's got some sort of chemical on it. It looks like he treated it, like someone would treat animal hide."

Jenny flipped it back and forth, studying the nipple. Who was walking around without a nipple? But she had a better question. Why didn't she know about it?

"Let's get some pictures of this place and catalog everything in the apartment. I'm almost afraid to look in the closet." Nancy peeled her gloves off. "Call me if you find anything else."

"Where are you going?"

"The hospital. I need to check in on a witness and find out if anyone's missing one of those." She tossed her chin in the direction of the nipple still sitting in Jenny's palm. An injury of this type had to require a hospital visit. It just had to.

"Agreed. I just can't imagine someone not seeking medical treatment for this, let alone not reporting it. It had to be painful, and the victim could die if not treated immediately."

Nancy rubbed her thumb against her eyebrow and squeezed her eyes shut. What the fuck was this world coming to?

"I'll call you with a report after we've logged all of this in and run some tests." Another young man walked into the room and scooted around Nancy. "Now shoo, so I can do my job," Jenny ordered her, pushing her out the door.

"Call me. I don't care how late it is."

"Don't you mean early?" Jenny looked down at her watch.

"Late, early, it's all the same to me." Nancy held her finger and thumb up to her head and mouthed, "Call me."

It was going to be hours before she hit the sack, so she might as well check in on Greyson and talk to the ER doctors. Surely someone had come in with some weird injuries, if you could call losing a nipple weird.

Chapter Thirty-nine

Greyson cringed as she tried to open her eyes. The light in the room was killing her. Throwing her arm over her face, she tried to open her mouth, but she could only squeeze a moan through. She rubbed her face and flinched as she felt the bruises and wires running through her mouth.

Christ, how long had she been out? Looking out from under her arm, she could gradually see someone lying on the edge of her bed.

Addie.

Gently, she ran her fingers through Addie's hair, smoothing out some tangled strands. Addie stirred at Greyson's touch. She looked up at Greyson and smiled.

"Greyson, you're awake." She stood and ran her fingers over Greyson's jaw. "How bad does it hurt?"

If it did, she couldn't feel it at the moment. She leaned into Addie's touch, her eyes watering as everything that had happened to Addie came rushing in on her. All she could think about was scooping up Addie and holding her close. Her heart lurched as Addie started to cry too.

"Don't cry," she forced out, barely audible.

"Oh, Greyson, I'm so sorry this happened to you."

She held Addie's hand tight against her face. Suddenly, she felt a deeper connection to Addie.

They'd both been victims of evil people. Addie had suffered through her injuries with such dignity that it had quickly drawn her to Addie. Addie had gotten that twinkle back in her eyes only recently, but looking at her now, Greyson couldn't see it anymore. It had vanished.

Kissing the inside of Addie's palm, she smiled and whispered, "I'm fine."

"I'm so sorry."

"You didn't do this." Greyson swung her hand down her body. "Jarrod."

"I can't believe it. He seemed so…normal."

Greyson tweaked her eyebrows and shook her head.

"Okay, he seemed so weird. It was like he had the hots for you."

"He did," Nancy Hill said, walking into the room. "Sorry, I didn't mean to intrude."

"You're not. Greyson just woke up. Your timing couldn't be better, Detective," Addie said, stepping away from the bed. Greyson didn't let go of her hand, so she couldn't move very far. She wasn't about to let Addie go, not yet. Her mind swelled with all the things she wanted to say to Addie. Detective Hill's timing couldn't have been worse.

"I should be going." Addie let go of Greyson's hand and scooped up her things. "I have to get to work. If you'll excuse me."

"Peez don't go," Greyson pleaded. Looking at the detective, she said, "Can you give us a minute?"

"Of course. I'll just wait outside." Detective Hill slowly left the room and pulled the door shut behind her.

"Greyson, I've brought enough trouble to your

door." Addie didn't look at her.

"NO. You didn't do this." Greyson reached for Addie's hand again. "I...I want you to stay, peez... don't go."

Greyson smiled as Addie's gaze mapped every bruise, cut, and mark left behind from the attack. Gone for now was the self-assured, dynamic entrepreneur. The beating had taken its intended toll. In her place was a softer version that she wanted to share with Addie. They'd shared a lot of moments together, and Greyson didn't want those to just be a memory because Addie was afraid. Actually, Addie was everything Greyson wasn't. Addie was the ying to Greyson's yang. Soft, kind, alluring, even if Addie didn't know it. Greyson was attracted to every facet of Addie Blake, and she didn't want to lose her because Addie might think she needed time to come to terms with what had happened.

"Greyson, I should probably leave the house. I..." Addie bit her lip. "I feel like I'd be a constant reminder of what's happened to you, of what Drake did to the company—"

"Stop," Greyson whispered. How could Addie think that she would hold a grudge? Addie was just as much a victim here as anyone.

Addie tried again. "But—"

"Stop. I don't know how to say this, so I'm going to say it one more time. I'm not sure if you remember, but when we were sitting in front of Drake's garage, I told you how I felt about you. I still feel that way. Addie, I'm attracted to you, and I'd like to see where this takes us, but I'll understand if you don't feel the same way. If you still want to leave, I won't stop you, but I just had to let you know." Greyson wanted to say more, but the door swung open and Detective Hill

stood looking at them both.
	"Okay, got a minute?" She pulled her phone and walked toward them

Chapter Forty

If subtext was a language, Greyson Hollister and Addie Blake were shouting it. Nancy hated to interrupt whatever was going on between them, but she needed to get back to the station and brief the chief. She was almost positive they'd caught the elevator rapist and Addie's attacker. She just wanted to give Hollister a little information. Well, actually ask some more questions and quell her sneaking suspicion about Jarrod Bennet.

"Ladies, sorry to interrupt, but I'd like to ask you some more questions and give you a brief update." Neither woman said anything. "Okay. Ms. Hollister. Was Jarrod always your date for those events like the Chamber dinner?"

Greyson nodded twice, as Addie moved to stand near her. Subtext was flowing even stronger, and Nancy could feel it now.

"I see." She pulled out her pad and her phone, then slid her finger across her phone and correlated the dates with what she had written down. Turning her pad toward Hollister, she asked another question. "Do these dates look familiar?"

Hollister looked and then motioned for the pad. Holding it closer, she stared at each date, closed her eyes, and then looked again.

"I think so. Why?"

"These are the dates you were at dinners and events where Jarrod Bennet accompanied you." Turning her phone around, she flashed the picture of the boxes found in the medicine cabinet. "These are boxes I found in his medicine cabinet."

Addie gasped.

Hollister didn't express any emotion. "You're thinking I had something to do with all of this?"

"Actually," Nancy scratched her scalp and selected another photo to show her, "I did until I saw this." She turned the phone around, and Hollister's eyes widened at the sight of the pictures of her plastered all over Jarrod's wall.

"What the…"

"Exactly. I think he was fixated on you and raped other women until he was sure he could get to you. I don't know if tonight was just a lucky guess or if he planned it."

"He told me he was leaving the company, that he had another offer," Hollister said, rubbing her jaw. Clearly she was in pain, but Nancy wasn't quite done with Greyson Hollister, yet.

She spent the next half hour lining out her suspicions, sharing the photos that weren't too graphic, and then explaining why she knew Bennet was the elevator rapist. Finally, she popped the final surprise.

"The rapist is Hep C positive. We're running the tests now, but if Jarrod is Hep C positive, he won't have any wiggle room for a plea deal. Did you get any of his fluids on your…in you?"

Hollister went pale. She shrugged and then asked for some water. Addie's hands shook as she poured her a glass and handed it to her. Obviously, the news had stunned both of them.

"It's possible. I hit him and stabbed at him. Fuck."

Addie kissed the side of Hollister's head and whispered, "It'll be all right. Don't worry. We'll get the best medical attention possible."

Nancy quirked her eyebrows and suddenly felt sorry for these two women. Both victims, both would fight their own demons, but at least they had each other.

"Well, I need to scoot. I have a chief breathing down my neck for some closure, and now I can finally give him that. Don't be surprised if the news media start breaking down your door for interviews." She stuffed everything into her pockets and turned to leave. Stopping at the door, she looked back at them. "I don't have to tell you to stay in town, do I?" The puzzled look on their faces said it all. "I didn't think so. I'll be in touch. Tell your legal eagle to give me a ring in the morning. I'd like to talk to him about Ms. Blake's case."

With that, the case and the door shut behind her. She almost slapped her hands together signaling a finality of sorts, but it wouldn't be completely over for months. At least this was one and done, as they said. Nancy whistled as she bounced down the hall. She felt good. She always felt good when she caught the bad guys.

Epilogue

*G*reyson stood on the platform waiting for the last train of the night. It had been a bitch of a day, and all she wanted to do was crawl into bed and forget the last ten hours of work. The familiar skid of the brakes on the metal rails drew her from her thoughts of Integrated Financial. The door swished open with authority, and she climbed into the familiar empty passenger car.

Empty.

It was always empty at this time of night. Sliding into a seat, she tossed her briefcase into the seat next to her.

Relax, she told herself. It was a forty-five-minute ride to the park-and-ride, and all she wanted to do was close her eyes and sleep. Leaning her head back, she wanted to just rest her eyes for a few minutes.

Just a few.

A familiar scent wrapped itself around her, and a warm breath caressed her ear.

"Greyson."

She was dreaming. She had to be.

"Greyson."

If she didn't open her eyes she wouldn't have to be tortured again tonight. A hand threaded through her hair, another hand down the front of her shirt. She could feel the tug of buttons being undone.

"Grey. Open your eyes, sweetheart."

Slowly she opened them and instantly recognized the woman straddling her lap.

"I've missed you," she said, so low and seductive that the sound pierced her heart. "How was work today?"

Just as she was about to answer, someone covered her mouth. Warm lips and a searching tongue dueled with hers. She pulled at the coat that separated her from what she desired and then pushed her shoulders back. She wouldn't let herself be tortured like this again.

Sitting up, she was stunned when she discovered that Cate wasn't sitting on her lap. Instead, Addie was smiling back at her. "What's wrong, tiger?"

"Nothing, not a thing," Greyson cooed, scooping Addie closer. "I've been waiting for you for a while," she said around kisses.

❧❧❧❧

The warmth of three bodies kept Addie from falling asleep again. She buried herself closer to Greyson's neck and inhaled a scent so familiar it made her body ache with anticipation—until Ben's head popped out from underneath the covers.

"Addie?"

"Hmm." She ran her fingers through his soft, downy hair.

It'd been two months of adjustment for all of them. The court trial for Drake had taken the shortest amount of time. As Detective Hill had predicted, Carl wasn't about to take the fall for attempted murder. The charges against him were dropped. But Drake, well, Drake was going away for a long time, thanks to Carl's testimony.

However, Jarrod wasn't going to go away so

easily. He'd been identified as the elevator rapist because he was, in fact, Hep C positive. The hang-up had been tracking down all of the other evidence in those little boxes he'd saved. Unfortunately, the detective's job wasn't over. She needed to track down those women, or at least get it out on the wire that they had possible evidence in other rape cases, and that was assuming they weren't homicides. No one lost a nipple and didn't say something. Unless they couldn't.

Addie shivered when she thought about all the things he'd done to women.

"Are you cold?" Ben's voice was still laced with sleep.

"No, honey. You should go back to sleep. Mommy has a big day tomorrow."

"Yep, and she's not going to get any sleep if you two talk all night," Greyson said, pulling Addie closer.

"You're awake, Mommy." Ben squeezed in tighter between them.

"I am, sport, but I need my rest. I'm going back to work." Greyson smiled at Addie and then winked. "I can't keep working from home, now can I?"

"Yes, you can. You have your 'puter here." Ben huffed. Clearly, he was afraid of being home alone.

"But you're going to school tomorrow. You're a big boy now." Addie tried to lessen the blow of Greyson's inevitable absence.

After listening to testimony in the courtroom, they'd found out that Jarrod was an only child with a mother who doted on him incessantly. She still did. Attending the trial daily and sending dirty looks at Greyson had been her way of showing her displeasure. After that testimony, Greyson had decided that preschool was in order for Ben. She'd explained to

Addie that too much time without social interaction was starting to create a few antisocial tendencies.

"Can I take you to school tomorrow?" Addie asked, trying to divert Ben's attention.

"How about we all go to school tomorrow," Greyson said, pulling them both closer.

Ben laughed. "You can't go to school, Addie."

"Can I go to school?" Greyson rested her chin on Ben's head and looked at Addie, smiling.

"No, silly. School's for me." Ben hugged Greyson tighter.

Addie smiled and winked at Greyson. Life had a way of working itself out, it seemed. Now if she could just get Paul married, she'd have a complete circle.

About the Author

Isabella lives on the central coast with her wife, and three sons. She teaches college and in her spare time, which there seems to be little of lately, she is working on her writers retreat in the Sierra foothills. She is a GLCS award winner for Always Faithful and a finalist for Scarlet Masquerade. She also a finalist in the International National Book awards and has two honorable mentions in the Rainbow Awards.

She also writes under the nom de plume - Jett Abbott. A darker, rogue who's a motorcycle enthusiast and loves people watching.

Like her fan page for the latest in news on readings, appearances and books.

https://www.facebook.com/isabella.sapphirebooks

or

www.sapphirebooks.com/isabella.html

or

www.isabella.rocks

Check out Isabella's other books

Award winning novel - Always Faithful - ISBN - 978-0-982860-80-9

Major Nichol "Nic" Caldwell is the only survivor of her helicopter crash in Iraq. She is left alone to wonder why she and she alone survived. Survivor's guilt has nothing on the young Major as she is forced to deal with the scars, both physical and mental, left from her ordeal overseas. Before the accident, she couldn't think of doing anything else in her life.

Claire Monroe is your average military wife, with a loving husband and a little girl. She is used to the time apart from her husband. In fact, it was one of the reasons she married him. Then, one day, her life is turned upside down when she gets a visit from the Marine Corps.

Can these two women come to terms with the past and finally find happiness, or will their shared sense of honor keep them apart?

Forever Faithful - ISBN – 978-1-939062-75-8

Life is what happens when you make other plans, and Nic and Claire have just found out that life and the Marine Corps have other plans for their lives. Nic Caldwell has served her country, met the woman of her dreams, and has reached the rank of Lieutenant Colonel. She's studying at one of the nation's most prestigious military universities, setting her sights on a research position after graduation. Things couldn't be better and then it happens; a sudden assignment to Afghanistan derails any thoughts of marriage and wedded bliss. Another combat zone, another tragedy, and Nic suddenly finds herself fighting for her life. Claire Monroe loves her new life in Monterey. She's finally where she wants to be, getting ready to start her master's program at the local university, watching her daughter, Grace, growing up, and getting ready to marry the love of her life. What could possibly derail a perfect life? The Marine Corps. Will Nic survive Afghanistan? Can Claire step up and be the strength in their relationship? Or will this overseas assignment and a catastrophic accident divide their once happy home?

American Yakuza - ISBN - 978-0-9828608-3-0

Luce Potter straddles three cultures as she strives to live with the ideals of family, honor, and duty. When her grandfather passes the family business to her, Luce finds out that power, responsibility and justice come with a price. Is it a price she's willing to die for?

Brooke Erickson lives the fast-paced life of an investigative journalist living on the edge until it all comes crashing down around her one night in Europe. Stateside, Brooke learns to deal with a new reality when she goes to work at a financial magazine and finds out things aren't always as they seem.

Can two women find enough common ground for love or will their two different worlds and cultures keep them apart?

American Yakuza II - The Lies that Bind - ISBN - 978-10939062-20-8

Luce Potter runs her life and her business with an iron fist and complete control until lies and deception unravel her world. The shadow of betrayal consumes Luce, threatening to destroy the most precious thing in her life, Brooke Erickson.

Brooke Erickson finds herself on the outside of Luce's life looking in. As events spiral out of control Brooke can only watch as the woman she loves pushes her further away. Suddenly, devastated and alone, Brooke refuses to let go without an explanation.

Colby Water, a federal agent investigating the ever-elusive Luce Potter, discovers someone from her past is front and center in her investigation of the Yakuza crime leader. Before she can put the crime boss in prison, she must confront the ultimate deception in her professional life.

When worlds collide, betrayal, dishonor and death are inevitable. Can Luce and Brooke survive the explosion?

America Yakuza III- Razor's Edge - ISBN - 978-1-943353-81-1

Luce Potter lives by a code of honor. Push her and she shoves back, harder. There's only one problem: Luce has just found out that revenge is a knife that cuts both ways. Now that her lover Brooke has survived the attack on her life, Luce has only one thing on her mind, and his name is Frank. Unfortunately, someone walks into her life that she didn't see coming. Brooke Erickson has survived an attack so brutal it's left a permanent scar on her soul. All she wants to do now is go home and finish recuperating with her lover, Luce Potter, by her side. An unexpected event puts Brooke at the head of the Yakuza family. Can she command the respect necessary to lead it through the crisis? Luce and Brooke's worlds are upending. Can each do what's necessary to survive and return to a new normal

Executive Disclosure- ISBN - 978-0-9828608-3-0

When a life is threatened, it takes a special breed of person to step in front of a bullet. Chad Morgan's job has put her life on the line more times that she can count. Getting close to the client is expected; getting too close could be deadly for Chad. Reagan Reynolds wants the top job at Reynolds Holdings and knows how to play the game like "the boys." She's not above using her beauty and body as currency to get what she wants. Shocked to find out someone wants her dead, Reagan isn't thrilled at the prospect of needing protection as she tries to convince the board she's the right woman for a man's job. How far will a killer go to get what they want? Secrets and deception twist the rules of the game as a killer closes in. How far will Chad go to protect her beautiful, but challenging client?

Surviving Reagan - ISBN - 978-1-939062-38-3

Chad Caldwell has finally worked through the betrayal of her former client and lover, Reagan Reynolds. Putting the pieces of her life back in order, she finds herself on a collision course with that past when she takes on a new client, the future first lady. Unfortunately, Chad's newest job puts her in the cross-hairs of a domestic terrorist determined to release a virus that could kill thousands of women. Reagan Reynolds has paid for her sins and is ready to start a new life. Attending a business conference in Abu Dhabi gives her the opportunity to prove to her father and herself that she's worthy of a fresh start. Her past will intersect with her future at the conference when she accidentally comes face-to-face with Chad Caldwell. Time is running out. Will Reagan confront Chad? Can she convince Chad she's changed, or will death part them forever?

Broken Shield - ISBN - 978-0-982860-82-3

Tyler Jackson, former paramedic now firefighter, has seen her share of death up close. The death of her wife caused Tyler to rethink her career choices, but the death of her mother two weeks later cemented her return to the ranks of firefighter. Her path of self-destruction and womanizing is just a front to hide the heartbreak and devastation she lives with every day. Tyler's given up on finding love and having the family she's always wanted. When tragedy strikes her life for a second time she finds something she thought she lost.

Ashley Henderson loves her job. Ignoring her mother's advice, she opts for a career in law enforcement. But, Ashley hides a secret that soon turns her life upside down. Shame, guilt and fear keep Ashley from venturing forward and finding the love she so desperately craves. Her life comes crashing down around her in one swift moment forcing her to come clean about her secrets and her life.

Can two women thrust together by one traumatic event survive and find love together, or will their past force them apart?

Scarlet Assassin - ISBN - 978-1-939062-36-9

Selene Hightower is a killer for hire. A vampire who walks in both the light and the darkness, but lately darkness has a stronger pull. Her unfinished business could cost her the ability to live in the light, throwing her permanently back into the black ink of evil.

Doctor Francesca Swartz led a boring life filled with test tubes, blood trials, and work. One exploratory night, in a world of leather and torture, she is intrigued by a dark and solitary soul. She surrenders to temptation and the desire to experience something new, only to discover that it might alter her life forever.

Will Selene allow the light to win over the darkness threatening the edges of her life? Two women wonder if they can co-exist despite vast differences, as worlds collide and threaten to destroy any hope of happiness. Who will win?

The Gate - ISBN – 978-1-943353-93-4

Valhalla is for warriors that die in battle. What of those who don't have a hero's death? Where do they go? The inter-world is in chaos and has become the heart of the battleground in the war between Paladins and Gatekeepers. Harley doesn't know it yet, but she's at ground zero. A night of drinking, to forget a cheating girlfriend, is about to change her life forever. A birthmark—or a birthright—sets her on a direct path to a woman who claims to have known her for centuries. Not ready to accept her Paladin mantel, she needs proof—and that proof is out to destroy her. A protector by birth, Dawn was bred to preserve the delicate cycle of life and death. Protecting a Paladin is to be mated for eternity, usually without the sex, but Harley's allure is universally compelling. Harley's rise in status to The Chosen complicates things further as Dawn finds herself fighting for her own heart, as well as battling her biggest nemesis and brother, Lucius. Lucius, lord of the Gatekeepers, is out to kill souls moving to their next life. He wants Harley in his corner and he isn't about to let a little sibling rivalry stand in the way, no matter what it takes. Harley find herself caught up in Lucius's tempting promise of power, but cannot shake the soul-tugging love she feels with Dawn. Will Dawn convince Harley in time to embrace her Paladin destiny and save the souls looking for their gate, or will Lucius be able to sway Harley to throw in with the Gatekeepers?

Writing as Jett Abbott

GCLS Finalist - Scarlet Masquerade - ISBN - 978-0-982860-8-6

What do you say to the woman you thought died over a century ago? Will time heal all wounds or does it just allow them to fester and grow? A.J. Locke has lived over two centuries and works like a demon, both figuratively and literally. As the owner of a successful pharmaceutical company that specializes in blood research, she has changed the way she can live her life. Wanting for nothing, she has smartly compartmentalized her life so that when she needs to, she can pick up and start all over again, which happens every twenty years or so. Love is not an emotion A.J. spends much time on. Since losing the love of her life to the plague one hundred fifty years ago, she vowed to never travel down that road again. That isn't to say she doesn't have women when she wants them, she just wants them on her terms and that doesn't involve a long term commitment.

A.J.'s cool veneer is peeled back when she sees the love of her life in a lesbian bar, in the same town, in the same day and time in which she lives. Is her mind playing tricks on her? If not, how did Clarissa survive the plague when she had made A.J. promise never to change her?

Clarissa Graham is a university professor who has lived

an obscure life teaching English literature. She has made it a point to stay off the radar and never become involved with anything that resembles her past life. Every once in a while Clarissa has an itch that needs to be scratched, so she finds an out of the way location to scratch it. She keeps her personal life separate from her professional one, and in doing so she is able to keep her secrets to herself. Suddenly, her life is turned upside down when someone tries to kill her. She finds herself in the middle of an assassination plot with no idea who wants her dead